Enchanted Series Book Two

Sophie

Trish Moran

Chapter One

Sage and Sophie sat down at the canteen table with some other students from the sixth form at Briar Lane High School.

'Our last year of school,' Sage commented.

'It already feels like we've been back for ages, and it's only the first day of the school year,' Sophie added.

One of the other girls sighed. 'Yes, the long summer holiday is already just a distant memory.'

Bridget turned to her. 'Did you go anywhere interesting, Tracey?'

'London for a few days, then France, camping for a week with my family.'

Layla pursed her lips. 'Still holidaying with your family? Can't think of anything worse! Me and Sasha had an awesome time in Spain, didn't we? Sun, Sangria, good looking lads and no parents!'

Henry looked up. 'Actually, me and Bridget enjoyed our holiday in Silversands with my family.'

'Silversands? Not exactly the Med, is it?' Layla laughed. She turned to Sophie and Sage. 'What about you two? Did you go anywhere interesting?'

'We visited some family friends,' Sage answered. 'We had a great time.'

'Yes, it was one of my best holidays ever,' Sophie agreed, thinking wistfully of their time in Aurum, the world created for magical creatures and now open to the Gifted people from Earth world.

'You're all so unadventurous!' Layla shook her head. 'Come on, Sasha, I want to freshen up before History. The new guy in the class looks rather interesting.'

'Unadventurous? If only she knew,' Tracey whispered to Sophie. 'I heard all about your trip to Aurum! I can't wait to go there. Me and Mum have applied for visas to visit over half term.'

'It's definitely worth it!' Sophie nodded.

As the others were leaving the canteen shortly afterwards, they passed by Callum Hunt with a group of his friends. He gave her a dark look as she walked past him.

'I hope he's not going to cause trouble this year,' she muttered to Sage.

'We have to be very careful we don't give him or anyone else any clues about our Gifts,' Sage reminded her. 'Even if he is annoying.'

Sophie scowled. 'He's not just annoying, he's a bully.'

'You're right about that, Sophie.' Tracey nodded as they headed up the stairway to their classes.

Sophie swung her rucksack onto her shoulder, giving a cry as her water bottle slipped from it. She watched it turn and twirl through the air, then quickly moved herself to the foot of the stairs in time to catch it before it hit the ground.

'Good catch!' Tracey said admiringly.

'And good luck that there isn't anyone else around right now,' Sage added. 'You can't Transpose here in Earth world, Sophie.'

Sophie banged her forehead. 'It was just an impulsive reaction; I completely forgot where we were! I promise I'll be more careful in future.' She looked around before hurrying back up the stairs.

As the girls continued to their class, no-one noticed Callum stepping out of a nearby doorway. 'I *knew* there was something weird about you,' he murmured to himself. 'And at last, I have proof!'

That afternoon, as Sophie took her books from her locker Callum appeared in the corridor. He glanced about him then seeing there was no-one else nearby, he headed towards her.

'I saw what you did on the stairs earlier.'

Sophie gave him a questioning look.

'The way you moved when you dropped your water bottle.'

'I'm sorry, Callum, you've lost me there.'

'When I tell my friends what I saw…'

'That I dropped my water bottle?'

'That it wasn't normal, the way you moved to the bottom of the stairs to catch it!'

Sophie fixed her eyes on his. 'Callum, what you saw was…'

He shook his head and backed away. 'You're not going to get to me! I saw the stuff you did last year and I'm determined to prove to everyone what you and your weird friends really are!'

He turned on his heel and strode off.

Sophie repeated the conversation to Sage as they walked home that afternoon. 'I don't think anyone would take him seriously but we'd all better be a bit more careful.'

***

'Oh, come on, Callum! You're not still obsessing over that girl, are you?' his friend, Roy, said as they made their way home. 'How could she move that quickly? Most likely, she was downstairs and her friend dropped the water bottle and she caught it.'

'I'm telling you what I saw. And after the things that happened last year, I know it's not normal; she's weird. And it's not just her; some of her friends are the same.'

'What? They all have superpowers?'

'You can laugh now,' Callum said as he headed towards his front door.

His mother was folding laundry into a basket when he entered the kitchen. 'Hi, love. How was your first day as a sixth former?'

'Not bad.' He made himself a cup of coffee and opened the biscuit tin. 'Mum, what do you think about…magic and stuff?'

'Mmm, I don't know about magic but there are lots of things we can't explain. Mind you, The Valley has a history of magic going back centuries. You know the carved stone beside the old crossroads? That's supposed to be the place where the last Valley witch was burnt at the stake.'

There was a knock on the door and Mrs Hunt let in their next-door neighbour, Brenda.

'Sorry to bother you, but I've forgotten my key and Mum's out at the moment. Have you still got the spare?'

Mrs Hunt took it down from a hook on the wall. 'Here you are. Have you time for a cup of tea?'

'I could do with one after the boring afternoon I've had.' She joined them at the table, pulling the biscuit tin towards her. 'I don't blame you staying on at school for another couple of years, Callum. Put off going out into the real world of work for as long as possible.'

'I thought you enjoyed working at The Valley News,' he said. 'You've always wanted to be a reporter.'

'Usually I do, but as the newest reporter, I get stuck with the most boring jobs. Today, I had to attend a demonstration on lacemaking at the Willows Care Home. And somehow, I have to write an interesting article on it!'

'Well, you've only been there a few months. You have to work your way up and show them you can handle the more interesting stories,' Mrs Hunt commented.

'If I could get just one story that would grab people's attention, I'd be made; but there's not a lot that happens here in The Valley.'

'Callum just reminded me of the history of magic in The Valley. That might be worth looking into. There are still lots of shops that sell magic related articles in the town even now. They might be able to tell you a bit about The Valley's history of magic.'

'Most of the shops just sell tacky stuff for the tourists. I suppose I could do a bit of research, though. There's not much else going on at the moment.'

'Maybe you could find out if there are people who can do real magic today,' Callum suggested.

'Now that would be a scoop!'

Callum leaned forward. 'I actually saw some strange stuff at school last year and today I got proof that there's at least one girl who's definitely not normal!' He went on to describe how quickly Sophie had moved to catch her falling water bottle.

'There are probably simple explanations for what you saw, Callum,' his mother commented.

He spread his hands. 'One second, she was halfway up the stairs and the next she was catching her water bottle at the foot of the stairs. Don't tell me that's normal!'

'Your mum's right, it probably *appeared* to happen like that,' Brenda nodded. 'But I'll take a look around and see if I come up with any other evidence of modern day magic.'

Chapter Two

'I never thought it would be so hard to hide my Gift,' Sophie complained to Sage on their way home from school a few weeks later. 'I envy my Mum and Mary and your grandparents going to Aurum this weekend.'

'Nan and Grandad are really looking forward to it.'

'So's Mum, she has her case packed already!'

As Sage pushed open the front door, she saw a brand-new suitcase standing in the hallway.

'That's pretty big for just the weekend, Nan. Is it for both of you?'

'No, that's for my things. I wanted Jim to buy a new suitcase, too, but he insists his old one will do. I don't want the people of Aurum to think we're just the poor relatives here in Earth world, but he won't listen.'

'My bag is fine, Ellen. No-one is going to be scrutinising our luggage, anyway,' Jim said as he came down the stairs.

'Denise said her husband, Paul, will drive us to the portal where Lupe will be waiting to take us to the hotel. She said they are fine about Sophie staying here with you while we're away and that if either of you need anything, you can ask her husband. If you felt nervous and you preferred to stay at their house, Sage...'

'Ellen, Sophie and Sage could be going off to college themselves next year. I'm sure they'll be okay for a weekend on their own,' Jim interrupted.

On Friday afternoon, Sophie and Sage stood by the door as Paul helped Ellen into the car. She turned to call out last minute instructions to the two girls.

'We'll be fine, Nan. Just enjoy yourself,' Sage assured her.

'Where's Jim?' Paul asked.

'Coming. I was just having a last minute chat with Adam and Elvis. They're both on the garden bench. Adam likes to watch the other ants at work on the pathway. Elvis still joins them sometimes. He says he likes to make himself useful, but I suspect it's more to annoy Adam, who can't mix with the other ants anymore. I've warned Elvis to be a bit kinder to Adam; he can make quite hurtful comments about his injured leg. Keep an eye on them, Sage.'

'I will, Grandad' she promised him.

She gave a wave as the car finally drove off. 'I'm glad it's the weekend. What time is Paris coming over tomorrow?'

'He's playing football in the morning, so he said he'd meet us at Alora's. I wonder if there'll be many new Gifteds there tomorrow. I remember what a mess I made of my first Transposing lesson at Alora's! I could move quickly, but I didn't always land where I intended to!'

Sage laughed. 'And you landed on Wilf's lap!'

'Thank goodness I've improved since then! You were much quicker developing your Gifts – first as a Snare; then finding you were also an Animator like your Nan and a Communicator like your Grandad.'

Sage looked serious. 'I'm starting to get used to things, but sometimes I feel quite nervous about being a future Spell master. That's why I've decided to take a gap year before thinking about university. I'll spend some time here in Earth world and some time in Aurum. There's so much I need to learn about both worlds.'

'I'm glad I'm just your average Transposer! Though I envy you being able to orb, being half fae. What does it feel like when you're a tiny glowing sphere?'

'Like being myself but smaller and faster. It's strange how quickly you get used to your Gifts, isn't it?'

'That's true. At first you think you'll never get the hang of it, then suddenly it seems natural.'

***

At Alora's the next morning, Sophie found herself relaxing as she went through the first set of Transposer routines that Rhandra had set for them.

'Sophie you've really come on over the last few months,' Rhandra told her. 'How about you take over as coach for our three newbies while I carry on with our advanced group?'

Sophie smiled at the two boys and girl. 'Okay, we'll start with something easy.'

The taller boy shrugged. 'I've been practising quite a bit since I got my Gift last week. I don't know about Joy and Freddie, but I'm ready for a bit of a challenge, really.'

'Trust Alfie to think he knows it all already.' Joy rolled her eyes.

'Let's start with you, Alfie.' Sophie placed a chair on the far side of the room. 'Take a seat.'

Alfie quickly transposed and landed seated on the chair. The two others completed the first task easily.

Sophie arranged three chairs. 'Now, Alfie, take the middle chair.' He gave a smug smile as he landed neatly on the seat. Joy found this easy, too, but Freddie landed on the floor when it was his turn.

'Don't' worry,' Sophie reassured him. 'I didn't always land where I was aiming for at first.'

'Can we start on the cards, now?' Alfie asked.

Sophie nodded, handing them out. 'You can work at your own pace. It's not a race to begin with, we're more concerned with accuracy at this stage. There are ten moves and you get a point for each move you make successfully. You lose two points if you miss your landing mark.'

She watched as Joy and Freddie carefully considered each move while Alfie raced through the first five moves.

'Don't rush things, Alfie,' she warned him as with a cursory glance at the next card, he launched himself across the room. There was a resounding smack as he hit the door.

'Oh dear.' Joy stifled a giggle as she helped him to his feet. 'You lost two points and gained a large bruise!'

Alfie smiled sheepishly, gingerly touching his forehead. 'Okay, maybe I need to take it a bit slower.'

By the end of the morning session, Sophie was pleased with the progress of her three students. 'You've all worked hard and earned your lunch today,' she said as they made their way to the kitchen.

Most of the others were seated around the long wooden table when she slipped into the seat between Sage and Paris.

'Before we start eating, there's something I have to tell you,' Alora said. 'Petronella, who runs 'Petronella's Potions' in Main Street, called by to speak to me yesterday. She told me that last week Brenda Dickens, a reporter at The Valley News, has been asking questions about modern day magic in The Valley after her neighbour, a young lad, told her he had witnessed strange happenings at his school. This kind of thing has happened a few times before and it will probably all come to nothing as on previous occasions, but we must all be alert.'

Sophie put down the bread roll she was holding. 'Alora, this is all my fault! The boy must be Callum Hunt. Last term, twice I used my Gift to teach him a lesson. I couldn't stand back and watch him bully some of the younger kids. On the first day back this term, I completely forgot where I was and Transposed. I didn't think anyone had seen me, but he cornered me later and told me he had seen what had happened.'

'Why didn't you muddy his memory?' someone asked.

'He didn't give me the chance. He wouldn't hold my gaze.'

Casper cleared his throat. 'Thank you for being so honest, Sophie. I know we're not meant to use our Gifts lightly, but I must admit to…erm…bending the rules a bit sometimes myself. Mainly on the dog next door, actually. It just keeps on and on yapping. I quite often give him some happy thoughts to shut him up. I came close to being caught out by his owner a few times. And had to give her the same treatment.'

'I very nearly got caught in the supermarket last week,' another girl said. 'I couldn't reach the juice I wanted; why do they make these shelves so high, anyway? There wasn't anyone around to help me, so I Animated the bottle; but just at that moment little boy came around the corner. He tried to tell his mother, but of course, she thought he was making it up.'

Alora shook her head as three others began to confess to similar lapses. 'I think we can stop there. I know it is very tempting to use our Gifts but we must always remember how important it is to keep them hidden for the safety of all our community. So, let's make a determined effort to do just that. If anyone hears any more stories about Callum Hunt or anyone else, let me know straight away.'

Chapter Three

'What a weekend!' Ellen said as she took a cup of tea from Sage on Sunday evening. 'Aurum is such a wonderful place, isn't it? The hotel Lupe and Saffron have set up on the Plains is really magnificent, though we didn't spend too much time there, of course. We met a lovely couple from York, June and Bob – he's a Communicator like your grandad and she's a Transposer. A group of us were invited to dine with Mai Lin at the castle on Friday evening – and she showed us around. Your grandad was really taken by the suits of armour and the stained-glass windows in the Great Hall. I rather liked Flavia's old kitchen, though as Mai pointed out, the rooms in her own modern apartment in the castle are much more practical. On Saturday morning, June and I went on a tour of Faeville and then spent the afternoon with Mercy and Peridot in Goblin Glen while Jim and Bob went with Sylvan to Dragon land.

'Those dragons are pretty impressive. Abraxus and Mimosa had a great deal to say about the last few centuries of their lives,' Jim added. 'Don't worry, you're wonderful, too, Jet.' He smiled as the black cat on his lap gave a disgruntled yowl.

'I was a bit wary of our invitation to Delbert's mansion for Sunday lunch,' Ellen continued, 'but I've quite changed my mind about vampires after meeting some of them, especially Vinnie. What a lovely well-mannered girl she is.'

'If you can call someone who is several hundred years old, a girl,' Jim chuckled.

'As vampires don't eat, some of the shifters supplied the food. Chrysta and Petra send their love, they were full of praise for you, Sage and your friends. Saffron came with Lupe, too. I'm so glad they are settling in there.'

'Did you ride in the carriage with Malbeam?' Sage asked. 'And did Ernesto sing for you?'

Ellen shuddered. 'I can't say I enjoyed the bumpy carriage ride but we both enjoyed the entertainment, didn't we Jim? What a lovely voice Ernesto has. Saffron played her harp for us and a group of the younger shifters gave us a very impressive gymnastic demonstration.'

'Mai said she hoped you and your friends could visit for a few days over the half term holiday, if you haven't too much school work,' Jim told Sage.

'I'll make sure I get it done before then!'

***

'I'm not missing out on a trip to Aurum,' Sophie said when she told her the next day. 'I'll keep on top of things in the next two weeks.'

'Me, too,' Sage agreed. 'But what about Paris? It would seem strange to go there without him.'

'I'll see what he says when he phones this evening.'

After the incident with Callum, Sophie deliberately stayed out of his way at school. She felt a sense of dismay when he sat down opposite her in the library one morning.

'I've found out quite a lot about you people.'

Sophie shrugged and continued typing on her laptop.

'Don't you want to know what?' He pulled a notebook out of his bag and opened it. 'The Valley has a history of witches and magic that go back several hundred years. Do you know that the carved stone beside the old crossroads…?'

'…is supposed to be the place where the last Valley witch was burnt at the stake,' Sophie completed his sentence. 'Yes, everyone knows that. They use a picture of it on the town website. Haven't you seen the tourists taking selfies next to it?'

'Hmm. Did you know that The Valley has the widest range of herb plants in all of the country?'

'About two hundred plant species grow here that can't be found anywhere else in the UK.'

'And how do you know that?'

'The town website has an article about the famous Kitchen Nursery.'

'Oh. Well, Jessica Godwin's grandmother, who runs Petronella's Potions, told me that all her potions are the real thing. While I was there, Roy's older brother came in to buy a good luck potion. He said the last one had helped him win at the races the day before.'

'I didn't know Roy's brother was a gambler.'

'That's not the point! Petronella insisted that her potions are genuine magic.'

'She would say that, wouldn't she? How could she sell stuff if she told everyone it was all fake?' Sophie packed away her books and laptop and stood up. 'Let me know if you find out any other ground breaking news. And let me know if the good luck potion works for Roy's brother again. I might try some myself!'

'I need hard evidence!' Callum muttered to himself as he watched her walk away. 'If only I had a video of what happened the other day. That's it! I need to collect photographic evidence.'

He kept his eye on Sophie and her friends in the canteen that lunchtime.

'It would be good if she could perform magic on the canteen food, wouldn't it?' Roy joked as he put down his tray and sat down beside him. He turned to another boy and was soon engrossed in a conversation about an up-and-coming football match.

Callum frowned as he saw a girl from his year group, who seemed upset, talking to Sage. She glanced around before leading the girl outside. He tossed his half-eaten lunch into a bin and followed them. The two girls were sitting in a sheltered spot, talking quietly. Every now and again, Sage would spread her hands and seemed to grasp something from the air; then the girl imitated her. Slowly, the younger girl seemed to become calmer. He pulled out his mobile and videoed the strange interaction. Finally, the two girls stood up and headed towards him. He drew back out of sight behind the concrete steps.

'That's all you have to do; just relax and you'll be fine,' he heard Sage say to the younger girl.

'I can do it here with you, but when I'm in class...'

'What do you have this afternoon?'

'Geography.'

'Fiona is in your class, isn't she? Let's go and find her. She'll help you. Don't worry, you'll soon be on top of this. I remember when I first...' Her voice faded as they turned a corner.

Callum hit the stop button on his mobile. 'On top of what? When she first what?'

'Well, it's not exactly hard evidence I'm afraid, Callum,' Brenda told him that evening after watching his video. 'All they're doing is moving their hands about.'

'But what did Sage mean by "she found it hard at first" and that "she'd soon be on top of it"?' Callum persisted.

'School work? A sport? It could be anything,' Brenda suggested. 'I didn't get many original thoughts from any of the magicky type of shops in town either. They all said they were the real thing, without concrete evidence to prove it. The chief editor wasn't impressed with the idea for an article on modern day magic; he said it's been done too many times before; so there's no story there, I'm afraid.'

Callum scowled as she went into her house. 'I *know* I'm right and somehow; I'm going to *prove* it!'

Chapter Four

'I'm so pleased you can come too, Paris,' Sophie smiled as the three friends made their way to the portal at the start of their half term break.

'Yes, luckily, I got a week's study leave. I'll have quite a bit to catch up on when we get back.'

Sylvan was waiting for them as they stepped onto the grassy plateau in Aurum.

'It's so good to see you all again. Mai and Saffron are waiting for us at the castle.' He turned and gave a shrill whistle. Sophie beamed as a dark shape in the sky grew larger as it approached them. 'Sage and I can orb; how about you two ride over on Mimosa?'

'A ride on a dragon! It's *so* good to be back in Aurum!' Sophie said.

A short while later, they were all seated around the kitchen table in the castle.

'Mum and Mary haven't stopped talking about their trip,' Sophie turned to Saffron. 'She said the new hotel you set up is very impressive.'

'Yes, it's been pretty busy since it opened. Luckily, we have quite a few young fae and goblins happy to work there. They enjoy hearing stories about Earth world. Some of the fae are planning trips there themselves.'

'Nan and Grandad had a great time here. Grandad loved the dragons,' Sage said. 'He's planning a return visit with Axel in the near future.'

Mai nodded. 'Yes, he really enjoyed his visit to Dragon land.'

'I'm hoping to get the chance to take Jim and Axel to Lilac Brae,' Sylvan added. 'Being Communicators, I think the wood nymphs will accept them.'

They chatted for a while until Saffron yawned and stood up. 'I'd better get back home. We've an early start tomorrow. Come over and see the hotel tomorrow morning. And you can call by and see Peridot. She's looking forward to seeing you again.'

'I'd better go, too,' Sylvan said. 'I've training until mid-morning, then I'm free for the rest of the day. I'll join you at the hotel.' He gave Sage a wink as he left.

'I often look around in Earth world and think how lucky I am to be Gifted, to lead such an incredible life,' Sophie said as they cleared the table. 'Then I think of you, Mai. You travelled all the way alone from China to England when you were even younger than we are now; you must have some amazing stories to tell.'

'Tell us about your childhood, Mai. Are your parents sorcerers? Do you see them at all?' Sage continued.

'Yes, you told us it was a story for another time; maybe this is the time,' Paris added.

'It's a long story, so make yourselves comfortable.' Mai smiled as they all settled themselves down on the soft armchairs and sofas.

'I grew up in a tiny village in China with my adopted parents, Jul and Peng. Jul told me how one cold winter night she heard a cry coming from the garden. Peng said it was just the wind rushing through the trees, but when Jul ventured outside, she found me in a wooden crib near the front door. There was already a scattering of snow on the blanket I was wrapped in.'

'Did she see who had left you there?' Sophie said.

Mai shook her head. 'She looked around but there was no sign of anyone so she carried me inside and sat with me near the fire. She said my hands and feet were like blocks of ice. Peng found a dry blanket and warmed up some milk for me. He said I could stay for the night but the next day he would take me to Chen, the elder of the village, and he'd know what to do with me They were very poor and my father was reluctant to have another mouth to feed, especially as they were both getting on in years and would find it difficult to bring up a child. But luckily for me, Jul had always wanted a child and had already decided that I was going to be part of their family. She said the gods had placed me outside their door that night. When I was fed and changed, she put me into Peng's arms while she sorted out clean, dry bedding for me. As he watched over me, I clung to his finger with my tiny hand and smiled up at him. Jul said that was the moment that I won over Peng and he became my new father. That same night they gave me my name, Mai after Peng's mother and Lin after Jul's mother. So, I became Mai Lin.'

'Later known as Merlin,' Sophie commented.

'Did you every discover anything about your birth mother and father?' Paris asked her.

'Not for many years, and not from Jul and Peng. All I had of my previous life was the blanket I was wrapped in when they found me. I would not go to sleep at night without it. Let me show it to you.'

Mai disappeared into her bedroom and returned a few moments later with a small cotton cover. Inside was a worn yellow blanket which she carefully spread out on the sofa. Ghostly images began to appear. A woman who looked very much like Mai herself smiled down at the infant she cradled in her arms. She caught a tiny flailing hand and brought it to her lips as the child laughed in delight. Mai had a sad smile on her own face as she looked at her mother. 'It was many years before I understood its true significance. I'd always assumed my parents could see the images, too; but, of course, they couldn't, they weren't Gifted.'

'A beautiful memory of your mother,' Sage whispered. 'You can see how much she loved you.'

'And your adopted parents seemed very kind,' Paris added. 'What was your life like as a child?'

'Life was hard but full of love. And there were plenty of happy times, too. I was quite a tomboy when I was young. Several times I got my parents into an argument with the village elder, Chen.' She shuddered. 'He was a horrible man!'

'What did they think about you being Gifted?' Sophie asked.

'They didn't realise I was different to the other children. I didn't myself until I was twelve years old. I remember that day very clearly. It was very cold; Papa was out looking for work on the larger farms nearby and I was collecting wood for the fire. I had just added to the small pile by the door when Papa arrived home, empty handed. He looked so dejected, but Mama was doing her best to stay optimistic. Let me show you...'

She turned to the wall and spread her hands. Slowly an image of a small hut appeared. Two people were talking:

'Don't worry, Peng,' Jul said, patting her husband's shoulder. 'Something will turn up. Tonight, we have two eggs and some rice. Mai Lin, you go and milk the goat and we can all have a cup of fresh milk. I'm sure there are others who have less than we do.'

She was still chatting as Mai Lin made her way to the shed. She patted the goat's head and placed the bucket underneath her.

'You don't have much for us today, do you, Rona?' she sighed as the slow trickle of milk stopped, hardly covering the base of the bucket. She patted the animal's rump. 'Never mind, Rona, you've done your best.'

Suddenly, without warning, the goat stepped back and knocked the bucket over and the precious milk spread across the ground. Mai Lin felt a wave of panic wash over her.

'It's okay; it's okay. I will fix everything.' A shiver ran through her entire body as she stretched out her hands and watched the bucket right itself and the spilt milk flow back into it. She stood motionless until the goat nudged her hand. Absently patting the animal's head, she murmured, 'I did fix it, didn't I?' In a daze, she picked up the bucket and walked back to the house in silence. She decided that her eyesight had played tricks on her; she must have caught the bucket before it overturned. Her imagination was running away with her.

'Not much milk tonight,' Peng commented as Mai Lin shared the milk between three cups.

'It's better than nothing,' his wife replied.

'The goat is getting old, past her useful days. Perhaps she'll serve us better in a stew,' Peng continued.

Mai Lin was horrified. 'No, Papa! We could never eat Rona! She's part of our family.'

Her father shook his head. 'We can't afford to feed her if she's not useful. We can barely afford to feed ourselves at the moment.'

'But…' Mai Lin began.

Jul placed a hand over hers and gave Peng a warning look. 'Let's not talk about this now. Let's enjoy the food we have.'

The next evening, Mai Lin felt tears sting her eyes as once again the goat yielded very little milk.

'Rona, you must try and give us more milk even though you're getting old and tired, please, for your own sake.' She ran her hands along the goat's rough coat and narrowed her eyes. 'I wish I could give you some of my energy.' Her eyes widened as she saw a gentle orange light pass from her hands into the body of the animal.

She returned to the house as her mother was stirring a few shrivelled vegetables into a thin gruel boiling over the fire. 'Mai Lin, did you find any eggs today?'

'Only one; but Rona gave us nearly half a bucket of milk today, Mama. She smiled, pouring the milk into a large jug.

'Perhaps our luck has changed and your father will have found work today,' Jul commented. However, the expression on his face as Peng pushed open the door a short while later, told a different story. Jul continued to chatter with a false brightness as they sat down to the evening meal. She exchanged an anxious look with her husband as there was a sharp rap on the door.

Mai Lin stood up and opened it. Chen, the village elder, stepped inside.

'I'm so sorry to disturb your meal, but I was hoping thar you would have called by earlier this afternoon, Peng, to pay this month's rent.,

'Please, sit down, Chen. Would you like a cup of fresh milk?' Jul began. 'And you're most welcome to a bowl of soup.'

Chen picked up the cup and nodded appreciatively but turned up his nose at the thin gruel. 'I also wanted to talk to you about the behaviour of young Mai Lin, here. How this young lady has been indulging in horseplay with the village boys.'

'What?' she exclaimed indignantly. 'I have never...'

Chen leaned forward, waving a finger in her face. 'You were seen on no less than three occasions joining in with martial art contests with four young lads near the water pump. Don't try and deny it!'

'Oh, that.' Peng smiled. 'Mai Lin is showing great skill in martial arts. Why only yesterday, she managed to beat young Gan by several points...'

'You mean you condone such unladylike behaviour?' Chen's eyebrows drew together. He turned to Mai Lin. 'How old are you, young *lady*?'

'Twelve years old.'

He nodded slowly. 'I say this as I only have Mai Lin's interest at heart. In a year or two, you will be seeking a husband for her. What man wants a woman who does not know how to deport herself in public? Especially with such a background as she has and, we must admit, her dowry won't be of a size to attract many suitors.'

Peng's breath quickened. 'Let me tell you...'

Jul patted his hand. 'Thank you for your advice, Chen. We will bear this in mind. Our daughter's welfare is of the upmost concern to us.'

'Good.' Chen stood up and pulled a thick cloak around his shoulders. 'Well, if you can just let me have this month's rent, I'll leave you to your meal.'

Peng did not meet his eye as he placed a pile of coins in his hand.

The older man gave a short laugh. 'This is four pieces; the rent, as you well know, is six pieces.'

'Yes, I will pay you the other two pieces as soon as I get work, Chen. I'm hoping...'

Chen shook his head. 'You live in my property; you pay the rent on time.' He held up a hand as Peng began to speak. 'There are plenty of people waiting to rent a house like this. If you can't afford the very reasonable rent I ask; may I suggest you find a new place to live.'

The silence that followed was broken by a gentle tap on the door and Yet-Sen, the village scholar and tutor, stepped inside. 'Good evening, everyone. Ah Chen, good evening to you, too. I have come to ask a favour of you, Jul. I wonder if you and your daughter could come and help out for a few weeks at our house. My sister, Suyin, has slipped and twisted her ankle. We've no-one to cook and clean and fetch the shopping from the market. In fact, if you would be so good as to oblige, I could make an advance payment tonight – would two pieces be sufficient?'

'We'd be more than happy to help out, Yet-Sen,' she said as he placed the two pieces in her hand.

'Well, that's a great relief to myself and my sister. We'll see you tomorrow morning.' He turned towards the door and then stopped. 'I nearly forgot, Peng. I was talking to Huang, who has the farm north of the river. He is looking for workers to mend the fences brought down in last week's storm. I gave him your name.'

'Oh, that's great news,' Peng stammered. 'I'll go and speak to him this evening.'

As Yet-Sen walked off into the darkness, Jul held out the two pieces to Chen. 'That's the rent paid up in full, Chen.'

'Chen was a horrible man!' Sophie said as the images faded from the wall. 'What was it like at Yet-Sen's house? I hope he and his sister were nicer people.'

'They were lovely. I didn't realise what a difference they were going to make to my life.' She turned back to the wall as new images appeared.

Chapter Five

Mai Lin felt herself cower under Suyin's critical gaze the next morning when Yet-Sen ushered herself and her mother into the main room. The stout old woman looked formidable as she lay back in an overstuffed armchair with a heavily bandaged foot propped up on a stool.

'You can start off in here. I didn't even get the chance to clear up our breakfast dishes when I took a tumble yesterday,' Suyin told Jul. 'The young girl can fetch some water from the pump. But don't spend all morning giggling with your friends down there now.'

When she placed the full bucket in a corner of the room a short while later, Mai Lin smiled to find the two women chatting together happily.

'Don't just stand there catching flies!' Suyin reprimanded her. 'Pick up that broom and the cloth over there and make a start on tidying Yet-Sen's study. But don't move any of his books or papers - he's very fussy about his things.'

Mai Lin stood in the centre of the study and looked around her in awe at the shelves full of books. On a large table in the centre of the room, a leather-bound book lay open. She traced the inked letters that curled across the page. She picked up a quill that lay beside an ink pot beside it. Placing it gently back on the table she lifted the inkpot and stared at the dark blue liquid inside the glass container.

'I'd *love* to be able to read and write,' she whispered longingly. A movement out of the corner of her eye made her lose her concentration for a moment and the glass container slipped from her grasp, scattering ink across the table. Her hand flew to her mouth.

'I must fix this! I must fix this!' she muttered to herself. Taking a steady breath, she stared at the glass bottle and narrowed her eyes. The bottle rose and twisted and turned through the air, collecting droplets of ink as it travelled, until it was back in her hands with no evidence of the earlier accident.

'Well done, my dear.' The voice behind her made her jump. A hand shot out and grabbed the ink bottle from her which was wobbling precariously.

'I don't know if the undo spell would work twice,' Yet-Sen chuckled, returning the inkpot to the table.

'Spell?' Mai Lin whispered.

Yet-Sen raised his hands and the papers arranged themselves in neat piles on the table while the books flew back to the shelves. 'I'm just showing off really. What else can you do?'

Mai Lin shook her head wordlessly.

'Well, there was the goat. Giving her some of your own energy is pretty impressive for a beginner; especially as most of us don't get our Gifts until we reach sixteen.'

Mai Lin looked own at her hands. 'How do you know about Rona?' She looked up at him. 'What gifts? What do you mean by "us"?'

Yet-Sen sat down in the large wooden chair and motioned for her to sit down opposite him. 'People who can cast spells, Mai Lin. Your family, your birth parents' families have a long history of magic. When your mother left you here, she asked me to watch over you and to guide you in your studies.'

'You met my mother? What was she like? Why did she leave me here? Where did she go? Where is she now?'

'You have much to learn about your family and your Gifts. Little by little, over the next few weeks I will answer all your questions. And I will teach you to read and write. You will need these skills in the future. But it will mean a lot of hard work.'

Mai Lin's eyes shone. 'I can work *really* hard.'

Yet-Sen's thick eyebrows drew together. 'Yes, I know you can. I will speak to your mother, Jul. But we will have to keep your learning a secret for now. A village girl educated beyond her station could be seen as a threat by some. Especially one who is a match for the village male champion in martial arts.'

'Papa and I agreed that it is better if I'm not seen taking part in those games anymore.'

'Oh?'

'So we practise together in the scrubland away from the village where no-one can see us and be offended.'

Yet-Sen gave a deep chuckle as they exchanged a grin.

Jul looked alarmed later that morning as Yet-Sen explained his plan to teach her daughter to read and write. 'I'm sure it's most kind of you to offer, Yet-Sen, but what man will take a wife who is cleverer than he is himself? Peng and I are not young and we need to know that Mai Lin will have a good man to look after her when we are no longer here.'

'Knowledge is a great gift, Jul. And I am sure Mai Lin will use her knowledge wisely. But I do understand your fears and I have suggested we keep this to ourselves for the moment.'

'Please, Mama,' Mai Lin begged. 'I promise I won't let anyone know.'

Jul sighed as she reluctantly agreed. In her heart she hoped that her daughter's thirst for knowledge would be short lived.

By the end of the second week, Suyin was able to walk about once more and she asked Jul to accompany her to the market one morning.

'You won't be needing us soon,' Jul said with a sad smile.

'Oh, I couldn't do without you now.'

'Indeed,' Yet-Sen agreed. 'And I would like to continue to teach Mai Lin. She is an extremely bright girl and a quick learner.'

Jul blushed. 'She is indeed. Peng and I are so proud of her.'

Yet-Sen motioned for Mai Lin to sit down opposite him as the two women headed for the village.

'They should be gone for a while. Suyin is anxious to catch up with the village gossip first hand. That gives me a chance to tell you more about your background, Mai Lin.'

Mai Lin leaned forward and nodded eagerly.

'No doubt you have heard the story of how you were found outside Peng's door on a cold, snowy night.'

'Yes, I still have the blanket I was wrapped in. It has a sort of picture…but no-one else can see it.'

'Only Gifted ones can see the memory your mother left for you, my child.'

'People who can do spells?'

The old man nodded. 'After your mother, Hoshika, left you on Peng's doorstep, she came here. She was distraught at having to leave you, but she knew it was the only way to keep you safe.'

'Safe from whom?'

'Your uncle, Kano. He is a wicked man who uses his Gifts entirely for his own benefit.'

'But why would my uncle want to harm me?'

'Kano was jealous of your mother. As she grew up and her Gifts were revealed, it was clear that she was destined to be a much more powerful sorcerer than he was. When she married your father, Zeyo, who was also a powerful sorcerer, all Gifted ones believed that their child, you, Mai Lin, was destined be one of the greatest sorcerers of our times.'

He went on to explain how Zeyo had died in a tragic accident while out hunting with Kano. Kano took his sister and her young child into his house, vowing to care for them. At first, Hoshika was grateful to her brother as she mourned the loss of her husband, but after a while she began to find his constant presence stifling.

Yet-Sen shook his head. 'When she heard him turning a friend of hers away from the door without letting her speak to them, she became angry. He insisted he was only thinking of her welfare; but the feeling of unease did not leave her. She packed up her belongings and asked him to order her stableman to be ready to take her home the next morning. Kano tried to persuade her to stay for a while longer, but eventually agreed to her wishes.

'As she prepared for bed that night, a young kitchen maid brought a drink to her room. Her hand shook as she placed the tray on the table. Glancing around, she put a finger to her lips and tipped the contents of the cup into a plant nearby. Hoshika watched in horror as the green leaves shrivelled before her eyes. The maid explained that Kano planned to kill her and keep the child with him to use her future powers for his own ends.

'That night, with the girl's help, she crept from the house and summoned Martej and asked him to take her to a place of safety. Martej and his donkey, Kosmo, are often called upon to carry people to safety. He brought you and your mother here to me. Hoshika knew that Kano could not track you down until your Gifts were revealed, but she knew he could easily trace her through her Gifts. That meant that she could not keep you with her. As Gifted myself, it was also dangerous to keep you here, so I took you to Peng and Jul. I knew they would be good parents for you and I could keep an eye on you until I was able to be of use to you.'

'And my mother…?'

Yet-Sen shook his head. 'She…she was heartbroken; first she had lost her husband and now she had to give up the child she loved. She…asked Martej to take her to the mists…to After world…'

Tears glistened in Mai Lin's eyes. 'My mother did love, me. She didn't abandon me...'

Yet-Sen nodded. 'Yes, your mother loved you very much.'

Chapter Six

As the weeks turned to months and the months into years, Mai Lin learnt so much from Yet-Sen; reading and writing Chinese and Latin.

'Latin is a language in which you will be able to communicate with many other Gifted ones from all four corners of the earth,' he told her.

'But when will I ever meet people from all four corners of the earth?'

His face grew serious. 'Before too long, you will be ready for the next stage.'

A thirteen-year-old Mai Lin was laying the table for the evening meal at Yet-Sen's house as Suyin fussed over a pot of soup on the hob.

'It just needs a little more pepper, then it will be perfect.'

Jul shook her head. 'Why can't you just admit that it is perfectly fine as it is? Always, it's "you need another bay leaf..." or "a little less salt..."'

'Jul, why can't you accept good advice? I've been cooking for many more years than you have. Mai Lin, put some soup in the small pot to take home with you. Your father will be home from work soon and he'll be glad of something hot.'

A short while later, as they made their way home Mai smiled listening to her mother grumbling about Suyin's constant needless advice; well aware that the two women had grown as close as sisters over the years.

They were surprised to find Peng already home when they pushed open the door.

'You're home early today. Is everything going well?' Jul asked him.

He rubbed his face. 'I felt a bit off colour, so Huang told me to get an early night. I think he was ready to stop work himself, to be honest.'

'I'll heat up the soup for you, Papa,' Mai Lin said.

'I think I'll just have a lie down for a while,' he replied, pulling the thin blanket around his shoulders.

'You're not going to work today and that's final, Peng,' Jul told her husband as he struggled to get out of bed the next morning. 'You're not well. You didn't eat any of the soup Suyin sent for you last night.'

'But if I don't work, I don't get paid.'

'I sent Mai Lin to Huang to tell him you need a day or two in bed. He'll understand.'

'He'll find someone else and that'll be my job gone!' Her husband protested weakly as he lay back against the pillow.

At that moment, Mai Lin stepped inside, closing the door against the cold wind.

'What did Huang say?' Peng asked her.

'He didn't say anything. He's very ill himself. His wife is very worried and has sent for the healer. Two of the other workers are ill, too. I met Gan on the way home and he says his mother has been in bed for three days and is getting worse each day. They say the winter sickness has hit the village.'

She noticed the look of fear that flashed across her mother's face as Peng gave a rasping cough.

'Mai Lin, you must go to Yet-Sen yourself today while I stay here with your father.'

Suyin took one look at the young girl's face when she arrived at the house.

'The winter sickness.' She nodded as Mai Lin told her about her father. She took down several dried herbs from the kitchen shelf and crumbled them into a small calico bag and placed it into her hands. 'Go home and take this with you. It's a blend of healing herbs to reduce fever. Make a paste with hot water and rub it onto Peng's chest.'

Mai Lin thanked her and clutched it tightly as she hurried home. She pushed open the door to find Jul sitting by Peng's bedside, gently stroking one of his hands. His eyes were closed as he struggled for each breath.

'Mama, Suyin gave me this. It will help reduce Papa's fever. I will make up a poultice.' She quickly made up the paste and watched as her mother gently spread it on his shivering chest.

For the next few hours, they both sat by his bedside until Mai Lin found herself drifting off to sleep. A husky voice made her sit up.

'Jul, I was truly blessed to find such a good wife as you. Then the gods smiled on us again when they brought Mai Lin to our door.'

Jul put a cup of water to his lips as he began to cough. 'Hush now, save your strength to get yourself well again.'

He shook his head and held out a hand to them. 'You must look after each other now.'

'No, Papa, you'll get better.'

With a slight shake of his head, Peng lent back on the pillow and gave his last breath. For the next hour, all Mai Lin could hear was the sobbing of her mother. The first light of day was visible in the sky when Jul finally stood up and pulled the sheet over her husband's face.

A dark cloud hung over the village over the next few weeks as Mai Lin and Jul along with a number of their friends and neighbours arranged the burials of many of the villagers. Just as the terrible winter sickness seemed to have run its course, Mai was awoken one morning by a rasping cough. Jul sat on the edge of her bed, shaking as she tried to pull herself to her feet.

Two days later, Mai felt a cold numbness as she stood once again by the graves of both her parents. She was hardly aware of those around her as she made her way back to her lonely home. Dishes of food were brought and left untouched on the table. Suyin offered to stay with her for a while, but Mai Lin shook her head. Even the offer of books by Yet-Sen failed to rouse her from her grief.

One evening a few days later, there was a firm rap on the door. Without waiting for her to respond, Chen entered.

'Mai Lin, I realise you have suffered a great loss and that you must be finding it hard to find motivation in these sad times.' He sat down opposite her at the rough wooden table. 'There are many others who are also suffering as you do this winter. You must realise that we all have to move on. As the village chief, I feel it is my duty to help you to find a way forward and be able to enjoy a comfortable living.'

Mai pushed her hair back from her eyes. 'I will go back to work with Yet-Sen soon so I can pay the rent I owe you, Chen, if you could just give me a little more time.'

He gave a sad smile, shaking his head slowly. 'Mai Lin, don't be deluded. Your work with Yet-Sen will not make you enough to pay the rent owing, let alone feed you.'

'I can find extra work, maybe helping out at the market, or on one of the farms…'

'No. Who will employ a young girl when there are strong, young men available for work?' He stood up and paced around the room. 'I *would* suggest a husband. You are a fine looking young woman; but with your background…a foundling, no dowry; even *I* would be hard pushed to find you a match.' He sat down again and put his hands over hers. 'There is however a way you can stay here, in your own home…if you accept my …protection…'

Seeing the look of naked lust in his eyes, Mai Lin pulled her hands free of his and stood up, the wooden stool clattering to the ground behind her. 'No! Never!'

His face hardened. 'Don't dismiss my offer so quickly! Do you really have a choice?' He walked around the table, backing her up against the wall. 'Would you rather take your luck on the streets? How long would a young girl like yourself last? There are men out there who would take you and offer nothing in return.'

Mai recoiled in disgust as his face neared hers. He gave a harsh laugh as she pushed her hands against his chest. A surge of anger washed over her as she stared at her hands. Seconds later, Chen drew back abruptly, clutching his chest where two burning handprints were visible.

'You...witch...daughter of the devil!' he screamed as she gazed down at her two glowing hands. He stumbled to the door still screaming. Several villagers had come outside on hearing the commotion, all watching in horror as Chen continued tearing at the welts on his chest. He pointed a shaky finger at Mai Lin as she appeared in the doorway, hands still glowing. 'She's a witch! *She* is the one who has brought the sickness to our village! Fetch the holy man!'

Mai Lin ran back inside the house and pushed the door closed, pulling the table in front of it although no-one had dared come close. She stood trembling, staring at her hands, which had now returned to their normal colour.

'They will kill me. I must get away from here.' She flung her few clothes into a bag and grabbed the cotton case that contained her mother's blanket, then slipped through the narrow window at the back of the house.

'Come, child.' Yet-Sen was standing nearby. He quickly led her through the village garden plots to his own house where Suyin was waiting.

'Have you alerted Martaj?' Yet-Sen asked her.

'He'll be waiting at the crossroads.' She took Mai Lin's hands. 'My poor child. That awful man...'

'He didn't get a chance to harm her. It was as I said; her powers saved her. I didn't have to intervene myself,' Yet-Sen interrupted.

His sister gave a sigh of relief as she pulled Mai Lin inside the house. 'Quickly, put these on,' she said, shaking out a pair of leather trousers and a jerkin. 'They may be a bit big, but we didn't think you would need them so soon.

'But these are boy's clothes.'

'Yes, it is safer to travel alone as a young man than as a young woman.'

'Why does this jacket have so many tiny pockets?' Mai asked as she pulled the jerkin on.

'They are to keep your special things safe.'

Yet-Sen held out the leather-bound book that he and Mai Lin had been studying over the past few years. 'This is yours now. You are destined for great things, Mai Lin. It has been an honour to be the first to help you on your pathway.'

Suyin pointed to the jerkin. 'That first pocket is for your first book.'

Mai Lin was amazed to watch the book shrinking to fit inside one of the many pockets.

'Where will I go?' she asked.

'You will stay with Leisha, a friend of ours who lives in India. She will guide you in the next stage of your learning.'

The old woman hugged her in a tight embrace. 'May the elements embrace you and guide you through your future life. You will always be in our hearts, Mai Lin. Remember that when life is harsh.' She put a bag in the girl's hands. 'There's enough food and water to keep you going for a day or two.'

A short while later, Yet-Sen and Mai Lin stood at the crossroads. Mai Lin looked around at the familiar scenery. There was the old tree where she had pitted her martial arts skills against Gan. How many times over the years had she led Rona up the muddy pathway to graze on the sparse clumps of grass further up the hillside? The sound of creaking wooden wheels and the clip of hooves brought her back to the present. A rough, wooden cart pulled by an aged donkey appeared. The driver, an old man, gave them a toothless smile. 'Greetings. Who is my passenger today?'

'Mai...Merlin,' Mai said.

'Welcome aboard, Merlin.' His eyes crinkled as she climbed up beside him.

'Take good care of her, Martej. She is very precious to us.'

The old man laughed. 'She is in safe hands with me, Yet-Sen.' He flicked the reins gently. 'Let's go, Kosmo.'

Mai Lin bit back the tears that threatened to spill as she settled herself on the rough wooden seat beside Martej. Her eyes looked out at the only home she had ever known, long after the figure of Yet-Sen had disappeared into the darkness behind them.

***

Mai Lin shook her head as the images on the wall faded. 'And that was the start of my travels.'

'You must have been terrified,' Paris said. 'How long did it take you to get to your destination?'

'A few days. I was scared at first, but if Yet-Sen and Suyin trusted Martej, I knew I could, too.'

'Did you meet anyone on the journey?' Sophie asked.

'We did, but the strange thing was, they couldn't see us. Martej told me while the cart was moving, we were invisible.'

'Wasn't Martej the man who had taken your mother to Yet-Sen?' Sage said. 'Did he tell you about her?'

'I asked him, but he said his name said it all. In his language Martej means "forget". He never remembered any of his passengers, where they came from or their destinations. This meant they were safe from their pursuers. And he was safe from people questioning him.'

'How long did you stay in India? What was it like?' Sophie asked.

'How many other places did you visit on the way to England?' Paris added.

Mai stood up. 'Come with me.'

She led them up to the turret room which held the shelves of books and the display of crosses. She picked up the book filled with Chinese writing and placed it on the table.

'This was the first of my collection, from Yet-Sen.' She turned and chose another book from the shelf and laid it next to the first one. 'The second one is in Hindi, a leaving present from Leisha, in India.'

Sage, Sophie and Paris watched as she scanned the shelf and placed five more books alongside the first two. Mai put her hand on the third book. 'Book three, from Omar in Arabia. Book four, from Liriope in Greece. Book five, from Delbert in Romania.' She smiled as she saw their expressions. 'Yes, the Delbert you know. Book six from Gautier in France and finally book seven from Kelrug in England. There it is, the history of my travels and of the great teachers I met on the way.'

'Did you learn different skills from each one?' Sage asked.

'Mainly, although some skills overlapped.' Mai put her hand on the second book. 'I stayed with Leisha, for five months. She is a healing master. During my time with her, I learnt how to mix medicines and potions, deliver babies, mend broken limbs and cure a fever. And plait a love charm!'

She placed her hand on the third book. 'When it was time for me to leave, Martej took me to a port on the west coast of India. He spoke to the captain of one of the merchant vessels setting sail for Arabia. It was both exciting and terrifying! I had never seen a ship before or the sea! When we disembarked in the Arabian port, I could hardly stand upright on firm land. I sat down for a while in the busy market square and looked around me in wonder. The two quiet villages I had stayed in in China and India were nothing like this. There was so much colour, so much noise, so many people! I felt very nervous, and had started to worry that I was in the wrong place when a young couple came up to me and addressed me by name. They introduced themselves as Zia and Babur. They said they worked for Omar and that he was expecting me.'

'And you trusted these strangers?' Sophie raised her eyebrows.

'I was wary at first, but Zia pulled out a mirror from her bag and handed it to me. An image of Yet-Sen appeared. He smiled and told me Zia and Babur were good friends and that all was well, so I felt it was safe to go with them. They took me through the town up the hillside to a huge marble palace; the home of Omar, where I was to spend the next six months. I learnt so many amazing things! The first was that Zia and Babur were genii.'

'Did they live in lamps?' Paris asked.

'No, they preferred the comforts of the palace. Often, when Babur became too mischievous, Omar would threaten to banish them to their lamps.' She smiled. 'But he never carried out his threat.'

'What else did you learn in Arabia?' Sage said.

'Omar taught me how to charm snakes and tame tigers and how to levitate myself and others – even non-Gifted people. I became skilful at sword fighting and fire throwing. Zia taught me spells to protect myself, like conjuring up a swarm of bees and making it rain frogs. Babur taught me how to freeze an enemy or a wild animal in their tracks, usually involving the use of brightly coloured powders or loud explosions. Some days we caused havoc in the market square. That's when Omar would get angry, as he was the one who had to calm people down and muddy the memories.

'One morning, Omar told me that Martej had come to take me to my next place of learning.'

'Were you sad to leave your friends?' Paris asked.

She nodded. 'I was very sad to say goodbye to them. But we agreed that we would meet up again in the future, when my learning was complete. And we have met up a few times over the years.'

Mai put her hand on the fourth book. 'Martej took me from Arabia to Greece where I spent nearly seven months with Liriope, a water nymph in a quiet glade deep in the countryside. At first, I thought I would find it dull after my stay in Arabia, but I soon learned to love the peace and the creatures that she introduced me to – wood nymphs, air nymphs, centaurs and unicorns. The only ones who were not so peaceful were the satyrs; they reminded me of Babur! Liriope taught me how to communicate with all kinds of animals.

'My next teacher was completely different to the soft-spoken nymph. Martej took me to Romania, into a dense, dark forest and left me outside two huge iron gates. As his cart disappeared, the gates swung open and a small, black carriage drew up beside me. The driver jumped down and opened the coach door for me.'

Sophie nodded. 'Ah, it was Malbeam, to take you to Delbert, wasn't it?'

'No, it wasn't Malbeam; it was one of Delbert's earlier drivers. I must admit I was terrified as we drove up to a huge black castle and stopped outside the foreboding wooden doors. I had never met a vampire before and knew very little about them. An old woman came to the door and led me into a large reception room. Everything seemed so dark, the wood panelled walls, the dim candle lit chandelier in the middle of a high, yellowing ceiling. At one end of the huge room there were two black, leather sofas near a fire blazing in the hearth, but the room still felt very cold. The woman motioned for me to sit down and she left me there. After a while, the door creaked open and Delbert appeared. He gave a brief nod and introduced himself. He seemed so cold and arrogant that my spirits sank at the thought of spending the next few months with him in that gloomy place.'

'Yes, Delbert can be quite intimidating at first, can't he?' Paris agreed as the two girls nodded.

'I soon got used to his ways and he taught me so much about vampires, shifters and wraiths. And how they aren't really that scary at all. I found the darkness of the house quite depressing, until one of the shifters, a girl around my own age, taught me how to ride a horse and we would go for long rides across the countryside. We never ventured into any of the villages or towns as many of the local people were afraid of Delbert and his acquaintances, although over the years they had built up a quiet tolerance of each other. Later, Delbert spoke to me about creating Aurum, when his people had had enough of persecution by ignorant humans.

'After spending six months with Delbert, Martej once again appeared and transported me to Gautier in France. Gautier was a sorcerer who was a bit too much into dark magic for my taste, but I knew I had to learn about it even if it was just to defend myself against it. For five months, I lived in a crumbling chateau high in the mountains and spent my days with witches, goblins and fae that had turned against humans because of their cruel treatment over the centuries. Not a very happy group! I was relieved when I was on my way to England with Martej.'

'England, your final destination!' Sage said.

'Whereabouts in England did you land, Mai?' Paris asked.

'In Camelot, near where you live now.'

'Did you know that this was the end of your travels?' he continued.

'Not at first, but I realised it very soon after my arrival.'

'Tell us about your time in Camelot, Mai,' Sage urged her.

Mai stood up. 'Not today. It's getting late. I think we have enough of my memories of the past. Let's think about the present and what you are going to do on this visit.'

'We showed Sylvan how we enjoy ourselves on Earth world when he visited us there. I hope he'll give us a taste of what people get up to here in Aurum,' Sage said.

Chapter Seven

The next morning, Sage was the first to join Mai in the kitchen. She was sitting at the table with several large yellow leaves in front of her. Sage poured a cup of coffee and sat down beside her.

'What are these?'

Mai held up one of the leaves. 'Talking to you last night reminded me that I haven't been keeping in touch with some old friends as often as I should. I decided to catch up on correspondence.'

Sage picked up one of the leaves and turned it over. 'I can't see any writing.'

'No. Only the person it's addressed to can read it.' She gathered up the pile of flat, yellow leaves and walked to the window. Opening it, she breathed on the pile of leaves in her hand and watched them flutter away in the breeze. Returning to the table, she smiled at Sage. 'I noticed that you and Sylvan are getting on very well.'

Sage blushed. 'Yes. I like him very much.'

'And he obviously feels the same.'

'What about you, Mai? Is there someone you care about?'

'Yes. He's the reason I stayed in Camelot all those years ago.'

'Was he a sorcerer, too? Where is he now?'

Mai bit her lip. 'I can still see him but he's out of my reach until I...' She stopped and shook her head. 'No more memories for now. Here are Sophie and Paris. Let's talk about your plans for today. Mimosa will be here to take you, Sophie and Paris to the new hotel once you have had your breakfast. Sage and I can orb. I've a few things to do in Faeville this morning.'

An hour later, Mimosa landed gently outside the hotel where several Earth world guests gazed in astonishment.

'Will we get the chance to ride on a dragon?' a young girl asked Saffron.

'We have tours scheduled for this afternoon. Put your name down on the list in reception.'

'You won't get me on one of those,' the girl's mother commented. 'Is there another way of travelling around Aurum?'

Saffron smiled. 'Don't worry, there are several goblin and fae carriages available, too.'

Vinnie came out of the hotel and walked over to Sophie and Paris as Mai and Sage appeared beside them. 'Hi there. I just called with a message for two of the Earth world vampire guests. Delbert has arranged for Malbeam to collect them and take them on a tour of the Dark Forest this evening.'

'We've come to take a look around the hotel. It's certainly impressive,' Sage said, looking up at the large, ornate, white stone building. A wide driveway swept up to the main entrance. French windows on either side revealed a spacious lounge to the left and a dining room to the right. Several people could be seen in each of the rooms. On the top floor was a row of six windows with a view of the front gardens. There was a turret at each end that gave a panoramic view of the area.

Lupe joined them, smiling. 'Yes, Peridot is responsible for the design, with input from Saffron. The outdoor areas are the work of Leaf and Flora. There is a large garden and two games courts at the back of the building. The second building over there is for workshops and there are activities arranged by all the different people in Aurum, open to everyone who visits. Let me show you around.'

'I'm so pleased to see the different groups mixing and enjoying themselves,' Mai said as they walked past a group of goblin and shifter youngsters playing together. Some of the guests were climbing into goblin and fae carriages with signs showing the different locations they were heading for.

'How is Samar coping with his punishment?' Mai asked Vinnie.

'Very well. He works hard and actually seems quite happy these days. Delbert said he was talking about working here at the hotel when he is free in two months' time.'

Once they had finished the tour of the hotel, they headed for Peridot's house, where they found her busy in her art studio working on a portrait of a regal looking fae dressed in a robe in a sumptuous gold thread fabric.

'Do you recognise the dress, Sophie?' she said as they entered her studio. 'We've had orders for seven more already; the same material but different designs of course.'

'It looks beautiful,' Sophie said.

'And she commissioned me to do her portrait wearing the dress – probably to remind everyone that she was the first to have Brunswick's latest material! I'm hoping that I'll get a few more portrait commissions too. It means I get to work here instead of at Brunswick's, which suits me and keeps Uncle Brunswick happy.'

As they were leaving, Mai turned to Peridot. 'Saffron, Lupe and Sylvan are coming to eat with us this evening. Will you join us, too?'

A smile broke out on Sage's face when she saw Sylvan walking towards them as they left Peridot's house.

'Saffron told me you were here,' he said as they made their way towards Faeville.

'I'll see you back at the castle later,' Mai told them as an older fae waved her over.

'Have you any suggestions on what we can do in Aurum today, Sylvan?' Sage said. 'What sort of thing do you get up to here?'

He looked around. 'Let's go and ask Zephyr. He always has interesting ideas.'

'Before we go, I want to say hello to Mercy,' Sage said. She left the others talking to a group of young fae and goblins and headed for the older fae's house.

Mercy greeted her with a hug. 'Sage, I'm so glad to see you again. I had such a lovely chat with your grandparents the other week. I hope it's not too long before they're back for another visit.'

'They're very keen to return. Grandad was thrilled to talk to the dragons. Sylvan said he's going to arrange a visit to Lilac Brae for Grandad and Axel when they are in Aurum.'

They chatted for a while longer, before Sage went to rejoin her friends to find Flame and Flora with the group.

'I'm sure Saffron would be glad of an extra pair of hands at the hotel, Flame,' Flora was saying as Sage walked up. 'You finish gossamer duties in two months' time, don't you?'

Flame nodded. 'And I really want to have something to keep me busy.'

'And out of mischief!' her friend added.

'The new Flame has turned her back on mischief. I've learnt my lesson this time.'

'So, what are the plans for this afternoon?' Sage asked Sylvan.

'Zephyr recommends grass surfing on Mount Nuage.'

'That sounds like fun!' Sophie said.

'I have to get back to work. But I'll walk up to the main street with you,' Flame said as she fell into step with Sage. 'Two more months of unravelling gossamer before I start work at the hotel! I'm looking forward to it.'

'I hear that Samar is thinking of working there, too,' Sage commented. 'You'd be working together; would that be a good thing?'

Flame blinked rapidly. 'Oh, it won't be a problem. I'm sure we've both learnt a lot from our mistakes and have moved on. Here's my work place; bye for now.'

Sage looked thoughtful as the fae disappeared into the shop doorway before turning back to her friends.

***

A short while later, Sage and her friends, Sylvan, Zephyr and the two goblins, Lichen and Herb, stood at the bottom of Mount Nuage.

'It's pretty high,' Sophie commented.

'Don't worry, we'll start on the nursery slope,' Sylvan said, leading them through a gateway. 'Grab a board from the stack over there.'

'The grass isn't so ferocious here,' Zephyr said. 'Just watch what that girl does.'

A tall goblin put her board on the ground and stepped on to it, slowly drifting down the gentle slope. She spread her arms for balance as a swathe of grass lashed out, tipping her board backwards. Frowning, she leaned forward and steered a zigzag pathway to avoid several further grass attacks on her board. A smile passed over her face as she neared the bottom of the slope, but at the last moment a huge grass wave tipped her to the ground.

'Hard luck there, Zelen. You were so close!' someone called out.

'Let's have a practise run for those who haven't tried this before,' Sylvan suggested. 'I'll go first, Sage, you follow me.'

'Don't let the grass tip up your board, Sage,' he advised as she was tossed off within the first few minutes. 'If you see any waves coming at you, steer away.'

'Easier said than done!' she complained as she climbed back onto the board only to find it pushed upright making her slide to the ground once more.

'Show the grass who's boss!' Zephyr told Sophie as she struggled to avoid a grass wave edging towards her.

'Yes, I'm going to do this!' she said desperately swinging her board out of its path, but it was immediately tipped up by a long, thick, grassy tendril.

'This is great!' Paris called out as he swept passed them, skilfully steering his way down the hillside.

An hour later, Sage groaned as she rubbed her shoulder. 'I think the grass has definitely got the upper hand here.'

Sophie nodded. Yes, I think I've had enough grass surfing for today.'

'How about you watch as the rest of us go on the higher slopes?' Sylvan suggested.

'Yes, come and see how it's done!' Zephyr grinned.

'I wouldn't mind trying out a higher slope,' Paris said.

They all stepped onto a wooden travelator that took them several levels higher on the hillside.

The girls watched in amazement as two surfers rushed past them, weaving and dodging to avoid huge waves and snaky grass tendrils that threatened them from every angle.

'There's Sylvan, just setting off,' Sage pointed to a figure higher up the hill. He sped past them, riding one of the bigger grass waves and crouching low as a snapping tendril lashed out at him. Halfway down the slope, a wave emerging suddenly from one side knocked him to the ground. He stood up and grinned as he watched his board continue without him.

Not long after starting out on the second level, despite his best efforts, Paris was swept from his board. Laughing, he moved out of the way of the more experienced surfers and joined the girls as Zephyr set off from a higher level. The fae had a determined expression on his face as he sped downhill, crouching, jumping and twisting to avoid the barrage of grassy onslaughts. Several onlookers cheered as he finally drew to a halt at the base of the hillside, punching the air in triumph.

Sylvan appeared and put his arm around Sage's shoulders. 'Zephyr's in a class of his own when it comes to grass surfing.'

Zephyr made his way back to them, exchanging comments with several other surfers on the way.

'You're really good at that,' Paris said.

'I've been doing it for years now. I'm impressed with you, going for the second level on your first day.'

'I could really get into this.'

'Do you want to join me tomorrow morning?'

Paris glanced at Sophie who shook her head. 'You go, Paris. I'd like something a little more relaxing tomorrow.'

'It's time we headed back to the castle,' Sylvan added. 'Maybe Mai will have some suggestions.'

Chapter Eight

When they reached the castle, Saffron and Lupe were sitting in the kitchen with Mai.

'How did grass surfing go?' Mai asked them.

'Paris was the only one who could remain upright for more than a few seconds.' Sophie eased her shoulders. 'I need a hot shower for my bruised limbs, never mind my bruised ego!'

'You really have to keep focused,' Saffron said. 'Keep one step ahead of the grass.'

Paris nodded eagerly. 'You're always second-guessing which way it's going to move. It's a real challenge. Level two was too much for me at the moment but I'm sure I could do it with more practise.'

'You tried level two on your first day? That's really good. When I first started surfing, I didn't get any further than the nursery slope but I knew I wasn't going to give up until I mastered it!'

After showering and changing, the three friends returned to the kitchen to find Sylvan, Peridot and Vinnie there.

Mai placed a casserole in the centre of the table as they all sat down. There was silence for a while as they filled their plates with one of Flavia's fragrant stews and passed around the basket of freshly baked bread.

Mai turned to Sophie. 'Jay came to see me while you were out. He told me about Callum's interest in magic in The Valley.'

Sophie blushed. 'Oh, it's all my fault...'

'Don't worry, Sophie. You're not the first Gifted one to accidently reveal your talents. When I learnt his surname, Hunt, I realised that we do need to keep a careful eye on the family.'

Vinnie, who was seated on a sofa nearby, stiffened. 'Hunt?'

Saffron saw the puzzled expressions on the faces of Sage and her friends. 'The Hunt family could be descendants of the hunters who pursued and killed anyone they believed to be involved in magic.'

'Well, we definitely need to keep an eye on Callum and his family,' Sage said.

'Yes, we must be careful but we don't need to overreact,' Mai assured them.

Sophie noticed the troubled look on Vinnie's face and changed the subject. 'Any ideas on what Sage and I can do tomorrow while the others are grass surfing?'

'I'm going to see Holly at the Art Museum in Goblin Glen tomorrow. One of Delbert's friends has commissioned me to obtain a particular Paul Gaughin to add to her collection. She's ready to donate one of her other paintings, a Monet, to the museum to make room for it. The older fae and some of the vampires have donated some beautiful works of art over the centuries,' Vinnie said. 'Why don't you come with me and see what treasures we have collected over the years?'

'It's certainly worth a visit,' Mai added. 'Delbert and Vinnie were the ones who set it up all those years ago, but these days, Delbert leaves Vinnie to track down and collect new artwork from Earth world.'

'It looks so impressive from outside; I'd love to take a look around inside.' Sophie replied as Sage nodded in agreement.

***

'Delbert wanted the building to be modelled on the Taj Mahal,' Vinnie explained as they stood in front of the towering marble building the next day. 'Luckily, he agreed to a simplified, scaled down version!'

'It took quite a few spells to complete even this simplified version until Delbert was happy with it!' Mai laughed.

'It's amazing!' Sage said, looking up at the intricate carved stone that surrounded the entrance.

Holly Brunswick appeared. 'Vinnie, and you've brought our Earth world friends too! I was so excited to hear that we'd be getting a new Monet in the gallery. We've been arranging the perfect viewing spot for it! Come inside.' She led them into a domed, high-ceilinged hallway. Four corridors led away from the centre. 'Let's take you on a tour of our museum. We're very proud of the works we have here.'

Sophie's eyes widened as they followed her into the first gallery. 'Isn't that a Gustav Klimt? There's a copy of this picture near the staffroom at school.'

'And that's a van Gough, isn't it?' Sage said.

Vinnie smiled and nodded. 'Yes, the originals. Of course, they are replaced with perfect copies in Earth world.'

They walked slowly through the gallery, stopping to admire individual works.

'And through here, we have our sculpture gallery.' Holly showed them into a courtyard. In the centre was a fountain surrounded by flower beds and trees. Statues and wood and stone carvings were arranged around the garden.

Mai sank down onto one of the benches near a tinkling fountain. 'This is such a peaceful place to relax.'

'I recognise one or two of these; that's Rodin's Thinker over there,' Sage said.

Sophie pointed to three figures. 'And they're part of the Terracotta Army.'

Holly sat and chatted with Mai and Vinnie as the two girls strolled around the garden. When they joined them, she pointed to a pathway that led to a long stone building. 'In this gallery, we have our earlier works.'

She pushed open a heavy wooden door and they stepped into a cool, dimly lit interior. 'Some of these paintings are very old. When they were brought here many of them were in poor condition so we keep the room cool and dark. We have a team of restorers looking after them.'

Sage and Sophie peered at the first few paintings.

'I've never seen any of these pictures before,' Sage commented.

'There are a lot of religious themed ones,' Sophie said. 'And medieval battles.'

'I think I prefer the later paintings,' Sage admitted.

'You must see the Egyptian artefacts,' Vinnie said. She led them into a smaller room off the main gallery and pointed to a glass case where several gold objects were displayed. She sighed. 'These bring back so many memories. Delbert and I collected these on one of our Middle Eastern trips. We had spent a while in Jerusalem locating a medieval church that Arthur may have visited on his travels. That's where we found one of the first crosses. On our journey home, we decided to visit a village just outside Cairo in Egypt. They had recently discovered a new burial chamber and it was obviously someone important. Delbert was completely taken by these jewellery items and decided to add them to his own collection. It took a while for Cornelia to create the copies to replace them so we joined in one of the digs. It was very interesting.'

'I thought only fae could travel to Earth world. How come you and Delbert travelled so much?' Sophie asked.

'When Delbert first rescued me and took me under his wing, he was living in a spectacular castle in Romania just outside the village of Rasinari. He had a collection of artworks, similar to the ones in the last gallery and over the next hundred years, spent most of his time building up his collection. As his protegee, he wanted me to learn about art appreciation too and we often travelled to distant lands to seek out new items. Rasinari was a quiet village. The villagers treated us with caution, but we lived peacefully alongside each other. Of course, we needed to feed, but we never harmed any of the villagers or their families or friends; we fed on wild animals and on very rare occasions, a visiting stranger. Some of the people were quite friendly when I took a stroll around the market place. There was a young man in particular, Timur, who had a vegetable and flower stall with his father. When his father wasn't looking, he would give me a small bouquet and a wink.' She smiled at the memory before her expression grew serious again.

'All that changed when a group of newly changed vampires rampaged through the village one night and several young people were found dead the next morning. As you can imagine, there was a great outcry; and overnight we became the spawn of the devil. Delbert tried to reason with the head of the village but feelings were running high. Delbert ordered his housekeeper to secure all the doors and windows of the mansion. He hoped we could sit it out and that it would all blow over. But that didn't happen. It grew worse, until two nights later there was a hammering on the main door. I was terrified. We all stayed silent, hoping whoever it was would give up and leave. Then there was a shout from the kitchen door. I recognised the voice, it was Timur. He told us we were in grave danger and that we must leave immediately; a mob was heading towards us at that moment. Despite Delbert's suspicions of Timur, I opened the door. The shouts of the villagers were getting louder and angrier. We could see their flickering torches as they came up the hill towards the house. Timur pressed a purse into my hands and urged us to flee. We scrambled up the rocky mountain path behind the house and didn't stop until we reached the summit. The night sky was filled with an orange glow as our home was set alight. 'That was the first time I had ever seem Delbert near to tears. He had lost his home and all the treasures he had collected over the years.' Vinnie paused. 'I often wondered what happened to Timur. Did he go on to lead a fulfilling life with a wife and family or did someone realise that he had been the one to help us escape?'

Sage let out a long breath. 'That sounds terrible! Where did you go?'

'We travelled westwards until we reached France. We heard and saw so many atrocities committed against anyone suspected of being connected in any way with magic, they labelled it all the "Dark Arts". In Paris, we met an old crone who had met Mai Lin many years previously. She said that only Mai Lin was capable of saving the Magical and Gifted of Earth world. When we learnt that the last known place where she had been seen was Camelot, we headed there.'

'Did you find Mai there?' Sophie asked.

'No. Camelot was falling into ruins. We had to ask several people before we learnt where she was living. She was shocked when we explained how much suffering was going on in the Magical and Gifted community.'

Mai shook her head. 'I'm ashamed to say, I was so taken with my own private grief that I hardly took any notice of the world around me. All my life I had known that magic was frowned upon but I hadn't realised how serious the situation had become until Delbert and Vinnie brought me to my senses. We set out a plan to create Aurum where the Magical and Gifted could live safely.'

'Once Aurum was established and Delbert had built his home, he began to make plans to rebuild his art collection which meant we would need to spend some time in Earth world. Mai confided in us that she wanted us to collect certain artefacts from Earth world for her, too,' Vinnie continued. 'Delbert and I had the opportunity to spend time in many different cities in Earth world and add new treasures to Delbert's growing collection and to look for the artefacts that Mai wanted.'

'What artefact were you interested in, Mai?' Sage asked.

'Crosses. Well, one cross in particular.'

'The second cross,' Vinnie nodded. 'The one we have yet to locate.'

Sophie exchanged a puzzled look with Sage. 'Why did you need this cross?'

Mai spread her hands. 'It's linked to Camelot, to Arthur.'

'I know some of your background in Camelot, Mai, but I would love to hear the full story,' Holly said.

'It's quite a long story.'

'Well, I know the ideal place for us to settle down and listen,' Holly continued. 'We've arranged an alcove for the new Monet where people can sit back and enjoy it. It's just a blank space at the moment. Follow me.'

She led them to a glass conservatory where several plush sofas were arranged in front of a blank wall. 'This is the perfect setting for your story. If you feel you want to share it with us?'

'It will be good for you to remember the happy times as well as the sad ones, Mai,' Vinnie added gently.

Mai nodded. 'That's true. Where did we get to the other night?'

'When you arrived in England.'

'Ah, yes. My first impression, when I stepped off the French merchant vessel, was of a busy port.' Mai began. 'Lining the town wall were rows of stalls selling fresh fish, vegetables, herbs, spices, bread and cakes. Once again, I felt overwhelmed and was wondering which way I should head when an old man tapped my arm and said my name.'

She turned to the wall and raised her hands.

***

A younger Mai was standing in the busy street facing an old man. He smiled. 'Mai Lin, or shall we keep to Merlin? I'm Kelrug, the king's physician. I'm looking for an apprentice and you come highly recommended by several of my acquaintances – Omar, Gautier, Yet-Sen...'

'I'm very pleased to meet you, Kelrug,' Mai Lin smiled.

'Let me take you to your new home.'

They entered the gateway in the high stone walls surrounding the castle grounds, Mai Lin struggling to keep sight of the old man who hurried on ahead through the crowds. Finally, they neared the main part of the castle and she followed him up a narrow pathway around the side of the towering building to a small kitchen garden filled with vegetables and herbs. A stone cottage covered in ivy, stood against one wall. Kelrug pushed open the creaky wooden door to reveal a room furnished with one table, two chairs and a shelf containing dried herbs, a row of coloured glass bottles and several leather-bound books. At each end of the room was a curtained area.

'That's my bedroom there, you can take the other one, Merlin,' he said pointing to one curtain. 'I expect you could do with a bite to eat after your journey.'

She was tucking into a bowl of thick vegetable soup, when there was a knock on the door. A woman opened it without waiting for an answer. 'Kelrug. Gliff said he saw you with a young lad back in the market place.' She scowled at Merlin. 'Not much of him is there? Still, needs must. We've just heard that King Arthur is on his way home now. He'll be here before nightfall. I'll need the lad to help in the kitchens. The king and his men will want feeding, so your herbs and potions will have to wait.' She turned towards the door. 'Gliff is taking care of the roast boar; we'll gather some vegetables on the way. Come on, boy.'

'Go and help Sanda out and make your way back here when you've finished your kitchen duties, Merlin,' Kelrug said as Mai Lin was ushered from the room.

For the next two hours, Mai Lin peeled and cut up vegetables and plucked several chickens while the others around her were hard at work, turning a pig on a spit and baking pastries. Finally, Sanda patted her shoulder. 'You might be a scrap of a boy, but you're a good worker, Merlin. Help Jenk take those trays of bread to the main table. I think we're about done here.'

Mai Lin picked up a tray of loaves and followed a tall, sallow faced youth along a corridor to the main dining room. Her eyes opened wide as she entered the room. A long table lit by several candelabra took up one side of the great hall. It was already laden with baskets of fruit and flagons of wine. Tapestries and portraits lined the walls around it, their images seeming to flicker with life in the light of the tapers fixed to the walls. Jenk and Merlin had put down the trays and were about to make their way back to the kitchen when loud cries and cheers came from outside. They ran to the windows and looked out so see a group of knights ride into the courtyard. A young blonde man waved and smiled at the crowd. He glanced up and for a moment, Mai Lin felt his eyes on hers.

'King Arthur himself,' Jenk murmured reverently.

They both watched the stable boys rush forwards to take the horses' reins as the knights dismounted. Mai Lin stood transfixed until the knights had entered the castle and the crowds had started to disperse. Jenk had already left when she turned around and made her way back along the corridor.

'Here, boy!' a woman shouted as Mai Lin neared the kitchen. She pushed a pile of clean towels into her hands. 'Take these to the king's room. His valet should have done it, but he thinks that's too far beneath him! Quickly now.'

'But where…?'

She pointed down a long wood panelled corridor. 'See that man with the velvet cap up ahead? Follow him. Look sharp now.'

Mai Lin hurried after the well-dressed man as he made his way along several corridors and finally reached a pair of tall carved doors. The man said something to one of the two armed soldiers standing guard. One of the soldiers stepped inside, then reappeared to let him enter.

Nervously, Mai Lin approached with her pile of towels. She cleared her throat. 'These are for the king.'

One of the soldiers gave a brief nod. 'When the king has finished talking to his advisor, you can take them in.'

Mai Lin stood and waited for several minutes until the advisor reappeared. The soldier once again disappeared into the room, returning a few minutes later to usher Mai Lin inside.

She felt her heart beat wildly as she slowly walked forward. Arthur was peeling off his dusty clothes and throwing them onto the floor. 'Ah, good. Clean towels. Put them on the chair near the bathtub.'

Mai felt her face flush as she kept her eyes averted from the near naked king.

'And check the water temperature will you, boy? Not too hot, nor too cold, I hope.'

She stuck her fingers in the bathtub. 'It's just that, not to hot, nor too cold, sire.'

She watched as from the corner of her eye she could see Arthur shed his last garment.

'Good heavens, boy, you're blushing like a girl! Surely you've seen one of your own kind naked before?' Arthur laughed as he lowered himself into the water. 'Maybe I should ask you to scrub my back for me?'

Mai Lin let out a short cry.

'Just go, boy!' Arthur laughed. 'Run home to your mother!'

***

Over the next few weeks Mai Lin spent the mornings helping Sanda in the castle kitchen and the afternoons with Kelrug, learning about new plants and herbs and preparing simples - medicines for common ailments. During the afternoons and evenings, many people would call to seek advice from Kelrug who was greatly respected by those in the castle and in the village nearby.

After supper, she would sit with Kelrug and learn how to mix the various balms and potions for the simples he used.

Late one afternoon, as she was about to close the door after the last patient, a young girl, clutching a puppy, ran towards her. Mai Lin grimaced as she saw the tiny creature with its fur matted with blood and its hind legs twisted.

'Wait! You have to help me,' the girl sobbed. Mai Lin stood back as she came in and placed the still figure of the puppy on the table. 'It's Patch. He ran under a cart. I couldn't stop him. Can you help him? Please say you can...'

Kelrug looked at the tiny animal lying in front of him. 'I'm not sure there's a lot we can do for him, I'm afraid.'

Seeing the child's stricken face, Mai Lin thought of her own precious Rona and the energy she had been able to give her that had saved the old goat's life. She leaned over the dog, shielding it from the child's view. Could she do it again, with a creature that had already nearly lost its life? Concentrating, she placed her hands on the battered body and willed the energy to pass into the tiny form. 'Come on,' she whispered. 'Feel the warmth. Take my energy.' Several minutes passed before the puppy stirred, giving a soft whimper as his damaged limbs clicked back into place.

'Patch?' the girl looked up. 'Is he going to be alright?'

Mai Lin lifted the dog up and ran her hands over its healed body. 'Yes, he's had a very nasty shock but I think he's going to be fine.'

The girls took the dog in her arms as it yapped and licked her face. 'Thank you so much! Patch, you must never run out in the road again!'

She was still thanking them as Kelrug closed the door behind her. He pushed a heavy bolt across it. 'Yet-Sen was right when he told me that he believed you are destined for great things. But I must warn you to keep your Gifts well hidden. Arthur's father, Uther, was vehemently opposed to magic and passed a law to proclaim anyone found practising what he called the Dark Arts was to be given the death sentence. Arthur still upholds this law; so, you must be very careful.'

He went to his bedroom and reappeared with a large, silk bag. Almost reverently, he placed it on the table and gently pulled out an old, leatherbound handwritten book, its pages yellowed with age.

'This is a collection of charms and spells from some of the greatest sorcerers in all of the country. Many years ago, my mentor used it to teach me my craft just as I am ready to teach you now, Mai Lin.'

She carefully turned the pages, reading the titles of Latin incantations. The first half of the book dealt with everyday magic - spells that could be used to promote fertility or bring about a good harvest. Another chapter explained how to banish a mischievous house imp or repel the unwanted attentions of a satyr. In the last few chapters, the spells dealt with more serious issues, such as how to release someone from an evil curse or build the strength to withstand the wiles of a daemon.

Kelrug patted Mai Lin's arm as she shuddered. 'Don't worry; I haven't had to use many of the spells from the final section of this book; but it is better to be prepared for any eventuality, isn't it?'

Chapter Nine

'Just one more task for you before you go, Merlin' Sanda told her one morning. 'Take the besom and clean up the rushes in the Great Hall and replace them with fresh ones. King Arthur will be entertaining an important French gentleman and his entourage this afternoon.'

Mai Lin took up the besom and headed for the Great Hall. She flinched at the stench of old food and bones as she swept up the rushes and tipped them into a large sack. Once she had removed them, she grabbed an armful of fresh rushes and made her way back down the corridor to the hall. Her view was obscured by the pile of rushes and she slammed into a figure who let out a stream of curses in French. Dropping the rushes to the floor, she quickly apologised to him in his native tongue. She looked up to see a richly dressed man standing beside Arthur.

'Do you teach your kitchenhands to speak French?' the man said to Arthur. 'Or has the boy been kidnapped from our shores? Though he does not have the features of a French boy.'

Mai Lin shook her head. 'I learnt French on my travels. I was fortunate enough to spend time in a…magnificent chateau in the beautiful French countryside.'

'And fluently, too. Guinevere will be greatly relieved to know she will have someone to converse with, if she accepts your offer, Arthur.'

Mai Lin felt Arthur's eyes on her as she gathered up the fresh rushes and hurried on to the hall.

When she sat down with Kelrug later that day, she asked him about Guinevere.

'She's the youngest daughter of one of the most powerful men in Brittany. Rumour has it that if a marriage can be arranged between Guinevere and Arthur, it will be beneficial for both sides, strengthening their resistance against other monarchs who would like to extend their own kingdoms.'

Mai Lin told him what had happened in the hall earlier. 'If she does come here, I may be called upon to converse with her, maybe even act as translator at times.'

Sanda looked flustered as Mai Lin entered the kitchen the next morning. 'King Arthur has sent for you. I do hope you haven't been annoying or upsetting his lordship.' She straightened up Mai Lin's tunic. 'Go to him now; and remember your manners.'

The guard outside the king's room nodded at her as she reached him. 'The king is expecting you. Enter.'

Mai Lin felt herself tremble as she walked into the room. Arthur was seated behind a desk, writing in a ledger. She listened to the scratching of the quill on the heavy vellum. Finally, he put down the quill and looked up. 'I was impressed with your grasp of the French language yesterday, Merlin. It will be a great help in my quest to win the hand of Guinevere. I have written a letter to court her. I don't expect you can read and write French, but if I read it to you, can you help me hone it and correct any glaring errors? Pull that stool up beside me.'

Gingerly, Mai Lin sat down beside Arthur and glanced at the letter, reading it quickly. 'You need to use the feminine article there,' she pointed out. 'And maybe change the verb tense there? To give it a more …caring…tone. And maybe…' She stopped as she felt Arthur' eyes on her. 'Forgive me, Sire. I'm letting my tongue run away with me. I'm sure your original choice of words will be most acceptable.'

'On the contrary, I have asked you for your help. How come a lowly kitchenhand can also be somewhat of a scholar, Merlin?'

'Not much of a scholar, my lord. I just happen to have picked up some skills on my travels.'

'I would be most interested to hear about your travels.'

'But not today, sire. You have a lady's heart to win.'

Arthur raised an eyebrow as they turned back to the text.

A week passed before Arthur once again summoned Mai Lin.

'I have a reply from my lady here. It seems she is impressed with my, or rather, *our* letter. Here, read it.'

'She is very moved my lord, and also with your portrait her father brought back with him on his visit to Camelot.'

'A messenger from her father has brought a portrait of her to me. Come and take a look.' He led her to an easel in the window where Guinevere looked out at them. Although her face was solemn, Mai Lin could see a touch of laughter in her eyes. 'The messenger told me she is even more beautiful in the flesh.'

'She is indeed a beauty, Sire.'

'I'd like you to help me prepare a second letter today, Merlin. And I want you to be available for an hour a day to practice my French conversation. I am paying her family a visit next month and I will be formally introduced to her. It's a chance for me to make a good impression on her and her father.'

They sat down together writing a second moving love letter to Arthur's intended. At one point, Mai Lin's comments on Arthur's choice of words was quite critical.

'If you say that, my lord, she will think you are shallow and using words only for effect, rather than writing from your heart.'

A tense silence followed and she feared she had overstepped the mark.

Arthur cleared his throat. 'What makes you such an expert on a woman's heart? A scrawny young lad like yourself. I bet you have never even loved a woman, have you?'

Mai Lin shook her head. 'You are right, sire. I'm speaking of things way above my head. Leave the words you suggested.'

He grunted. 'No. We'll do it your way.'

As Mai Lin left Arthur's room that morning, she gave one last glance at the blonde head bent over the final draft as he signed his name with a flourish. A stab of jealousy went through her heart - she wished the letters he wrote were for her.

One morning, Mai Lin was surprised to hear Arthur talking with Kelrug as she climbed out of bed. She quickly dressed and pulled back the curtain to see the king leap to his feet. He held a letter out to her.

'I had to tell you first, Merlin! For you are the reason behind my happiness. Guinevere has accepted my proposal of marriage. We are to be wed here in Camelot in three months' time.'

Mai Lin fixed a smile on her face and congratulated Arthur. He slapped her shoulder. 'Now I must go. There is much to prepare. Merlin, I can never thank you enough for giving me the chance for such happiness.'

The day seemed endless to Mai Lin as she carried out her usual tasks, with talk of the upcoming wedding on everyone's lips. At midday, she made an excuse to slip away to her own room to ease her aching head. As she lay on the bed, she heard Kelrug come in and was about to join him when she heard a second, female voice.

'Who is she? Some light headed French girl who will be little use to Arthur.'

'She is his chosen bride, Morgana, who may very well provide a son and heir for our king,' Kelrug replied.

'Gossip has it that your new apprentice was involved in the courtship with his fine French words! As if a poor country lad could have such skills! He must have used some kind of sorcery. What have you been teaching him, Kelrug?'

'He has been working with me making simples to treat the common illnesses of the people of the castle and the local villagers. As have many young lads before him.'

'If the king knew of your real powers, Kelrug, you would not be living here. In fact, you would not be living at all.'

'The king knows that the medicines and potions we prepare are from the recipes of the holy monks who have lived on these isles for many centuries, Morgana.'

'You can fool the king, but you can't fool me. The same goes for your new apprentice.'

When Mai Lin heard the door slam, she stepped into the room.

'Who was that?'

'Morgana La Fay, a powerful sorcerer and the half-sister of Arthur. She believes that she should be the ruler of Camelot, not Arthur and is not happy with the news of the wedding. You must be extra careful to hide your Gifts from her and any of her followers.'

***

'It's a beautiful day for a wedding, is it not?' Sanda asked as she bustled around the kitchen several months later. 'I hear the bride is a great beauty; and so she must be to capture the heart of our handsome King Arthur.'

Mai Lin swallowed the lump in her throat and nodded carrying out her tasks mechanically.

Her husband, Will, placed a tray of baked meats on the table. 'I know one of the guests is not too pleased for the happy couple. If Arthur has a son, it will put the crown even further out of her reach.'

Sanda tossed her head. 'The crown will never be within Morgana's reach. What kind of queen would she make? She must accept Arthur as the rightful king of Camelot.'

'Come on Merlin, you should have taken those loaves out of the oven by now!' Jenks pushed her aside, grabbing the tray before the bread was burnt. 'Where is your head today of all days?'

'Take those flagons of wine to the Great Hall, Merlin,' Sanda told her. 'The wedding party will be heading there once the ceremony is over.'

Mai Lin stopped near the doorway of the castle chapel where a crowd of family and close friends cheered as the priest announced the couple man and wife. Moments later, the newlyweds appeared. Guinevere looked radiant in a red silk gown that clung to her curvaceous figure. On her head was a tiara studded with rubies that reflected the rich hues of her gown. Arthur, beaming as he clutched his new wife's hand, wore a padded red velvet jacket that emphasised his wide shoulders and narrow hips. On his head rested the simple gold crown passed down from his father. The couple were escorted to the Great Hall where they took their places at the head of the main table. Once everyone else was seated, Mai Lin, Jenk and a team of kitchen staff, began to circulate, filling and refilling goblets with fine French wine.

As Mai Lin returned yet once more from the kitchen with two more flagons of wine, she heard someone call.

'Merlin! Merlin! Come and meet my beautiful bride.' Arthur beckoned her to join them.

She put a smile on her face and walked towards them.

'Is she not the most beautiful woman in the world?'
Arthur kissed his wife's hand.

Mai Lin gave Guinevere a short bow. 'You are
indeed, my lady. Your portrait, though stunning, does not
reflect your true beauty.'

'And Merlin here can speak your mother tongue as
if he was a native himself. And can read and write fluently,
too.'

'Really?' Guinevere turned to Merlin and addressed
her in French. 'Where did such a youth learn our
language?'

Mai Lin replied in kind. 'I was lucky to spend some
time working for a scholar in a French village before
travelling to England, my lady. In return he tutored me in
your language.'

'One day you must tell me about your time in
France, Merlin.'

Mai Lin slipped away as the bride's mother came to
speak to her daughter. Soon the newlyweds were led to the
dance floor amidst cheers from the guests.

As she left the hall, she caught sight of Morgana
standing motionless in the shadows, staring intently at the
newlyweds. With her slender figure, pale skin and jet black
hair, she was a beautiful woman, but Mai Lin flinched as
she saw the vicious upturn of her lips and the smouldering
hatred in her piercing, blue eyes.

The wedding celebrations lasted for three days
filling the castle grounds and nearby village with music and
dancing long after dark. Each night, Mai Lin fell into an
exhausted sleep, sometimes on the kitchen floor, not even
making it back to her own little room.

By the end of the week, most of the French guests
had departed and life in Camelot began to settle back to a
more normal routine.

Kelrug poured a cup of tea for himself and Mai Lin one evening as they finished their usual work attending to the ailments of the local people.

'I can see that you are unhappy, Mai Lin. And I think I can work out the reason behind it. You were becoming a little too close to Arthur as you helped him to woo his bride.'

Mai Lin shrugged. 'It's all but a passing fancy. I'm sure such a fine-looking young man has turned many a young girl's head before.'

'I hope there is another fine-looking young man who will be in a position to give you all your heart desires, Mai Lin.'

She smiled at him. 'I'm sure you are right, Kelrug.' But in her heart, she felt these words were empty.

Chapter Ten

While Arthur and his bride spent their time riding and visiting or entertaining noble company, Mai Lin worked hard in the kitchen during the day and studied with Kelrug each evening. She had almost persuaded herself that she had her feelings for Arthur under control, until the sound of his voice as he spoke with his wife would awaken a pang in her heart.

One morning as she reached the couples' suite with fresh bed linen and towels, she paused before knocking on their door.

'Must you go, Arthur?' Guinevere sounded petulant. 'How will I manage here all alone without you?'

'You know as king that my job is to defend my kingdom and my people,' he replied gently. 'This morning, Osric brought me news of unrest from the northern hills. Anyway, you are hardly all alone here in Camelot, my love.'

'For how long will you be gone?'

'Hopefully, no more than a month or two.'

Guinevere sighed loudly.

'The weather is getting milder; you can walk in the gardens and take a ride with one of your ladies. Or with Merlin. I will tell him to be ready for any requests you have, my sweet.'

Guinevere laughed. 'As if big, strong Merlin can look after me! He looks as if a puff of wind would blow him over.'

'He may not be the strongest young man, but he has a kind heart and an intelligent mind and can provide stimulating conversation. And of course, my knights will always be here to guard Camelot and its precious inhabitants.'

Despite her pleas, Arthur left Camelot early the next morning.

Guinevere spent the next few days with her ladies, working on a tapestry, walking and receiving visitors from the local gentry. Some evenings she would send for Mai Lin and listen as she read from a selection of French poems. The weeks passed pleasantly and soon Arthur returned to the castle.

Three months later, Mai Lin heard the same conversation between the couple.

'But you knew when you married me, Guinevere, that as king, I would have to spend time away from Camelot.'

'Yes, but I didn't realise that sometimes you may be gone for nearly a year. What am I to do?'

'You found plenty to occupy yourself with on my last trip, my love. I will return as soon as it is possible and I will write to you whenever I can.'

For the first two months after Arthur's departure, Guinevere busied herself with her usual daily routines, However, by the third month she was becoming increasingly bored and short tempered.

'I can't believe such a pretty woman can have such a mouth on her. I don't need to speak French to understand what she is saying,' Sanda complained in the kitchen one morning.

'And there's worse to come,' Her husband added as he placed a basket of vegetables on the table. 'Morgana will be arriving later today.'

Mai Lin was surprised to see Morgana greet the young queen warmly that afternoon.

'I am sorry to see such a young and beautiful woman so out of sorts. Arthur would not like to see his wife so sad. What can we do to remedy this, my lady?

Come, let us take a walk in the gardens and enjoy the fresh air.'

Soon the two women were walking along the pathways, Morgana chattering away until she brought a smile to her companion's face.

'Look, here is entertainment for us,' Morgana said, looking down at the field below where a group of soldiers was exercising. 'Lancelot is putting his men through their paces. Let us stop and watch awhile.'

They watched as one group of men fought with swords and another practised their archery skills.

'I would like to try my hand at shooting an arrow,' Guinevere commented.

Morgana stepped forward and beckoned Lancelot over.

Soon, Guinevere was holding a bow, with Lancelot's hands guiding her as she lined up the arrow.

The images faded as the couple's eyes locked.

Sophie sat upright. 'Morgana set up Guinevere and Lancelot!'

Mai nodded. 'Yes. Four months later it became clear that Guinevere was pregnant. One night, the two of them just disappeared. Of course, Morgana was long gone by then.'

'Poor Arthur,' Sage said. 'What happened when he returned to find his wife had left?'

'He was devastated. We were all really worried about his health. He stayed in his rooms eating nothing just drinking wine. Finally, I decided as a good friend I needed to act. When he sent a request to the kitchen for another flagon of wine, I brought him a large jug of tea instead and gave him a good talking to about showing himself to be a true king and getting out to see to his subjects. Unsurprisingly, he threw me out of his rooms, and the jug of tea, too. But the next morning he came to Kelrug's cottage and apologised. He told me that he had decided to visit the smaller villages around Camelot, in disguise, to see what their life was really like and told me that I was to accompany him. The next few months were the happiest ones of my life, although things could have turned out much differently.'

'What happened?' Sage asked.

Mai blushed. 'Let me show you.' She raised a hand to the wall and two figures appeared, seated beside a fire in a forest.

'This trip has really opened my eyes, Merlin. I must keep in touch with my subjects,' Arthur said as he watched her stir a cooking pot over the fire. 'When we return to Camelot, I will order provisions to be sent to the northern villages where the crops have failed this year. And some of the boys in Cragshill could be trained to make fine knights, even if their parents aren't wealthy.'

They sat talking of the people they had seen and the plans Arthur had for his kingdom until the fire died down and they both slept.

As the sun rose the next morning, Arthur sat up and stretched. In the distance, he could hear a voice softly singing. Standing up, he followed the sound until he came to a river, where Mai Lin was bathing, humming softly as she did so.

'Ah ha,' Arthur smiled. 'You're in for a surprise, young man!' He quickly stripped off his clothes, leaving them in a heap beside Mai Lin's; then dived into the water and swam up behind his unsuspecting companion.

'Merlin, I …what…?' he spluttered as he came face to face with the young woman who gave a loud scream. She turned and hurried to the river bank, slipping her arms into her shirt, trembling as she fumbled with the lace ties.

Pulling on his trousers, Arthur grabbed her arm as she made to run.

'I planned to surprise you in the river, but I am the one who has been given the bigger surprise! Explain this deceit to me, please.'

Mai's face burned as the images faded once more.

'What a surprise! Did you tell him your secrets?' Sophie asked.

Mai shook her head. 'Not everything. Just that I had travelled from China in disguise to protect myself.'

'And were things okay with you after that?' Sage asked.

'Very much so,' Mai looked down at her hands, her face still tinged with pink. 'We became very close, although we decided to hide our relationship from those around us for a while. After the scandal of Guinevere, we were not sure that Arthur's next choice of a kitchen hand would be warmly received. I was also afraid of Arthur discovering the other big secret about me - my Gifts; especially as I knew how he felt about magic. But we were both convinced that one day we would live together openly.' She fingered a gold chain around her neck and pulled out the plain gold cross on it. 'He had this made for me as a token of his love.'

'What happened?' Sage asked.

Mai Lin closed her eyes for a moment. 'Over the next few months, Camelot prospered under Arthur. Morgana was furious that he had moved on so easily after the humiliation of his wife and continued to be loved and respected by his subjects. She turned to her son, Mordred and plotted with him to overthrow Arthur so she could take the throne.

'Arthur heard the rumours that Mordred was gathering an army and planning a surprise attack on Camelot in the night. He set out with his own soldiers for the camp where Mordred and his men were waiting. Before they left Camelot, I placed a safe charm on Arthur and his two closest friends. Morgana discovered this when she tried to bring him down as he neared Mordred's camp. She wasn't able to kill him and could only send the three men into an enchanted sleep but to everyone else, Arthur appeared dead and she could claim the crown.

'She stood beside me as his faithful followers pushed the burning funeral boats out onto the lake. As the mourners dispersed, she turned to me with a cold smile on her face. 'You may have saved his life, but he is as good as dead! He and his friends will lie sleeping under the island for all eternity!'

'That night I rowed out on the lake around to the other side of the island and found the passageway that led to the underground chamber. I could not get past the gates, and it broke my heart to think that he was being kept prisoner deep in the darkness. I made a vow that I would not rest until I had undone the spell that Morgana had cast.

'Morgana returned to Camelot and dealt ruthlessly with anyone who stood in her way. Most of Arthur's loyal followers fled. Kelrug set off to join his sister and her family in a town further north. He wanted me to go with him, but I couldn't leave Arthur. I disguised myself and waited nearby until I got the chance to steal into Morgana's rooms and locate her spell books.'

Sophie looked surprised. 'You managed to break into her rooms?'

'Once Morgana was queen, Camelot soon fell into a state of chaos. She had a very small number of trusted followers and her biggest rival, Constantine, was quick to act on this and stormed the castle within days of her taking the crown.'

'What happened to her?' Sage asked.

Mai Lin shrugged. 'Some say she was killed; some say she escaped. Once I had her spell books, I headed east until I reached a large town where I found work in a bakery. By day I baked bread and by night I studied Morgana's books.'

'And did you discover how to undo the spell?'

She nodded. 'After many a long year.' She raised her hands to the wall again and two hands appeared carrying a large, leatherbound book. The hands opened the book and smoothed down the pages. Mai read the ornate script aloud:

'Take the two crosses to where the king lies
The first will open the door
The second will open his eyes.'

'So that's why you have such a large collection of crosses.' Sophie nodded. 'I take it that the first cross must be the one Arthur gave you?'

'Yes, and I have been searching for the second cross, later with Vinnie's help, ever since.'

'And we won't give up until we find it,' Vinnie said, patting Mai Lin's shoulder. 'I've built up quite a few contacts over time and there's always someone with a new lead to follow.'

There was a thoughtful silence as they said goodbye to Holly and made their way back to the castle. Sylvan, Paris and Zephyr were full of their tales of grass surfing and didn't notice how quiet their companions were.

Finally, Mai stood up. 'I think it's time to get you back to Earth world.'

As they stood up to join hands, Sage asked her. 'Can I tell my grandparents the memories you and Vinnie shared with us this weekend?'

'And my family?' Sophie added.

Vinnie and Mai exchanged looks. 'Mary and your mother know the story. Mary has been keeping an eye on the archaeology group in The Valley. So far, they haven't unearthed a cross.'

'A cross?' Paris said. 'Have I missed something?'

'You can hear the rest of the story when Sage tells her grandparents,' Mai said.

It was Paris' turn to be silent later that evening as Sage recounted the story of Mai Lin's life to her grandparents.

'What a sad romance! She's been trying to awaken her lover for over a thousand years.' Ellen shook her head.

Sage nodded. 'And Mai Lin says she's not going to give up until she succeeds, even if it takes another thousand years.'

'I'm sure Vinnie will find the cross before then!' Sophie added. 'Who knows maybe one of us will learn something about the second cross.'

Sage nodded. 'Vinnie and Delbert have their own sad background story.'

'Yes, you'd never know they had been through so much before Aurum was created,' Sophie said. The others leaned forward as she launched into the harrowing story of their past life.

'I'm glad things are better now, for Vinnie and Delbert, at least,' Jim commented.

'And, hopefully, things will work out for Mai, too, before too long,' Ellen added.

Chapter Eleven

'How was your weekend?' Tracey asked as she joined them in the canteen the next day. 'Anything exciting happen in Aurum?'

'We tried out grass surfing,' Sage told her.

'And we visited the Art Museum in Goblin Glen. It's a really interesting place,' Sophie added.

Tracey screwed up her face. 'Museum? Tell me about grass surfing!'

'Painful!' Sage laughed.

'How was Alora's on Saturday?' Sophie asked.

'Good. I'm not up to your speed yet, Sophie, but I did better than last week. Two new Transposers joined us. They're not at this school though. But there's a new girl, a shifter, starting here soon. Alora wants you to look out for her, Sage. Her family have just moved into The Valley.'

'A shifter? Interesting,' Sage said. 'I'll go and see Alora on the way home.'

'What are you three talking about?' Callum asked as he neared their table.

'Well, it's actually girly stuff and a bit embarrassing…but if you'd really like to know…' Sophie cleared her throat.

Callum's friend pulled his arm. 'No, thanks! Come on. Leave them to it.'

He scowled as he turned away, knocking into a younger student who stammered an apology as he caught sight of Callum's face.

'I wish we could really put him in his place.' Sophie's eyes narrowed as he shot a last evil look over his shoulder.

'Like Alora says, we just have to ignore him,' Sage said. 'Don't let him wind us up. There's too much at stake, Sophie. The whole Gifted community.'

'You're right.' She nodded. 'So, a new Gifted family in The Valley? We haven't had shifters here since Mary and my mum were at school. I'll come with you to Alora's today.'

***

'Come on through to the kitchen,' Alora called out as the two girls reached the front door of The Coterie that afternoon.

She was seated at the large wooden table, weaving a twine bracelet. 'I knew you'd call by on your way home today. Sage, Sophie; meet Nick and Angelina Gouna and their daughter, Aliki. They have just moved to The Valley. Aliki is starting in the lower sixth at Briar Lane on Monday.'

Aliki and her father were both short and stocky. Despite the cool weather they were wearing shorts and tee shirts which showed well-toned legs and arms. Nick had olive skin and wavy black hair, flecked with grey. Aliki had darker skin and curly black hair that hung in a thick braid down her back.

Nick stood up and held out his hand with a warm smile on his face. 'We're very pleased to meet you. I've been working at the Castle Hospital for the past few years, and now my wife has taken up a post in the ophthalmic department, so we've moved to the area. I'm not sorry to say goodbye to commuting!'

Angelina smiled. She was slightly taller than her husband with dark brown skin and curly black hair tied back to show her high cheekbones. Her dark brown eyes were kind but held a hint of worry. 'We're pleased that Aliki will have a few friendly faces when she starts in the lower sixth next week.'

'Lovely to meet you.' Sage smiled. 'Aliki, is that a Greek name?'

The girl nodded. 'My father is Greek; my mother is from Barbados. Alora has told me all about you. I'm really glad to meet you before I start at school next week.'

'Are you all shifters?' Sophie asked.

Aliki nodded. 'I've just started to shift, actually. It's a bit hard getting used to it.'

Sophie rolled her eyes. 'Tell me about it, new Gifts; we've all been there!'

'Aliki is not too good at controlling her shifting at the moment. Whenever she gets angry, she can change,' Nick said.

'And lots of things seem to annoy her these days,' Angelina added. 'I'm not sure starting a new school is the right thing to do. I would have preferred it if Aliki would consider home-schooling until she is more in control of her Gift.'

Aliki sighed. 'But I've explained everything to you, Mum. I just want to fit in like everybody else. I'm planning on working with underprivileged youngsters in the future. I know what it's like to feel different to everybody else. Later, I don't want to tell the young people that I had a privileged background and when life got tough, I was home schooled. I want to be the sort of person they can identify with.'

'I can understand how you feel,' Angelina said. 'But you must also be aware that you have a responsibility to safeguard the Gifted community, too.'

'Put this on, Aliki.' Alora tied the woven band around her wrist. 'This charm will help you keep your temper but try to avoid situations that you find stressful.'

'If you need any help at school, we'll be there,' Sage told her. 'Which classes are you taking? There'll probably be a Gifted in at least one of them.'

'PE, Social Science and History.'

Sage and Sophie exchanged looks.

'Callum Hunt is in PE and Social Science.' Sage explained how his suspicions had been raised and his present quest to unmask the Gifted of The Valley.

Alora told her about the origins of his family name. 'You're going to have to be very careful.'

'There are lots of things that can help you while you get used to your Gift. My Aunt Mary has several kinds of teas that can keep you calm. We could call by her house on the way home today.' Sophie smiled.

'And on Saturday morning you'll get to meet some of the other Gifted from our school,' Sage added. 'Merc is in your PE class and Bess is in History. They'll be there if you need anything. And we'll see you at lunchtimes.'

'Well, I do feel more at ease about Aliki starting school now we've talked to Alora and the girls,' Nick said.

Aliki gave her mother a questioning look. Angelina sighed. 'Yes, I hope you will be okay, but if anything happens, we'll have to rethink things.'

***

The following Monday, Sage and Sophie smiled at Aliki and her mum as they waited in the reception area. Aliki gave them a nervous wave and fingered her wristband as they followed the secretary into the office.

The two girls were both pleased as Aliki arrived in the canteen at lunchtime, surrounded by a group of students.

'I've had such a great morning,' Aliki said as she placed her tray on the table. 'Everyone has been really friendly and helpful.'

Sophie nodded. 'Yes, it's not a bad school. Most of the students are friendly; though there are a few to watch out for.'

Sasha and Layla arrived with some other students and joined them.

'A new girl?' Layla said. 'It's unusual to get newcomers after the term has started.'

'My dad has been working at the Castle Hospital for the past three years. We didn't get to see much of him. When Mum was offered a post in the ophthalmic clinic, we decided to move here. It seems like a really nice place.'

'It's quiet; a bit dead socially,' a boy commented.

Layla nodded. 'Yeah, you have to go to one of the bigger towns nearby for any kind of nightlife.'

'Oh, I'm happy with a quiet life.' Aliki smiled.

They all turned around as there was the sound of shouting in the doorway.

'Callum Hunt making his presence felt!' Sage muttered.

'Callum's okay,' Layla said. 'At least he brings a bit of fun to the place.'

'He's not fun. He's an immature bully.' Sophie glared in his direction. He seemed to sense her attention and turned towards her. She groaned as he headed their way followed by two of his friends.

'Hey, new girl. I hear you're in our PE class. We've basketball this afternoon, I hope you're halfway decent.'

Aliki shrugged. 'I'm not bad.'

'We'll see if *not bad* is good enough for us.' Callum gave a condescending smile as he walked away.

The smile had left his face as he and Roy watched Aliki on the court that afternoon.

'The new girl is really something to look out for, isn't she?' Roy commented. 'I haven't seen anyone throw a ball so hard or so fast since the Titan was at school and he left over two years ago.'

'Yes, she is pretty good,' Callum conceded.

'We'll stand a better chance in the finals with superwoman on the team,' Layla commented. 'We've only managed to be runners up in the last three years.'

There was a loud whistle blast and the PE teacher pointed at Aliki. 'You're getting a bit carried away there, Aliki. Someone could be injured if you throw the ball that hard.'

'Sorry. Are you okay?' she said to a boy rubbing his shoulder.

'Well, we're playing to win, aren't we, Mr Bell?' Callum called out as he stood up. 'Can I take his place, sir?'

Aliki discovered him to be a formidable opponent as the game continued and began playing harder herself. Both were determined to be the winning team. There was a palpable tension in the air as they reached the last few minutes of the game and Mr Bell blew the whistle. 'It's a draw! Just think what we can do with both of you on the same side. Aliki, I'm signing you up for the first team for our match against St Piran's next week.'

'So how did your afternoon go?' Sage asked Aliki as they walked home that afternoon.

'Oh, really well. I'm playing basketball for the school next week. And I've also signed up for the Sports for All Club after school tomorrow. Merc said it's more for fun and it's a great way to meet new friends.'

'You've had really good first day, Aliki,' Sophie smiled. 'And you seem to be keeping on top of…everything.'

Aliki fingered her wristband. 'Yes; so far, so good.'

It was a different story at the Sports for All session the next afternoon. Miss Arnold, a PE teacher, had organised the students into teams and several games of football were being played.

She blew her whistle as she watched one of the games. 'Aliki, you must not be so aggressive. This is a friendly match, remember.'

Aliki helped a boy in the opposite football team to his feet. 'Sorry. I got a bit carried away there.'

For the next ten minutes she held back, allowing others to intercept the ball until the score was going against her team. She shook her head, feeling her competitive spirit rising. A boy in the opposing team had dribbled the ball towards the net and was readying himself to shoot. Aliki rushed forward, leaping high to intercept the shot before the goalie had a chance to react, kicking the ball with such force that several members of both teams dived out of the way.

'I'm so sorry,' Aliki muttered again.

'Hmm, you don't seem to know your own strength, do you, Aliki?' Miss Arnold frowned. 'How about we give Sue a chance to play and you sit out for a while?'

Aliki nodded and went to join a tall, skinny boy sitting on the bench. He was holding an ice pack to his cheek.

'Oh, dear, what happened?' she asked.

'The usual.' He shrugged. 'Some part of my body always seems to be in the wrong place at the wrong time. It happens most weeks.'

'Doesn't it put you off the Sports for All Club?'

'Sport isn't really my thing. But my mother thinks that this club gives me the chance to exercise, meet people and improve my social skills. We agreed to give it go until Christmas. But it's not really working out. Whereas, you definitely are the sporty type. I was very impressed watching that save.'

'You're right, I am the sporty type, but my problem is, I have to rein it in a bit. I've seen you in history class. Is history more your thing?'

'Definitely. I'm planning on studying archaeology at university. I belong to a group that does local digs and I spend most of my free time with them at the weekends. This area is really interesting from an historical point of view. We've found quite a few valuable artifacts in the past few years. Over the summer, as well as pottery shards, we unearthed a brooch and a comb that are well over a thousand years old, very well preserved. I'm really chuffed because it was me that discovered the brooch. It's heavy gold with a jewel encrusted design in the shape of a cross, so it would have belonged to someone of high rank; maybe a knight who would have used it to fasten his cloak. Can you imagine what kind of man would have worn such a valuable piece of jewellery and the places he would have visited? It's such a pity that these treasures can't talk, they'd have such interesting stories to tell us. In fact…' He stopped. 'Oh, I'm sorry, this is where *I* need to rein it in a bit.'

At that moment, Miss Arnold blew a whistle and a cheer went up from the winning teams. Merc came over as Aliki was pushing her clothes into her kitbag.

'You were brilliant, Aliki. Are you ready to go now?'

'Yes.' She turned to the boy. 'It's been really nice talking to you…'

'Radu. Nice talking to you, too, Aliki.'
***

'This is Radu, he's in my history class and in the Sports for All Club,' Aliki said as they both joined the others in the canteen the following day. 'It's jogging next week. Why don't you join us?'

Sage nodded. 'Actually, that's a good idea. I'm spending too much time sitting around these days. What do you think, Sophie?'

'As long as it's nothing too arduous…'

'If I can manage it, anyone can. I'm hoping I'll come out unscathed this week,' Radu joked.

At the next Sports for All meeting, Sage, Sophie and Radu sat down on a bench as Callum and Aliki jogged past them.

'Five laps and they still have the energy to talk to each other,' Sophie said, holding on to her side. 'Two did me in.'

'I saw you out running the other night,' Callum said to Aliki.

'Yes, I really enjoy running.'

'How about we go together one evening?'

'Yes, that would be good.'

'Tomorrow?'

'Oh, not tomorrow, I'm meeting Radu to go over some of the history I missed from the beginning of term.'

'I'm sure you could do that another day...'

'No, we've already arranged it. Are you free the next day?'

'No. Can't do, I'm afraid.'

'Oh well, another time that suits us both, eh? Race you to the finish line? Ready?'

Aliki was soon metres ahead of Callum. He stopped running and headed over to his own friends.

'Superwoman left you way behind, mate!' Roy said, patting his back.

'I don't think he's a particularly good loser,' Radu commented as he saw the expression on Callum's face.

'Did you enjoy the session today?' Aliki asked Sophie as they prepared to go home.

'I did. What about you, Sage?'

'Yes, though it made me realise how unfit I am.'

'Miss Arnold says she's booked the badminton courts for next week. Are you going to put your names down?' Merc said.

'Yes, that sounds like fun,' Sophie nodded.

'Badminton? Hey I might make it two weeks in a row where I don't get injured!' Radu smiled.

Callum bit his lip as he watched the group laughing and joking as they left the field. Any other student would have jumped at the chance to spend an evening with him. Why would she choose the geek's company?

Chapter Twelve

'So, that's about all we covered before you joined us, Aliki,' Radu said the following evening as he put together a pile of photocopied notes. 'It's all pretty straightforward, but let me know if there's anything else you need to go over.'

'Thanks, Radu. That's really good of you.'

hat have you got arranged for the rest of the evening?'

'I'm going for a run with my parents tonight.'

'In the dark?'

'It's fun in the dark, anyway, tonight's a full moon, so it won't be that dark. What about you? Are you going to get immersed in one of your history books?'

'I am actually. I've just had an email from the online archaeology library. They've sent an eBook I've been wanting to read for ages!'

Two hours later, Aliki and her parents left the house and began to jog towards the local park. As they turned into the gateway, Callum was leaving a café on the opposite side of the road.

'I wonder if superwoman's parents are as good as she is?' he murmured, running behind them and keeping out of their sight.

They picked up the pace as they headed uphill to a thickly wooded area, not seeming to have any trouble finding their way in the darkness, while Callum struggled to keep his footing, tripping over the branches and stones hidden in the undergrowth. He slowed down as the sound of their voices faded as they ventured further into the woods. Suddenly, he stopped hearing a noise that made his blood run cold. It was a long, drawn-out howl, followed by a second, then a third. Then the creatures began to howl together, splitting the night air with their eerie cries.

Callum turned and ran, pushing branches to one side and stumbling over rocks and stones; frantically trying to put more distance between himself and whatever was out there in the darkness. It was only when he reached the street that he felt he could slow down to ease his burning lungs. Even then, he didn't feel safe until he had reached home and closed the door behind him.

At the same time that Callum heard the first howls, Sage was sitting in her bedroom chatting on the phone to Sophie.

'What was that sound?'

'Stay on the line. I'll find out.' Sophie ran downstairs, the phone still in her hand. 'Mum? Mary? What was that noise?'

Mary smiled. 'It's a sound we haven't heard in The Valley for many years. Shifters are howling at the full moon.'

'Is it Aliki and her parents?'

Mary nodded. 'Yes. They must be up in Bleachers Woods. There's a clearing there so they'll get a good view of the sky on a cloudless night like tonight. Bleachers Woods used to be the place where shifters would hunt a long time ago. There hasn't been enough wildlife there to support even one family for quite a while now.'

'Do you think Aliki and her parents are out there hunting?' Sophie grimaced.

'No. Angelina said she'd prefer to buy their food the same as everyone else. They want to fit into their local community. But it looks as if they couldn't resist the shifter call of the full moon.'

***

'Hi Aliki,' Radu said as they walked into school the next morning. 'I'm glad to see you're okay. I was quite worried last night.'

Aliki frowned. 'Why?'

'Didn't you hear the howling?'

'Probably some stray dogs. Oh, I found this in the papers you gave me last night. She held out a photo.

'I've been looking for that! It's a photo of the gold brooch I was telling you about. I'm going to the town library to see if I can find out anything about it.'

'It's very beautiful. I'd love to see all these treasures you found.'

'They'll be going on display in the museum in January. The curators are still verifying the details of some of the finds we unearthed at the moment.'

Aliki handed the photo to Radu. 'I'll have to wait a while then.'

'You know, if you're really keen on seeing them; I'll see if I can get you permission to take you into the backroom where we prepare the items for the exhibition. I'm going there myself Friday afternoon. I'll speak to Natalie, she's the curator, and tell her that you're a history student, too. She might agree to let you have a preview of the artefacts.'

'That would be great!'

At that moment Sage and Sophie appeared. 'Hi there. What would be great, Aliki?'

'Radu was telling me about the treasures they uncovered in a dig over the summer. There's a brooch that...'

'Hey! Did you hear the howling last night?' Layla interrupted as she joined them.

'My dad said it sounded like wolves,' Sasha added.

'Probably stray dogs,' Sage said.

'No way!' Layla continued. 'It sounded more like a pack of wolves!'

A crowd had gathered in the hallway, all discussing the howling. 'Some people from the animal shelter and the police went up to Bleachers Woods to investigate,' a boy commented.

'Well, they didn't find any dangerous animals, did they?' Aliki pointed out. 'It was probably just some stray dogs.'

Callum glared at her. 'And how would you know?'

She shrugged. 'We'd have heard something by now if they had found anything, wouldn't we?'

As the others set off for their classes, Layla turned to her friend. 'Maybe it's the new girl who was doing all the howling. She looks like a bit of a dog, doesn't she?'

The two girls giggled as they walked away, leaving Callum frowning thoughtfully.

'All everyone seems to talk about today is the howling,' Bridget said as she sat down at the canteen table at lunchtime.

'Mr Phips told us we should think twice about going into Bleachers Woods at the moment. Apparently, the police and animal people didn't find anything, but he said it's best to be on the safe side,' Henry commented.

'I bet it was just a prank by some schoolkids,' Merc said. 'Do you remember the so-called UFO landing two years ago?'

Sophie laughed. 'And it turned out to be part of an old float from the carnival procession.'

'I wouldn't go into Bleachers Woods in the dark anyway.' Bridget shivered.

Radu turned to Aliki. 'I spoke to Natalie, earlier. She's fine about you coming with me to the museum to have a preview of the exhibition. Hopefully, in the next two weeks.'

'Oh good. I'm really looking forward to it.'

Chapter Thirteen

Aliki looked up from her locker door later that week to see Radu hurrying towards her.

He had a proud smile on his face as he pulled a sheaf of papers out of his bag. 'Take a look at this; I'm on page six. It's only the rough copy of the brochure, the final version will be on gloss paper.'

Aliki took the page he held out. 'You're famous! *"The youngest member of our society, Radu Munteanu, has made the most important find of our group to date. The gold brooch set with a cross of rubies was probably..."*'

'What have you got there, Aliki?' Callum peered over her shoulder.

'Radu is famous! He found this gold brooch on one of the archaeological digs!'

'Really?' Callum looked interested and read the caption. 'How much did they pay you for it, Radu?'

'Nothing. It's part of the dig. Anyone could have found it; I was just lucky that it was me!'

'So, you don't get anything for it?'

'His name is in the brochure...' Aliki began.

Callum gave a short laugh. 'Big deal! Why didn't you slip the brooch into your pocket? I bet you could have sold it somewhere for a good price.'

Radu's face reddened. 'I had no intention of slipping anything into my pocket! The exhibition is for everyone to enjoy and appreciate these historical artefacts.'

'There can't be much money in archaeology if you give everything away for free! Think I'll stick with my plan to get into one of the big IT companies. There's money to be made in future ideas rather than the past.' Callum walked away laughing.

'What has amused him?' Sage said as she and Sophie joined them.

Radu scowled. 'Callum can't understand why I didn't try to steal something valuable that I found on a dig. He has no morals whatsoever!'

'What did you find?' Sophie asked.

Aliki smoothed out the booklet in her hand. 'It's this brooch...'

A shout made them all look up as a girl hurried up to them. 'Aliki! So sorry to interrupt, but it's a life and death situation! Have you got any trainers I can borrow this morning? Mr Bell warned me if I forgot my kit again this week, I'd get a detention! Jill lent me a t-shirt and shorts but her trainers are too big.'

'Yes, I've a spare pair.' Aliki handed the brochure to Radu and turned to her locker.

Radu pushed it into his rucksack. 'I'd better get going, too.'

'I wonder what Radu found?' Sage commented to Sophie as they made their way to their classes.

'And so typical of Callum to feel it's okay to steal stuff from a dig! Making money isn't everything.'

'I don't think he'd agree with you.'

Chapter Fourteen

'All set for Alora's?' Aliki asked as she arrived at with Sophie at Sage's house a few weeks later.

'We're just waiting for Paris,' Sage told her. 'Come inside.'

Ellen smiled. 'You've time for a cup of tea before you go. Jim, can you ask Adam and Elvis to move over to the side?'

'Oh, I've heard of these famous ants. Which one is which?' Aliki asked as the two ants crawled onto Jim's hand.

Jim pointed to the quicker of the ants. 'This is Elvis. Hey, watch what you're saying!'

'What did he say?' Aliki looked intrigued.

'Elvis can be quite mean to Adam since he injured his leg. He said he has the swagger and Adam has the stagger.' He gave a nod. 'You're right, Adam, if Elvis is the beauty, you're the brains. Okay, how about you two continue your discussion outside?' He took the two creatures into the garden and returned a moment later.

'How are you finding things, Aliki?' Ellen asked her.

'I was so glad that people have stopped talking about the howling,' Aliki said as she picked up her cup of tea.

'You and your family are going to have to be more careful, aren't you?' Jim commented. 'Axel managed to convince the police that it was most likely to be a dog. He said it could be a farm dog that escaped and the owner was reluctant to say anything after all the fuss.'

'We definitely don't want all this fuss again,' Aliki said. 'Dad says we'll go further afield at the next full moon.

It's a pity we can't enjoy the full moon in our chosen home town. And this is such an interesting place to live. Yesterday, I went with Radu to the museum. They have this amazing backroom, the Lady Estelle Suite, where they prepare their findings for exhibitions. He showed me some of their latest artifacts, dating back hundreds of years. I actually got to hold the gold brooch that he found, wearing special gloves, of course.'

'Is that what Callum thought Radu should have pocketed?' Sophie asked. 'Is it really valuable?'

'Yes. It's solid gold with a cross design in rubies. It's quite heavy. Natalie Delta, who is the museum curator, said it was probably used by a knight or royal person to fasten their cloak. On the back it has the initials IC. Natalie said that could have been the owner of the brooch or the initials of the person who gave it to the knight.'

Silence fell around the table and Aliki was surprised to find all eyes on her.

'A cross?' Sage said.

'Hundreds of years old?' Ellen said.

A knock at the door made them all jump. Paris walked in. 'Sorry I'm a bit late, the train was delayed. All set for Alora's?'

'Paris,' Sophie squealed. 'Aliki has found the second cross!'

'Hey, slow down a bit, Sophie. We don't know that for sure,' Jim said.

'I just feel it *has* to be it!'

'What second cross?' Aliki asked.

'Of course, you don't know the significance of a cross, do you?' Sage related the story of Arthur and how Morgana had cast a spell on him.

'And Mai Lin needs the second cross to wake Arthur up,' Sophie concluded. 'It looks as if you've found it! I mean; *maybe* you have.'

'We need to speak to Alora about this as soon as possible,' Paris said.

Before joining their Gifted groups that morning, they sat down with Alora in a quiet room in The Coterie and Aliki explained how she had found out about the new cross.

She let out a long breath. 'Well, it sounds very interesting, but we mustn't rush to conclusions. Over the centuries, Mai Lin and Vinnie have unearthed many crosses that looked hopeful. Vinnie is in Wales at the moment, but she's due back here any day now. I'll tell her about this and she can make the necessary arrangements to procure the cross.'

Aliki looked unhappy. 'Will she just take it? It's part of Radu's great find. He's actually named in the exhibition catalogue.'

'Don't worry, when Vinnie takes a treasure from Earth world to Aurum, she leaves an exact replica in its place. No human can distinguish the substitute from the original.'

Over the next few days, they waited anxiously for news from Vinnie. On Tuesday evening, when Sage returned home from school, her grandmother met her with a wide smile.

'Alora has been in touch. Vinnie arrived at The Coterie about two hours ago. She wants you, Sophie and Aliki to go and see her this evening.'

A short while later, Alora ushered the three girls into the kitchen where Vinnie was seated.

'Ah, you're Aliki, a newcomer to The Valley.' She looked taken aback when Aliki flinched as she shook the girl's hand.

'I'm so sorry,' Aliki said. 'Please excuse my manners; your hand is really cold!'

Vinnie smiled. 'That's okay; shifters always feel so hot to us. Alora tells me you've found a new cross.'

'Actually, Radu found it,' Aliki explained about his involvement in the local archaeological group. She described the cross and gave the details about it that she had learnt from the museum curator.

Vinnie looked thoughtful. 'And where is it being kept at the moment?'

'In the Lady Estelle Suite, just behind the main exhibition rooms in the museum.'

'I've been in touch with a fae friend, Cornelia, who helps me substitute treasures that we want to take to Aurum. We'll visit the museum tonight. She'll need a few hours to create the substitute; then I can take the original to Aurum. I'm sure you'll be hearing from Mai Lin before long.'

'I do hope this is the second cross,' Sage said.

'I have a really good feeling about it!' Sophie nodded.

***

Sophie was to repeat similar words the following Saturday morning as she sat with Sage, Paris, Vinnie and Mai Lin in Mai's kitchen.

Mai's hands shook as she held the cross. 'It's Arthur's. He used it to fasten his cloak. I've seen it many times before.' She turned the brooch over. 'And here, the letters IC; they stand for Igraine Cornwall, Arthur's mother. She gave him the cross the day his father, Uthur, died. And shortly after that, she herself was killed.'

'This *must* be the second cross,' Sophie whispered.

Mai placed the cross on the table and stood up, wringing her hands together. 'We mustn't get too carried away. Don't forget, Vinnie and I have unearthed many crosses and had our hopes dashed many times.'

'But I think…'

Paris nudged Sophie's arm and raised an eyebrow.

'Shall we go and find out?' Mai strode towards the door and led them down to the edge of the lake. They climbed into the wooden boat moored there. Vinnie gave a final wave from the bank as Paris and Sage rowed out towards the island.

'No stormy weather or ghostly figures to turn us away like they did last time we were here. I think that's a good omen,' Sophie said as she stepped onto land.

Mai Lin led them along a rough pathway that continued into the mouth of a narrow passageway in the rocky hillside. She stopped to light a wooden taper fastened on the wall and held it aloft as they made their way ahead. They continued in silence, the only sound being the dripping of water above their heads. Finally, the pathway split into two separate ways, both encircling a central stone wall. Mai Lin led them around to a pair of tall, wrought iron gates set into the stone. A heavy padlock held them shut. Beyond the gates was a simple stone chamber. In the centre were three raised platforms, the middle platform being slightly higher than the other two. On each of them, a man lay sleeping.

'Arthur and his two closest friends, Osric and Maynard,' Mai Lin whispered.

The three friends watched as Mai Lin handed Paris the taper, unclasped the gold chain from around her neck and placed it against the padlock. It fell to the ground and the gates slowly swung open.

Breathing heavily, Mai Lin led the others forward until they were standing by the central figure.

'Arthur, my love. It's me, Mai Lin, come to take you home.' She unwrapped the cross from its linen holder and placed it in his motionless hands.

For a few moments, all was still, then suddenly, there was a flash and they found themselves lying on the ground outside the locked gates once again.

Mai Lin sat up and began to cry. 'No, no, no! Not again! I had so hoped...I thought this time there was a better chance...'

'This can't be right!' Sophie's voice echoed around the stone corridor.

Sage and Paris exchanged sad looks.

Mai Lin pulled herself up. 'Come, let's get back to the castle.'

Paris moved forward and helped her to her feet. 'I'm so sorry, Mai.'

'Wait! Wait! There must be something; we missed something...' Sophie closed her eyes. 'Of course!'

Sage gave her a warning look. 'Mai is really upset, Sophie. Perhaps it could wait until we get back to the castle?'

'No, no. We need to try it now. Can we get back inside, Mai?'

'Why? We've found that this isn't the right cross, so...'

'But can we go back inside?'

'Yes, I suppose we could. I don't know if it's a good idea.'

'Mai, please listen to me for a moment. There is one more thing we can try.'

Mai Lin looked at her.

Sophie turned to Paris. 'When I text you, or you text me, what does a cross mean?'

'Well, a kiss.'

'Exactly! Mai, have you ever kissed Arthur, I mean, there in the chamber?'

'No. As soon as I put a cross in his hands, I find myself flung back out here.'

'In all enchanted stories, the prince wakes up the princess with a kiss! Surely, it should work the other way round, too? A kiss could wake up a king or a prince?'

'It's worth a try,' Paris ventured.

'Maybe I'll just find myself back here again,' Mai Lin said.

'Then you haven't lost anything, have you?' Sophie continued. 'I really think it's worth a try.'

Mai Lin took another deep breath. 'I suppose I have nothing to lose.'

Once again, she touched her cross to the lock and the padlock fell to the ground. She made her way to Arthur's side and put her hands on his. Slowly she leaned down and whispered his name before placing a soft kiss on his lips.

Once again, all was still until suddenly Arthur's eyes flew open. He pulled himself up and looked around him.

Mai flung her arms around his neck and sobbed. 'Arthur you've come back!'

'Mai Lin? Where are we? Who are those youngsters?'

A deep voice sounded behind them. 'Yes, where are we?'

'In some kind of cave, I think,' a third voice answered.

Arthur's two friends had climbed down from the platform and were peering around in the dim light of the taper.

'What's that?' Sophie said as a rumbling noise grew louder.

A wall of water was pouring into the passageway.

'The place is flooding! We must get out of here quickly!' Paris shouted.

Grabbing Arthur's hand, Mai Lin led the group back towards a second passageway, but they soon realised that that exit was also filling up.

'We can't get out that way, we'll have to go up,' Mai Lin shouted. 'Hold hands.'

'What are you doing, Mai Lin?' Arthur shouted. 'Is this some kind of magic?'

'I'll explain everything later, Arthur, I promise, but for now we need to get out of here quickly.'

'But I do not countenance the use of magic!'

'Sire, with all due respect the lady is right. The water level is rising rapidly,' one of his men interjected. 'We must leave immediately - by any means.'

'Be it on your head, Osric!'

'Hold hands!' Mai shouted above the sound of the rushing water.

A moment later, they found themselves on the top of the hillside. Beneath their feet, the ground trembled. Mai put her fingers to her lips and gave a long, loud whistle.

'Dragons to the rescue!' Sophie smiled as three shapes flew towards them.

Arthur's face grew pale as the creatures drew close.

'There is no way I am getting on such a beast!'

'We'll take this fine specimen, Maynard,' Osric walked forward as the first dragon landed. He patted its muzzle and spoke softly to it. 'Come on, Maynard; we don't have a choice, do we?' He climbed on to the dragon and held out his hand to the second man.

'Abraxus can hold three,' Paris said, pulling Sophie up in front of him and helping Sage settle herself behind them.

'Arthur, please, trust me.' Mai patted the third dragon's neck. 'Mimosa is one of our gentlest dragons. She's come to our rescue'

As Arthur hesitated, there was a loud roar and a huge spout of water burst through the hillside. Mai grabbed his hand and pulled him up behind her a moment before the entire hillside began to crumble.

The three dragons soared into the sky, weaving around the fountains of water erupting around them. The riders looked down as the island disappeared beneath the surface of the lake.

The dragons eased their speed and slowly circled the now still waters.

Maynard looked down nervously. 'Whoever would have imagined that man could fly through the air like a bird?'

The dragons headed for the castle and landed gently on the parapet. Arthur watched warily as Mai Lin rubbed the snout of each one, murmuring softly to them before they flew off into the distance.

'Where is this place? Arthur asked. 'The castle seems familiar in some ways, but it is not Camelot.'

Mai Lin shook her head. 'No, it's not Camelot but I tried to make it feel homely for you. Come inside.'

'How about we show Maynard and Osric to their rooms, and explain any modern conveniences that might be new to them, while you show Arthur to his rooms?' Paris suggested.

Osric stepped forward happily while Arthur and Maynard looked less at ease.

'This new situation must be quite confusing for you,' Sage said to Osric as Maynard turned on and off the tap in the washbasin and peered underneath it. 'It's hot! Straight from this contraption with no obvious fire beneath it.'

'I'll show you how to use the shower,' Paris offered.

Osric looked at the three friends. 'I assume that you youngsters are all magically touched in some way?'

Sophie smiled broadly. 'Oh, are you all Gifted, too?'

He shook his head. 'Only myself. Now that we are in Merlin's – or should I say, Mai Lin's land, I'm assuming I won't have to conceal my Gift anymore. Although I don't know if Arthur will be so accepting.'

'I think he'll get used to things,' Sage said. 'He's going to find Aurum, this magical world, easier to accept than the changes in Earth world. A lot has happened in the last few centuries.'

'Is that how long we have been sleeping?' Osric gave a low whistle.

Maynard appeared in the room, towelling his hair dry. 'The boy says it's not magic, but I couldn't see how else there could be an endless supply of piping hot water. And the other facilities...much nicer than any I've ever seen in any land!'

Mai Lin decided they would eat in the Grand Hall rather than expose the newcomers to too much modern technology on their first day and led them to one end of the long table.

Arthur turned to his men as they sat down. 'It appears that not only did Mai Lin conceal her true identity as to her sex, but also failed to reveal that she is a sorcerer. And that this world – Aurum is the home to many other magical characters.'

'That's true. Long after Camelot had fallen, the persecution of those with magical powers continued until it seemed that they faced extinction if they remained in Earth world. They came to me for help and I created Aurum as a safe haven.'

Osric nodded. 'I wish that you had done so earlier. In my lifetime, I lost many Gifted family members and close friends.'

Arthur was astounded. 'All these years you served me, and I never even suspected you had magical powers, Osric. And you, too, Mai Lin.'

'With all respect, Sire, we were unable to reveal our true natures for fear of facing a painful death,' Osric pointed out. 'You must admit, neither of us was anything less than a loyal servant to you, Arthur.'

'You were indeed,' he conceded.

Mai Lin shifted in her seat. 'There's something else I need to mention. I put a charm on you to protect you and this stopped Morgana from harming you, but she was able to cast a sleeping spell on you. As all three of you spent several hundred years in a magical chamber; and now you are here in Aurum, a magical land.' She paused. 'You have all been affected by magic.'

'You mean, we now could possess magical powers?' Arthur asked.

'As you are now immortal, there is a strong possibility.'

'No, this can't be!' Maynard stood up. 'I want to be the person I was born to be – a normal human being!'

Mai Lin spread her hands. 'You do have a choice, Maynard. If you leave Aurum and return to Earth world, you can renounce any magical abilities as long as you live outside any town or village that is a crux.'

He sat down again, wiping his brow. 'I think the sooner we return to Earth world and leave magic behind the better, don't you agree, Sire?'

Arthur rubbed his chin. 'I really don't know what to think at the moment.' He looked around at the youngsters. 'And you also have magical talents?'

'Yes. I'm a Transposer. Sage and Paris are Snares,' Sophie told him. 'There are also Animators, Communicators and shifters in The Valley.'

'Osric raised his eyebrows. 'Shifters?'

'Are you a shifter?' Paris asked him.

'Yes,' he replied.

'I thought you were a Communicator when I saw how you were with the dragons,' Sophie said. 'They can sort of talk with animals, like Sage's grandad.'

'Well, I do have an affinity with many non-human creatures, I do feel I can communicate with them.'

'So, you have two Gifts,' Sage said.

Maynard's lips narrowed. 'Magic does not sit easily with me.'

At that moment, Flavia appeared in the doorway, followed by two young fae each carrying laden trays. Mai Lin introduced them to the newcomers.

'Welcome, Arthur and your two fine companions.' Flavia said as they laid the trays on the table. 'I trust your rooms are satisfactory?'

'Indeed, madam, I have never seen such splendid accommodation,' Arthur replied as his two friends nodded in agreement.

She beamed. 'For many centuries we have been preparing for the day we would welcome you to the castle. And if it had taken another few hundred years, we would have continued to do so most willingly.'

She ignored the slight cough from Mai Lin and continued.

'We thought some hot soup and fresh bread would be welcome after your adventures today,' Flavia said as they placed a bowl of soup in front of each of them. 'And a selection of the finest cakes that Aurum can offer.'

Her helpers placed jugs of water and wine on the table. 'Is there anything else we can get for you?' one of the girls asked.

'Hot tea would be welcome.' Arthur smiled. 'Mai Lin introduced me to that beverage. I find it is excellent for soothing the nerves. Perhaps it would help you, too, Maynard.'

After several more minutes of fussing, Flavia and her helpers left the hall. Conversation stopped for the next few minutes as they began to eat hungrily.

'A special request for tea?' Vinnie stepped into the hall carrying a tray with Peridot behind her holding a second tray of cups. The men began to stand up but she shook her head. 'Please carry on with your meal.'

Maynard's eyes were fixed on Peridot's hand as she placed a cup of tea down beside him.

'Goblin blood?' Osric asked her. 'And fae, maybe?'

She smiled and nodded as the two women sat down at the table, each taking a cup of tea for themselves.

'A warm welcome to you, Arthur, and your companions. I have travelled to many places in Earth world over the centuries, tracking down crosses that were linked to you and Camelot,' Vinnie said. 'So it was Radu's cross that released you from Morgana's spell?'

Mai shook her head and explained what had happened. 'Sophie showed me that the solution has been right under my nose, literally, all this time!'

Arthur nodded. 'Mai has told me an abbreviated story of your quest and gave me the cross Radu unearthed.' He pulled it from his pocket. 'I am most grateful to have this memento of my mother safely in my hands. I must have lost it in the last battle.'

'May I take a look?' Osric took the cross from Arthur's hand.

Peridot leaned towards him as he turned the cross over in his hands. 'It is a beautiful work of art. Brunswick would love to see this and to hear the story behind it.'

'Brunswick?' Osric asked her.

'My uncle, head of Brunswick Jewellers.'

'Is there much travelling between the two worlds?' Maynard asked Mai Lin.

'Until recently, few people ventured from one world to the other, but that's all changing.' Mai Lin began to explain her hopes of building closer links between Aurum and Earth world.

'I, for one, am ready to settle in Earth world,' Maynard said. 'Surely it will feel more like home than Aurum for someone like myself; no disrespect meant to you, Mai Lin, or to your companions.'

'Earth world has changed so much over the past few centuries; I think you will find it less like home than Aurum; and quite overwhelming. Of course, once you visit Earth world you can decide for yourselves where you want to settle.'

Vinnie spread her hands. 'Why don't I bring you books and pictures of modern life in Earth world, to give you an idea of what life is like in these modern times?'

'The perfect solution,' Mai Lin agreed. 'You'll need to be prepared to find many changes.'

'As you are probably aware, everyone in Aurum is anxious to meet you' Peridot said. 'Expect quite a few visitors over the next few days.'

Mai Lin patted his arm as a look of alarm crossed over Maynard's face. 'Don't worry, we'll arrange for you to meet a few people at time while you settle in.'

'And we'll be on hand if you find things too much; won't we Peridot?' Vinnie added.

'I wish we could stay longer.' Sophie sighed. 'But we have to get back to school and Paris to university.'

'But surely you are too old to be continuing your education?' Osric said to Paris.

'Are girls also educated in these modern times? Is that necessary?' Maynard frowned.

Paris gave a brief outline of the modern education system, while Maynard shook his head. 'I left home at seven to live in Camelot and learn to be a knight. At nineteen years old, I had achieved that distinction.'

'Seven years old? How awful. You were hardly more than a baby,' Sophie cried.

'I soon grew up and appreciated the great opportunity I had been given. Didn't you find it so, Osric?'

'At seven years old, I was running wild with my siblings and cousins in our mountain homeland. I joined Arthur's army when I was sixteen after an attack on our village left me homeless and alone.'

'But you knew magic was outlawed in Camelot, didn't you?' Sage said.

He nodded. 'I decided that it was best to hide in plain sight.'

'Now you don't need to hide anymore.' Peridot smiled.

Chapter Fifteen

Alora was at Sage's home when the three friends returned to Earth world the next day.

'Jay came here yesterday evening with the news! We could hardly believe it; after all this time. I just had to come and hear all about it.'

Sophie proudly explained her role in awakening Arthur and his companions. Paris added details of their escape from the collapsing island. Sage told them of their conversations the previous evening.

'Fancy going to sleep and waking up several hundred years later,' Ellen commented. 'It must be hard for them to understand what has happened.'

Paris nodded. 'Osric seems to be coping quite well. He's a shifter, so he's used to magic; but the other two are finding it harder to deal with.'

'Are they planning a trip to Earth world soon?' Jim asked.

'Yes,' Sage said. 'Mai Lin is a bit worried about how they will find Earth world with all the changes in the past thousand years.'

'Well, in Aurum and Earth world, we'll do all we can to support them,' Alora said.

Over the next few days at school, Sage and Sophie were often cornered by other Gifted students.

'What's Arthur like? How old is he? Is he good looking?'

'And his two friends...'

'Are they Gifted?'

'Will they be coming here?'

'Merc and Molly have visas to go to Aurum soon; they'll be able to give us the latest news.'

Callum was intrigued by the attention the two girls were getting. He approached Sophie at her locker. 'Who's Arthur? And where is he?'

She shrugged and walked away. 'He's obviously not someone you know so why are you interested?'

He pursed his lips. 'I'll find someone who will speak to me.'

At that moment, Aliki and Radu walked by and he fell into step beside them. 'Who's Arthur?'

Aliki looked flustered but Radu looked at him. 'Are you talking of a modern Arthur or King Arthur and the Knights of the Round Table.'

'There are loads of stories about King Arthur here in The Valley, but he's really just a legend, isn't he?'

'There is probably some truth in the stories about him, though there's bound to be a good deal of exaggeration, too. Some of the artifacts that we've dug up are from the period when he's supposed to have lived.'

'There was lots of magic back then, wasn't there? Dragons and wizards. Merlin was a wizard, wasn't he?'

Radu smiled. 'I don't know how much of the magical side was true; but there were mythical creatures and wizards mentioned. The wizards were probably the earlier doctors who used herbs and plants to cure different ailments of the people at that time. I suppose if they were successful, it might have seemed like they had magical powers.'

'Do you think there is any chance of there being magical people around today? I know it sounds daft, but there are so many shops selling potions and stuff and people saying they are witches and wiccans in The Valley.'

Radu shrugged. 'It keeps the tourists happy.'

'What do you think, Aliki?'

'Oh, it's just stuff for the tourists.'

Callum shook his head. 'I don't know, I've seen some strange things that can't be easily explained.'

'If you take a closer look, you'll probably find a simple explanation.'

He stood and watched as they walked away. 'Either they don't want to take me seriously; or maybe they've also got something to hide.'

After discussing Callum's continued interest in them; Sage and her friends decided to keep any further talk of Arthur and Aurum until they went to The Coterie on Saturday morning.

'That's a good idea,' Sophie agreed. 'Let's cool things down and a have a quiet week.'

On Thursday afternoon, Radu, Sage and Sophie went to watch Aliki play in the basketball team against St Martin's, another local high school.

'I hope we win this game,' she said as she dropped her kitbag down on the bench beside them. 'That would take us through to the finals.'

Both sides had excellent players and it was an exciting game with the score neck and neck as the game entered the last few minutes. Aliki had just intercepted the ball and was heading towards the net. As she swivelled to throw the ball, an opposing player knocked her off balance and she fell to the floor. Quickly, she pulled herself up to get back into the game, not noticing her wristband fall to the floor. A moment later, she was surprised by the surge of rage flowing through her body and reached for her wristband to curb her temper but was dismayed to find it missing. Clenching her teeth, she kept a rein on her actions and was relieved to hear the final whistle.

'A draw. Well played both teams,' said the teacher from the opposing team.

'Yes, well done everyone,' Mr Bell agreed.

As the others left the court, Aliki scoured the ground. Her friends went to join her.

'Well done, Aliki…' Radu began. 'Oh, have you lost something?'

'My wristband! It must be here somewhere!'

All looked carefully, but found nothing.

'Maybe it's on the bench,' she said. She had tipped out her bag and was rummaging through its contents when Callum appeared with a smile on his face. 'Looking for something?' He held up the wristband.

'Oh, thank goodness!' Aliki made a grab for it, but he held it out of her reach.

'Is this your secret weapon? I wonder what it would look like on me?' His smile faded as he tied the band onto his own wrist.

Aliki's friends hurried over to her.

'Hey, you give that back to Aliki,' Radu said, standing in front of him. 'You know full well it belongs to her.'

Callum's smile changed to a look of cold fury. 'Are you calling me a thief?'

'If you keep something that doesn't belong to you; well, yes, I am.'

A moment later, Radu went flying backwards across the floor, hitting his head on the edge of the bench. 'Don't mess with me!' Callum muttered as he turned and stormed away.

'Are you okay, Radu?' Aliki helped him up on to the bench. She glared after Callum. 'Now he's made me really angry!'

'Aliki…erm…Aliki…' Radu nodded towards her hand.

She looked down to see her hand slowly covering with thick fur and her nails curving into claws. 'Oh, no! No!'

With a cry, she sprang up and raced to the girls' changing room, locking herself in a toilet cubicle.

'I'll go after Callum,' Sage said. 'Sophie, you look after Aliki.'

'Slow breaths, slow breaths,' Aliki chanted as she crouched in the toilet cubicle.

Sophie knocked gently on the dor. 'Aliki, are you okay?'

The next moment, a group of girls entered the changing rooms. Sophie moved to the washbasins, pretending to wash her hands as she waited for them to leave.

'What was that noise?' one of the girls said as a low growl was heard.

'It's just the pipes, they often make that groaning sound,' Sophie said quickly.

'That wasn't the pipes. It sounded like a dog or something,' another girl said. 'It was coming from that cubicle.' She knocked on the cubicle door. 'Hello, who's in there?'

Her friend peered underneath the door. 'What the…? There *is* a dog in there.'

Now in full wolf shape, Aliki pushed under the door and dashed past the screaming girls as they scrambled to get out of the changing rooms. She leapt through an open window above the washbasins and raced up the playing field.

Sophie ran after the girls and bumped into Radu. Glancing around, he stepped into the changing rooms and looked out of the open window at the dog racing towards a clump of trees near the boundary fence.

'Radu…' Sophie began.

'She needs help,' he said, pulling himself through the window and hurrying after the animal.

With her breath coming in painful gasps, Aliki crouched down in the undergrowth listening to the sound of shouting from the school building. She had to escape before they found her. Scanning the wire fence, she saw a small opening that led onto the road nearby. She crept forward and started to ease her body through it when she felt a sharp pain as her leg became entangled in a length of wire. Her frantic struggles only made the wire dig in deeper. Aliki realised that she couldn't free herself in her present state, she must change back to human form so she could use her hands to unravel the wire. Closing her eyes, she breathed steadily and felt her body begin to change, then leaned forwards to free her still canine limb from the wire.

'Hey, are you okay?' The voice made her look up sharply. Radu was standing close by eyes wide as he looked down at her half-changed state. Aliki whimpered fearfully as he bent down over her.

'Hold still; you're making it worse,' he said as he carefully unwound the wire and freed her now human limb. Pulling his sweatshirt over his head, he wrapped it around her bleeding leg. 'You'll need to get that seen to.'

There was a shout from further down the field and Mr Bell appeared closely followed by Sophie. 'What happened?'

'Aliki was trying to free the dog that got into the school grounds and she hurt herself,' Radu said, helping her to her feet.

'Where is the dog?'

'It ran off, sir.'

'According to the girls who saw it, the animal was more like a wolf!'

'No, it was just a young, excited dog.'

'I think I'd better carry you back to the school, Aliki,' Mr Bell said as he carefully picked her up.

She mouthed a silent thank you to Radu over his shoulder as they made their way back to the school.

Sophie and Radu collected their bags and headed towards the gate where Sage and a subdued Callum stood rubbing his wrist.

'Are you sure you're okay now?' Sage asked him.

Callum nodded. 'Yes. I'll get off home now. And…erm…thanks for stepping in there.'

'That's fine.'

'What was that about?' Sophie asked her as he left.

'Whatever it was, I don't think anything would surprise me after this afternoon,' Radu commented.

'Callum lost his temper and took a bit of calming down. Luckily, he saw reason in the end, before he got himself into serious trouble, once I got the wristband from him' Sage said holding it up.

'Is Aliki's wristband the thing that keeps her…calm?' Radu asked. 'Will she be okay without it? Mr Bell told the secretary he was taking her to the hospital.'

'Her parents are both there, so she'll be fine.' Sage looked at the wristband in her hand. 'I'll call round and give this back to her tomorrow.'

'I'd like to come, too,' Radu said.

***

The following afternoon, Radu took a deep breath as Sage knocked on the door. Aliki's mother opened it, her expression growing wary as she saw the boy with Sage and Sophie.

'These are for Aliki, Mrs Gouna.' He held out a bunch of flowers and a box of chocolates. 'I've come to see how she is.'

'Hi guys, come in.' Aliki appeared beside her. 'This is Radu, Mum, he's the one I told you about, the one who helped me yesterday.'

Her father opened the door wider. 'Invite them in, Angelina.'

'But, Nick, don't you think…?'

'Radu is okay, Mum.' Aliki gave him a shy smile as she led the way into the lounge.

Her father cleared his throat as they all sat down. 'Thank you for helping Aliki yesterday, Radu. She got herself in a bit of a fix.'

'I was glad I could help her.'

'So, you know that our family...we're...different than many other people,' Nick continued.

'I know that Aliki is a good person; better than lots of the other normal people at school.'

'Not many "normal" people can handle our differences,' Angelina said drily.

Radu blushed. 'I'm sorry; *normal* isn't the right choice of word. Everyone has the right to be what they are.'

'In an ideal world, that would be true, but this isn't an ideal world,' Nick commented.

'Now that Aliki has shown her real self, it's not safe for us around here anymore.' Angelina sighed.

'Oh, please mum, I love living here. I love the new school. No other NGs know, only Radu. I'm sure he'll keep our secret...' Aliki began.

'How do we know we can trust him with such a big secret?'

'I swear, I'll never say anything to anyone, Mrs Gouna,' the boy insisted.

'It's just too dangerous. Even if we can trust you, there could be another incident at school. It's best if we move to a place where we can be safe until Aliki is on top of things.' She stood up. 'Thank you for coming today, Radu.'

'Mrs Gouna, if you are worried about any incidents at school, I promise you that I will take care of Aliki. If it's only when she gets angry that the incidents happen, we can be ready for it. You can count on me; I'll watch over her.'

'We all will,' Sophie added. 'And I'm sure Alora can make a new charm band for Aliki.'

'Please, Mum...? Dad...? Just give me a chance?'

Her father sighed and spread his hands. 'Maybe we could just see how things go, Angie. It would be good for Aliki to have a "normal" person amongst her friends.'

'How about a trial period of a month?' Radu suggested.

'We'll reassess the situation on a weekly basis. But if anything happens, even the smallest problem, we move,' Angelina said firmly.

Aliki and Radu grinned at each other.

'I have to call and see someone this evening,' Nick said pulling his jacket on. 'I'll give you youngsters a lift home on the way.'

***

'Are you sure that no-one else saw what happened, Aliki?' Alora asked on Saturday morning. They were sitting in the kitchen in The Coterie with Sage and her friends. She turned the wristband over in her hand. 'As you know, your father came to see me Thursday evening. He told me Radu said he was quite sure no-one else had spotted what happened.'

She grimaced. 'I must admit, I was too busy getting out of sight at the time, but Radu said he was pretty sure no-one else saw me.'

'If someone had seen anything, we would have heard rumours at school. No-one mentioned anything yesterday,' Sophie added. 'The talk was all about the wolf or dog, according to who was telling the story.'

'Didn't Callum see what happened?' Paris asked.

Sage shook her head. 'Once he put on the wristband, he flew into such a rage. After pushing Radu over, he ran out of the gym just looking for a fight. It was frightening. Everyone just leapt out of his way, except for his friend Roy. Callum was squaring up to punch him when I managed to grab his arm and pull the wristband off. Then his anger just evaporated and he seemed dazed. He told me he was ready to kill someone and he didn't know why.'

'He didn't associate his anger with Aliki or the wristband?'

'No. He was too shaken by how angry he'd been. He wasn't in school yesterday either.'

'Why did the wristband make him angry?' Aliki asked. 'It stopped my temper.'

'The spell took your anger and stored it in the wristband. And all your angry feelings were released into Callum.' Alora murmured a few words quietly before tossing the wristband into the fire. Blue and green flames shot up as the band sparked and crackled before disintegrating into a film of ash.

'Wow! You must have had some pent-up anger,' Sophie whispered.

Aliki sighed. 'I'm getting better at controlling it, but I still feel I need a charm to help me. Can you make me another wristband, Alora?'

'Hmm, we'll try something different. We don't want a repeat performance, do we?' Alora went to a tall cupboard and searched through several boxes on the shelves. 'Ah, here we are.' She opened a wooden box and took out a small crystal. 'Let me have one of your earrings.'

Her lips moved as she rubbed the earring and the crystal between her hands. The earring had a soft, bluish sheen to it when she passed it back to Aliki a moment later. 'That should do the trick until you feel confident enough to manage your feelings.'

'And Callum won't want to try this on!'

There was a light tap at the door and Jay came in. 'I heard about the incident at school the other day. Mai sent me to get the latest news.'

'No real damage was done and everything is under control now,' Alora told him.

Sage turned to him as he sat down. 'How are Arthur and his friends finding life in Aurum?'

'Osric has settled in very quickly. He spends a good deal of time at the goblin stables tending the horses. I think he has a soft spot for Peridot. They often ride out together. Maynard is keen on visiting Earth world as soon as possible. He has developed a great interest in motor vehicles from the magazines that Vinnie has brought from Earth world.'

'And Arthur?' Alora asked.

Jay frowned. 'Arthur is struggling. Now he knows he is no longer king and that Camelot no longer exists, he says he is finding it difficult to see his role in this new life. And the fact that Mai is obviously the unspoken ruler of Aurum is not sitting easily with him. Mai is hoping he can find inspiration when he visits Earth world. They're planning a visit here soon.'

Chapter Sixteen

On Monday, everything seemed to be back to normal at school. Talk of the wolf/dog had died down and Callum was back although he seemed subdued and made no reference to his outburst the previous week. Sage noticed him rubbing his wrist as he walked past her. He caught her eye, and looked away quickly. It was a relief to find him avoiding her and her friends over the next week.

She was sitting with Sophie in the library during the lunch break one day when Merc came to join them.

'Hey, how was your trip to Aurum?' Sage asked them.

Merc glanced around her to make sure no-one was within hearing distance. 'It was so good! We got to meet Arthur and his friends briefly. Later, Maynard came to find us and asked us so many questions about Earth world. He can't wait to come here and told us they're going to arrange a visit before long.'

'It should be happening soon. We helped Vinnie pick out some suitable clothes for their trip. I wonder what they'll make of all the changes in Earth world over the past few hundred years,' Sage said.

Sophie shivered as she watched the wind blow down the last few leaves from the trees. 'They'll find it colder here than in Aurum.'

'Yes, but when they lived here in Earth world, there was no central heating, or even glass in the windows,' Sage pointed out.

Radu and Aliki sat down with them.

'Who's Arthur?' Radu asked. 'Callum was asking about him last week.'

The girls exchanged looks.

'Look, I know about Aliki and I'm not sure exactly what you are, but I expect it's a bit out of the ordinary, too. You do know you can trust me, don't you?'

'Well, I certainly do,' Aliki said.

Sage nodded. 'I do, too.'

Merc frowned. 'It isn't just about us, is it? I'm sorry, Radu, but I think we need to speak to A…someone before we share anything else.'

'Shall we pay someone a visit on the way home today?' Sage suggested. Merc nodded.

Alora opened the door to the four girls that afternoon. 'I don't often get midweek visits these days. Have there been other incidents at school?'

Sophie shook her head. 'No, but we do need your advice.' She explained the situation with Radu.

'I feel bad about keeping things from him after all he's done for me. He's a really good friend and I know I can trust him,' Aliki said.

Alora sat down. 'Sometimes it's hard for you youngsters to keep your own secrets from everyone but you do have other Gifted who understand and who will look out for you. Just think how difficult it would be for a Non-Gifted.'

'We'll all look out for him,' Sophie countered.

'Haven't there ever been Non-Gifted who knew about us?' Sage asked.

'Over time there have been some who, after careful consideration, were let into our secret. I would like to see Radu for myself.'

'We could meet up at our house tomorrow after school,' Sage suggested.

***

'How about some tea and cakes?' Ellen said as she placed a tray on the kitchen table the next day. 'Radu, isn't it? Lovely to meet you.'

'Sage told us about your quick thinking the other day,' Jim added as he helped himself to a slice of cake.

Radu smiled and leaned down to stroke Jet as the cat curled around his legs, purring loudly. 'I was glad to help. It was amazing to find out about this whole community right here in The Valley.'

'What have you discovered so far?' Jim continued.

Sage got up as there was a knock on the door and Alora came in.

'I'll get another cup,' Ellen said. 'Jim, pull over the chair behind you.'

Alora nodded at the boy. 'Ah, you're Radu. I'm Alora.'

He held out his hand. 'I'm very pleased to meet you.'

'He was just about to tell us what he knows about life in The Valley,' Jim said as Alora sat down.

'Obviously, I know about Aliki and her family. I realised that Sage and Sophie had a different kind of background, too, by their reaction to what happened. And I'm assuming their families are the same. Watching the other students at school, I have noticed several that I suspect also have hidden talents, such as you, Merc.'

'Has anyone else revealed their Gift?' Alora asked.

He shook his head. 'A few of the ones in my year group seem a bit on edge at times, but when they are with Sage and Sophie, they become more relaxed, as if they feel safer somehow.'

'You're certainly very observant, Radu. I understand that you want to know more about us but you must realise that by keeping our Gifts hidden we are keeping ourselves safe. Not many people would accept us as easily as you seem to have done,' Alora told him.

'Aliki, Sage and Sophie are my very good friends and I would never give away their secrets. Before I got to know Aliki, I never really got close to anyone in school; in fact, my only friends were much older people from the Archaeology Society.'

'Radu is a really good friend and I would trust him with my life,' Aliki said.

Alora looked around the table.

'He seems like a reliable sort to me.' Jim smiled. 'Jet obviously like him and he's a pretty good judge of character.'

Ellen leaned forward and refilled her teacup. 'I think we can trust him.'

Aliki's face broke into a wide smile, reflected in her friends' faces as Alora said. 'I agree, I think we can. But you must remember, safeguarding our Gifts is vital at all times, Radu.'

'I'll never let any of you down, ever,' he promised as Aliki grabbed his hand.

'I'm sure you must have quite a few questions about us, Radu,' Alora continued

'Well, I'd like to know what your talents are.'

Sophie explained about the different Gifts they possessed. 'And Alora, as Spell Master, has quite a few Gifts, as does Sage.'

Sage spread her hands. 'I'm not quite up to speed with all of mine yet.'

'Do you use your Gifts a lot?'

Sophie leaned forward. 'They came in handy when we had to fight off a Daemon last year.' After prompting from Radu, she described the battle they had had with Nefarus and his sister, Diabella.

Finally, Alora held up a hand. 'I think that's enough questions for today.'

'Can I just ask one more question,' Radu pleaded. 'Who is Arthur?'

'Let Sophie tell you about that and the role she played in it,' Sage said.

Radu listened spellbound as he heard the story unfold. 'I can't believe you met the *real* King Arthur of Camelot! And to think that the brooch I found was actually his! And he's going to be coming here! I will get the chance to meet him, won't I?'

'As Radu is the one who found his brooch...' Aliki ventured.

Alora nodded. 'I'm sure Arthur would be delighted to meet you, Radu.'

Radu eyes shone. 'I've been researching Arthur Pendragon. Do you know what Pendragon means? *Pen* in Welsh means head or chief and *dragon* can mean an actual dragon, so Pendragon translates as Chief Dragon or Head Dragon; though most historians would go for the figurative sense that it means Chief Leader or Chief of Warriors. Their family motto is "Nosce Te Ipsum" which translates as "Know Thyself". This can be open to many interpretations; know your limitations *or* recognise how far you can go and what you are capable of achieving. Personally, I prefer the latter. What a man Arthur Pendragon must be! And I'm actually going to get to meet him!''

Chapter Seventeen

'Vinnie has brought you some clothes for your visit to Earth world,' Mai said as she placed a large holdall on the table and spread out a variety of casual clothes. 'Sage, Paris and Sophie helped her choose them.'

Maynard picked up a jacket and tried it on. 'This is a good fit; warm too.' He frowned. 'I can't find the buttons or laces to fasten it.'

'It has a zip,' Mai said as she showed him how to use it. 'Zips are used a lot in all sorts of clothes, boots and bags. In so many things, actually.'

He spent the next few minutes zipping and unzipping the jacket. 'Is it magic?'

Mai shook her head. 'No, look, this part makes the two set of teeth mesh, then come apart when you reverse it.'

'These working trousers have a zip, too. Much more convenient than buttons or laces,' Osric commented holding up a pair of denim jeans.

'What an ingenious invention.' Maynard continued to play with the zip.

Arthur frowned. 'Everywhere we look, we are going to come across so many new things in Earth world.'

Mai bit her lip. 'That's true; the modern world is so different to the world you once lived in. That's why we felt it was best for you to have these last few weeks in Aurum before you visit Earth world.'

'We've seen what the modern world is like in the books that Vinnie has brought for us. I, for one, am ready to embrace this new world,' Maynard said. 'Vehicles that travel way beyond the speed of horses, without the use of magic, on land and in the air! And one of the young Earth world visitors told me about small devices that allow you to see and speak to people from other countries at the click of a few buttons! Again, without the use of magic!'

Osric didn't look so impressed. 'I've also learnt that these fast moving vehicles can cause nasty accidents and the towns and cities are very noisy places with buildings crowded together.'

'They can't be any noisier than the towns we ventured into in far off countries,' Maynard countered. 'Or dirtier. You're getting soft with this new life.'

'Are you sure you're all ready to visit Earth world?' Mai asked. 'There's no hurry, if you want to wait a little while longer.'

'I think we need to make this trip,' Arthur said. 'To see our homeland; to see Camelot once again.'

Osric gave a brief nod. 'That is true.'

Maynard clapped Osric's shoulder. 'Come on, think of all the unknown territories we ventured fearlessly into in the past! This is just another exciting new adventure, a new challenge!'

Arthur exchanged a look with Osric, then nodded.

Mai looked at the faces around her. 'I'll speak to Alora and arrange the best day for you to go this week.'

'How long will our visit last?' Osric asked.

'Shall we leave that open for you to decide? Let's see how you find Earth world.'

The following evening the three men listened as Mai outlined the plan for their Earth world visit.

'So, we can go tomorrow afternoon,' she told them. 'Bert Melton will meet us at the portal and drive us to Alora's house.'

***

All three men were nervous as they stood on the castle parapet the following day and Mai instructed them to link hands. Each one gave a gasp as the cold mist surrounded them and they found them standing at the side of a leafy avenue. A car drew up beside them and a tall, grey-haired man stepped out. He held out his hand, first to Mai then to each of the others.

'Mai, friends! I'm Bert Melton; welcome to Earth world. There is a small group gathered to meet you at The Coterie. Not too many; Alora didn't want you to feel overwhelmed on your first day.'

Seeing Maynard's rapt expression as they walked towards the car, Mai suggested that he sat in front of the vehicle while the others sat in the back.

'So, this is a modern-day vehicle.' Maynard eyed up the dashboard. 'I see it's electrically powered.'

Bert raised his eyebrows. 'You know about modern vehicles?'

Maynard shrugged. 'Only a little, from the magazines and books that Vinnie brought to Aurum from Earth world. I would like to learn more, though. And how to drive a car.'

'You're talking to the right person, Maynard,' Mai said. 'Bert and his family run Melton's Motors, selling and repairing cars.'

Soon the two men were deep in discussion about modern day motor vehicles. Arthur and Osric seemed more taken by the view outside through the car windows.

'These houses would appear to belong to the gentry,' Arthur commented as they passed by ornate gates that gave a glimpse of large houses set well back in the leafy avenue.

'Well, not exactly gentry, but you'd have to be quite wealthy to afford property in this area,' Mai replied.

'And these dwelling must be for the workers,' Osric nodded as they drove down a street of smaller terraced houses.

'Where do the Gifted people of The Valley live?' Arthur asked. 'Are they wealthy?'

'They live in different parts of The Valley. Some are well off, others not. They blend in with the Non-Gifted in the community. It's only when they are in safe places with other Gifted that they let their powers show.'

'Here we are at The Coterie,' Bert said as he pulled into the driveway where several other cars were parked.

Alora was waiting at the door with a wide smile. 'It's good to see you again Mai and to meet you, Arthur, Osric and Maynard.'

As she ushered them into the hallway, Maynard jumped back as an old woman clutching a pile of heavy books hurried past them and faded as she reached the doorway.

'Don't worry, it's just Miss Fenella. She was the local librarian many years ago; she's not a ghost, just a memory,' Alora reassured him. 'You'll get used to them.'

A second woman appeared in the doorway, smiling widely.

'Ah, here's Mary. She's not a memory; she's actually here.'

'Welcome! Welcome!' Mary shook their hands firmly. 'I'll show you to your rooms, then when you're ready, you can join us in the rear reception room. We're all so excited to meet you all!' She caught a swift glance from Mai. 'But, don't worry, we won't be bombarding you with questions!'

Later that evening, Mai smiled at Alora as she surveyed the room where people sat around in small groups chatting happily. 'Thank you, Alora. What a lovely reception. I was a bit worried about how Arthur and his friends would find things on their first trip to Earth world. They seem to be enjoying meeting everyone.'

'They do. Let's go and see what they're talking about. Maynard has spent most of the evening talking to Bert and his wife, Venna. I think I'll join them.'

As she left, Mai made her way to Arthur who was deep in conversation with Jim and Ellen.

'Arthur has been telling us about waking up in Aurum and meeting you and Sage and her friends and what a shock it was for them all,' Ellen said.

'I think Earth world as it is today will hold some surprises for you, too,' Jim added.

'Yes, I'm sure it will. I am very curious to see what remains of Camelot, although I have been warned that there is not much of the original buildings left now,' Arthur told them.

'We've arranged for you to visit the site privately for two hours on Saturday before it's open to the public' Mai said. 'You'll have a chance to look around then.'

At that moment, Osric joined them.

'I have had a very interesting discussion with Nick and Angelina who are shifters. They are visiting some friends of theirs in a town a little further north to take part in a full moon run Friday night and they have invited me to join them. I am greatly looking forward to the event!'

'Mary, the librarian, and William Melton, Bert and Venna's son, have offered to give you a guided tour of The Valley tomorrow,' Alora said. 'William has suggested you might like a trip to London on Thursday and said he'd be very happy to be your driver then, too.'

An hour later, Ellen noticed the stifled yawns of the visitors and stood up. 'I think it's time we said goodnight. You must all be tired out after today.'

Osric rubbed his face. 'I must admit, that comfortable bed I saw in my room does seem to be calling to me.'

***

The next morning, not long after they had risen, Mary and a young man appeared at the doorway.

'This is William, our driver and tour guide for the next couple of days,' Mary introduced him as they sat down at the table.

'I thought we could drive as far as the lighthouse on the cliffside. From there, you can just about make out the site of the old castle, where Camelot once stood on the opposite bay. Then we can drive down to the sea front and take a look at the town centre. Some of the buildings there go back several hundred years,' William added.

'You have to remember that here in Earth world, we must keep our true natures hidden for our own safety and the safety of all the Gifted community,' Mai reminded them as they climbed into the car.

William drove along the coastal road, with Mary making occasional comments. She pointed to a weathered column at the side of the road. 'That stone marks the place where the last witch in The Valley was burnt, just before Mai created Aurum as a place of sanctuary for all Magical beings.'

'And can you see the large outcrop of rocks next to the lighthouse?' she continued as they headed towards it. 'It looks like a sleeping dragon, doesn't it? Legend has it that a powerful sorcerer summoned the dragon to his aid in a fierce battle, but his opponent was even more powerful and changed it to stone.'

William pulled up in a small car park close to the overhanging rock. 'We get a good view of the old castle from here and we can walk down to the sea front road along that track.'

Arthur and his friends gazed into the distance at the crumbling walls of the ancient castle before they headed towards the town.

At the same time, Callum was walking towards a nearby seafront café when his eyes fell on Arthur and his companions.

'It's very busy here,' Osric commented as they crossed the road at a set of traffic lights. Arthur stopped to gaze up at a tall office building before he followed them. There was a screech of brakes as a car sped towards him.

'Arthur!' Mai shouted. Raising her hands, everything around them froze and she hurried towards a stunned Arthur.

'I know I promised to try to avoid the use of magic as much as possible here in Earth world, but this was an emergency. Arthur, you must remember, you can only cross the road when the lights allow you to, otherwise the cars have the right of way.'

'Sorry, I forgot for a moment. There are so many rules to remember. And so many vehicles to avoid.'

Mai squeezed his hand. 'Just stay near me.' She frowned as she looked at the frozen figures around her. 'There's something not quite right. Someone is not completely frozen.'

Sweat stood out on Callum's forehead as he stood in the cafe doorway. For some reason, he couldn't move his body but he had a hazy picture of the world around him where everything seemed motionless. He was aware of a tingling sensation in one hand.

Mai clicked her fingers and people and traffic began to move again. No-one else seemed aware of the strange phenomenon.

Callum gave a gasp as his body came to life again and everything around him seemed normal once more. His hands were still shaking as he pushed open the café door to find his friends laughing and chatting in their usual corner seats.

'Hey, Callum! Get me a cappuccino, will you?' Layla called, pushing past him as she made her way to join their friends. His heart was hammering as Mai and her companions walked past the café window and she stared at him for a moment before turning back to her companion.

'Is everything okay?' Osric noticed the frown Mai wore.

'Everything's fine.'

William pointed out a row of grey stone shops. 'The buildings along this road are the oldest in The Valley.'

Callum stood and watched as they moved further down the street. 'Earth to Callum! What does a girl have to do to get a coffee round here?' Layla called out to him.

'Did you notice anything a bit strange out there Layla?' he said as he put their coffees on the table a short while later.

'Like what?'

Callum shrugged and gave one more glance out of the window. He was pretty sure the woman had called out the name Arthur.

Meanwhile, as they made their way along the road, Maynard commented on the number of shops promoting wiccan and witchcraft articles and potions. 'I thought you said that magic must be hidden here, yet these shopkeepers blatantly advertise their magical goods.'

'Most of these are for the tourists and have no link with real magic,' William replied. 'Some of them, like Petronella's Potions here, do have genuine magical articles, but they only work in the right hands.'

'Can we take a look inside?' Osric asked.

William nodded. The tiny brass bell above the door tinkled as he led them into a dimly lit, low-ceilinged shop. At one side of the room was a glass counter. The other three walls were lined with wooden shelves, each holding an array of bottles and coarse fibre bags labelled in handwritten ink.

Maynard's eyes widened as he picked up a small, blue bottle and it took on a gentle pulsating glow.

The old woman who appeared from a room behind the counter was smiling as she made her way towards them until her eyes fell on Arthur. 'Oh, my life! King Arthur and his knights! And Mai Lin! Here in my shop! Oh, my life!'

She held out a trembling hand towards Arthur, who guided her to a wooden chair. 'My good woman, please be seated.'

Mai disappeared into the back room and returned with a glass of water. 'Here, Petronella, take a drink.'

The old woman sipped from the glass and cleared her throat. 'You have done me such an honour; King Arthur himself in my shop. This must be the happiest day in my life.'

'It is a pleasure to meet you, Madam.' Arthur smiled.

'We knew one day you would awaken; you and your loyal friends. But I never thought that I would live to see the day. And here you are, in front of me!' She stood up. 'But where are my manners? You must have a cup of my own special tea.'

Soon they were seated around a table in the small backroom, with Petronella asking questions about their trip and supplying details about the other shopkeepers on the sea front. She was reluctant to let them leave the shop until two tourists entered and she had to give them her attention.

They continued walking along the road, Maynard stopping to take a closer look at a display of Goth outfits. A young couple came out of the shop; the girl wore a black lace blouse with a short, black taffeta skirt. Her partner wore a torn black tee shirt and tight black jeans. Both wore heavy black boots. The girl gave him a black lip-glossed smile as they went past. 'Is this modern-day witch attire?'

William shrugged. 'Goth fashion. It's been around for a while now.'

Mai stopped outside a shop with a large sign that announced "Belladonna's Tomes" and looked at the variety of books displayed in the window. 'Flavia would love that traditional Cornish recipe book.'

'Let's take a look inside,' William said, opening the door. They found themselves in a shop divided into several different alcoves, each one filled with shelves containing a particular genre of books.

Mary and Mai headed for the cookery section while Arthur and Maynard looked through a selection of the latest novels laid out on a table near the door. Osric was drawn to the art section at the back of the shop. He picked up a large hardback listing some of the most famous paintings over the centuries and the background details of the artists and their works.

'Peridot would love this.' He took it to the assistant as the desk where Mai was paying for the cookbook.

'A present for Peridot, Osric?' Mai nodded towards the book he held. 'It's perfect for her!'

As they stepped out of the shop into the sunlight, Arthur suggested a walk along the beach. 'The land has altered so much since we were here, but the sea and the sand remain the same.' He gazed at the distant outline of the castle ruins across the bay. 'I am greatly looking forward to standing on the grounds of Camelot once again.'

Mai linked her arm through his as they made their way along the beach. 'You seem more relaxed here.'

'The sound of the waves on the sand has that effect, doesn't it?' he replied. 'Whatever era you live in.'

That evening they discussed their planned visit to London the following day.

'We could drive around the main sights, such as the Houses of Parliament, Buckingham Place and the Cutty Sark in Greenwich and some of the modern sights, too, such as London's Eye. We could take a closer look at one or two of them if you find them interesting.'

'Buckingham Palace? Where the present day queen lives?' Osric said. 'Perhaps we could go there and meet her? I'm sure there would be some kind of affinity with Arthur, after all he was once an English ruler, too.'

Mary shook her head. 'I don't think that'll be possible. Anyway, the queen isn't at Buckingham Place at the moment. She's attending a conference with some of the European leaders.'

Chapter Eighteen

They set off early the next morning. At first all three men were interested in the passing scenery, commenting on the great changes in the landscape. After they had been driving along the motorway for half an hour, Osric and Arthur fell asleep in the back of the car, but Maynard was fascinated by the roads and the speed of the traffic and questioned William about some of the different vehicles they saw.

Mai gently nudged Arthur's and Osric's shoulders as they were nearing the capital.

They looked out at the tall buildings, heavy traffic and pavements crowded with people from all corners of the world.

'It's a lot bigger and busier than The Valley,' Mai said.

Osric drew a quick breath. 'We'll need to keep our wits about us.'

William pointed out various landmarks as they drove around the city. All three men gazed in awe at the towering glass buildings. As they passed the Tower of London, Arthur's face lit up. 'Just look at that castle! Who lives there? I would really like to take a look inside.'

'No-one actually lives there now,' Mai explained. 'It's like a grand exhibition site these days, for the public to see the treasures of royal history. It's definitely worth a visit.'

'And it's very popular.' William frowned as he saw the queue of people waiting to enter.

Mai smiled. 'Don't worry, I've a friend who could get us inside, avoiding the queue.'

'If we can find a parking space...' William began.

'Look, there's a car moving out just over there. What a stroke of luck.' Mai caught his eye in the mirror and gave him a wink.

They pulled into the space that had conveniently became available and made their way to the gate. Mai exchanged a few words with the woman at the ticket desk and they were soon led inside.

Following the lines of visitors making their way around the different parts of the tower, Arthur showed his frustration as he was prevented from spending more time at displays that particularly caught his interest. He turned to Mai. 'It is almost impossible to appreciate the finer details of each item before we are herded along like cattle.'

'We could use a little magic here, perhaps?' Osric said, half jokingly. 'What do you say, Maynard?'

He grinned sheepishly. 'I was thinking the same thing myself. Well, if we have the means…'

After exchanging a look with Arthur, Mai once again raised her hands and the scene froze.

All three men gave a sigh of relief, as they weaved their way around the motionless people to take a closer look at different artifacts that had caught their attention. Arthur stepped over a cord to examine a display of suits of armour. 'All this is considered history, yet it all happened after our time on Earth world.'

'Many of the later weapons were very similar to ones we used,' Maynard commented, picking up a sword and shield.

'Here was a king to be feared.' Arthur was standing in front of a portrait of Henry VIII. 'We were not always loyal in our relationships in our time, but we did not kill our wives and lovers.'

'Yes, a proposal from Henry wasn't always welcome news,' Maynard agreed, reading a plaque nearby.

Osric felt the thick fabric of one of the Tudor mannequins. 'These costumes were very ornate and very expensive. They remind me of some of the fabrics we would bring back with us from our eastern journeys.'

'Many of these poor prisoners had a lot more to worry about than their clothing.' Mai shuddered as she read the details next to the portraits of the Tower's more famous prisoners. 'Let's go somewhere more cheerful. I'd like to see the crown jewels.'

Arthur stood next to Maynard in front of the case displaying the Imperial State Crown. 'It certainly dwarfs the crown I wore, doesn't it?'

'It would be very uncomfortable to wear, weighing nearly five pounds!' Osric added.

Maynard was peering into the case that held the orb and sceptre when a sudden shout made them all turn around. A yeoman was running towards them holding a heavy baton in his hand. 'I will not stand back and watch you use your Gifts to steal the monarch's most precious treasures!'

'We are not here to steal anything.' Arthur spread his hands. 'We have only come to admire and marvel at such a collection.'

Osric stepped forward, frowning. 'Wilgred? It is you, isn't it?'

The man lowered his baton and walked slowly towards them. 'Osric…Maynard…and could it be…King Arthur of Camelot?' He knelt before him and bowed his head. 'Sire, forgive me. I did not recognise you…'

Arthur patted his shoulder and helped him to his feet. 'Stand up beside me, Wilgred. One of my finest knights!'

The yeoman's voice shook. 'We heard rumours that you were awakened but for so many centuries we clung to the hope of seeing you again, sire, that we didn't dare believe it could actually be true.'

Mai smiled. 'After such a long time, we finally managed to break Morgana's spell and bring Arthur and his friends back to us.'

Wilgred stood up, blinking as he looked at Mai. 'The men I remember and your face does seem familiar, somehow.'

'Mai Lin, but you knew me as Merlin in those days.'

'We always said Merlin had the complexion of a woman. We didn't know how true that was!' Maynard commented.

'She kept it well hidden. And her magical powers.' Arthur looked around him. 'Though it seems there were others with similar powers unnoticed in Camelot at the time.'

'You stood resolutely against the use of magic in those days long ago. How do you feel about magic now, Sire?' Wilgred motioned towards the queues of frozen visitors.

Arthur shook his head. 'So much has happened since we were wakened. We were nearly drowned in a cavern under a lake; flown to safety on dragons; then lived amongst a diverse community of magical people in Aurum. Somehow magic does not seem so outlandish anymore.'

'And the modern technology of today seems more like magic than anything we've encountered in Aurum,' Osric admitted.

'Ah, modern technology.' Wilgred shook his head. 'Anzetha and myself have had centuries to accustom ourselves to it, and yet developments over this past hundred years sometimes take us by surprise even now.'

'Anzetha from the kitchen in Camelot?' Mai asked. 'We worked together most days; she never mentioned a beau.'

'We found ourselves together when Morgana attempted to take over Camelot. Anzetha confided in me that her mother was half fae. Soon afterwards, we made our escape, joining a small group of other Magicals and made our way to a town on the south coast. We had heard the rumours of the spell cast upon Arthur and we spent several months searching for you, Merlin, I mean, Mai Lin. It was said that you were the only one capable of lifting the spell.'

'It was many hundreds of years before I was shown the solution by a young Gifted girl of these times.'

'So, while we slept through the centuries, what did life bring you, Wilgred?' Osric asked.

'Good times and bad times. As more people spurned magic in England, Anzetha feared for the lives of herself and her parents, so we fled to France and then travelled further south. That first summer a plague broke out and several of our community, including Anzetha's father, died. Her mother was heartbroken and decided to bequeath her immortality to me and join her husband in After world. They were sad times. I worked as a carpenter when I could find work. Anzetha made baskets which she sold on the markets. We could not stay too long in one place, being immortal. Ten years was the limit we gave ourselves before we feared our continuing youthfulness would come to someone's notice. Eventually, we made our way back to England. Life began to improve, even though we still had to limit our life in each new town to ten years. Later, it became possible for both of us to gain a reasonable level of education through evening courses. Having first-hand knowledge of much of what was written in the history books, I decided to take a degree in History which enabled me to get this post two years ago. Anzetha works as a nurse. You must come and meet her and our boys. She would never forgive me if you were so close and didn't pay us a visit.'

'Do you live here in London?' Mai asked.

'We live in The Hollow, a small village thirty miles south-west of London. There are ten Gifted families living there,' Wilgred replied. 'They would all be so pleased to meet you, Arthur.'

'We could make a detour on the way home this afternoon,' William suggested.

***

Two hours later, William drew up outside a small cottage. As Wilgred climbed out, the front door opened and a young woman stood there with two small boys either side of her.

'Anzetha!' Mai called out as she hurried towards her. 'I'm so pleased to see you again after all this time. Oh, what beautiful boys!' She turned and introduced Arthur and his friends.

Several people appeared at the garden gate. 'Anzetha told us we were to be honoured with a visit from King Arthur of Camelot himself!' a middle-aged woman gushed, grabbing Arthur's hand and shaking it vigorously.

The visitors were ushered inside a spacious lounge where a welcoming log fire burned in the hearth. More people arrived and they found themselves surrounded by an excited crowd.

Arthur stood up and spread his hands. 'It is lovely to meet you all. It warms my heart that you give such a welcome to myself and my friends. I must admit that we are still trying to come to terms with this strange new world after sleeping through the past few centuries. This quiet village seems like an oasis after the busyness of London.'

'The Hollow is a place where we can relax and be our true selves.' A man nodded.

Anzetha and some of the visitors set out dishes of food and passed around cups of tea and coffee. Arthur, Osric and Maynard listened with dismay as they learnt of the fate of Camelot after Arthur was believed to have been slain. Constantine succeeded Arthur, putting an end to Morgana's ambitions; then Camelot was ruled by a succession of kings until it was burnt down by the Saxons, leaving little evidence behind.

'We are to visit the site on Saturday,' Osric told them.

'There is not much left to see,' a woman said. 'I was there myself a few years ago.'

Mai confided to Anzetha, 'I'm afraid that Arthur and his friends will find the visit to Camelot disappointing.'

'Probably. But I think he has to see it for himself.'

Arthur joined Maynard who was standing by the window as the conversation turned to the changes in Earth world over the centuries.

'There's one of the good changes,' Maynard said pointing to a sleek motorbike parked on the driveway. 'Wilgred has offered to take me for a ride on it. Here he is.'

Wilgred joined them, handing Maynard a leather jacket and a helmet. Arthur watched as the two men mounted the bike and drove off along the road.

One of Wilgred's boys stood beside him with his brother close behind. 'I want to ride a motorbike like Daddy when I'm older.'

'Can you ride a motorbike?' the second boy asked Arthur.

'Kings don't ride motorbikes,' the first boy said. 'They have people to drive them around in cars.'

'Kings can do what they like,' his brother stated firmly. He turned to Arthur. 'Are you still a king?'

'I…I was once.'

'So, what are you now, then?'

Arthur raised his eyebrows. 'I'm not quite sure.' He was relieved when the sound of the motorbike caught the boys' attention and they hurried outside.

Shortly afterwards, William suggested it was time to head back to The Valley. Maynard was deep in conversation about cars and bikes with William and Osric was dozing in the back seat. Mai squeezed Arthur's arm. 'It was lovely to see Wilgred and Anzetha again, wasn't it? And meet their boys. So many visitors came to see you today, Arthur. You are still held in high esteem by so many people.'

He smiled. 'It is indeed heart-warming to be remembered so fondly.' A pained expression crossed his face as the young boy's words echoed in his head. *'Are you still a king?...So, what are you now, then?'*

Chapter Nineteen

Mai and Alora were chatting in the kitchen when Arthur came down the next day.

'Are Maynard and Osric still asleep?' he asked.

'No, they've both gone out. Maynard is spending the day with Bert and Venna at Melton's Motors. Nick and Anglina Gouna, Aliki's parents, picked up Osric about half an hour ago. They are going to spend today and tonight, a full moon night, with some friends who live further north,' Mai told him.

'I suggested a hack out on the moors for you both today,' Alora said. 'Friends of ours have stables just on the edge of the moors. I could drop you off there and pick you up this afternoon.'

'What do you think, Arthur?' Mai asked.

'It sounds a great way to spend the day; away from towns and cities.'

Mai smiled as Arthur gave a satisfied sigh two hours later as he drew his horse to a halt.

'Despite all the changes in Earth world, the moors have hardly altered.'

She nodded as she looked at the rugged scenery. Rocky outcrops were scattered among the tufts of springy grass and gorse bushes; a herd of wild ponies could be seen grazing between a clump of trees in the distance; white clouds scudded across a blue sky, making a dappled pattern on the land below.

Arthur turned to her. 'Do you remember our days together after Guinevere and Lancelot left?'

'Yes, I do,' she replied.

'I thought I was accompanied by my faithful manservant. What a surprise awaited me!'

Mai blushed and laughed. 'Yes, the revelation came as a bit of a surprise to me, too!'

Arthur leaned over and stroked her cheek. 'It turned out to be a good kind of surprise.'

'That was the best time of my life; until now, when I have you back with me again.' Mai squeezed his hand.

Arthur's horse pulled at the bit. He gathered up the reins. 'Let's make our way to the hilltop over there. My trusty steed needs some exercise. Race you to the summit!'

They galloped side by side towards the distant hillside. Arthur pulled ahead of Mai as the pathway became steeper.

'You win!' Mai laughed breathlessly as they drew to a halt on the plateau.

They stood in silence for a few minutes.

'The last time I gazed out over the moors I was King Arthur of Camelot.' Arthur sighed. 'I need to know who and what I am in this new life; I cannot wander aimlessly over the moors. I hope once I feel the soil of Camelot under my feet once more, I will find my direction.'

'Everything will work out, Arthur,' Mai assured him and received a slight smile in return. 'Well, I don't know about you, but this cold weather has given me an appetite! There is a village over there; I can just make out the church steeple. Alora said there's a pub that serves really good food and they have a place we can leave our horses, too.'

Arthur frowned. 'A pub?'

'A public house; a tavern.'

His eyebrows raised in surprise. 'I have never considered taking a lady to a tavern before.'

Mai smiled. 'A pub is not like the taverns you knew. Some can be a bit rough, but Alora recommends this one.'

Two young teenagers were happy to see to their horses when they reached The Shepherd's Inn. Arthur was pleasantly surprised when they entered the front door to find a cosy lounge with several other customers already there.

A young, smartly dressed woman came to greet them. She seated them at a corner table and handed them both menus. 'We've also today's specials listed on the board over there,' she told them. 'I'll be back to take your order when you're ready.'

'This is nothing like the taverns I was used to. Clean tables and floors; a choice of foods and smartly dressed staff.' He leaned forward and added quietly. 'And the other customers do appear to be decent folk and not roughnecks.'

He scanned the menu. 'Several types of meats and a wide choice of vegetables – some which are new to me. It's difficult to make a choice.'

A young couple sat at a nearby table. 'They do an excellent roast beef here. I'd recommend it,' the woman said.

'Indeed, it does look tempting,' Arthur agreed as the waiter set a large plate down in front of her. He nodded as Mai suggested they order the same dishes.

A companionable silence fell as they tucked into their meals.

'Did you enjoy that?' the young man sitting near them asked as the waiter cleared their plates away.

'It was delicious,' Mai answered as Arthur nodded.

'Are you going to order a dessert?' the man continued. 'I'd recommend the apple pie and custard.'

'I don't think I will,' Mai laughed. 'I won't manage the ride back if I eat anything else!'

'Are you here on holiday, like us?' the man asked. 'We've been coming here for the past three years now, haven't we, Lauren? Though this year is extra special for us; we're on our honeymoon.'

Lauren took his hand. 'Mike and I fell in love with the place when we first came here three years ago. We decided it would be the perfect place for our honeymoon.'

'The moors have always been a special place of beauty and tranquillity that can soothe the soul.' Arthur nodded gravely. 'I dare say they will be so for many future generations.'

'Wow! Are you a poet or something? You sound like Shakespeare,' Lauren laughed.

Arthur frowned.

'You know, *William* Shakespeare.' Mike raised his eyebrows.

'The world-famous playwright and poet, born in Henley Street, Stratford upon Avon on 23rd April 1564 and died on the same day in 1616,' Lauren continued. 'I still remember that from my school days.'

'1564? Ah, that would be after…' Arthur began.

Mai interrupted him. 'Unfortunately, Arthur had an accident recently and suffers from bouts of amnesia.'

Lauren's brows knitted. 'Oh, how terrible.'

'So we're here to make new happy memories,' Mai interjected and turned the conversation topic back to the young couple and their own lives. They needed little encouragement to talk about their wedding, with Mike showing them several photos on his mobile. By the time they were ready to leave, Mai and Arthur knew quite a lot about the young couple, although they themselves were selective in sharing their own personal backgrounds. Lauren gave each of them a warm hug as they parted.

Later, as they trotted side by side on the moor bridle path, Arthur sighed. 'Living from day to day in present day Earth world is a challenge. There are so many significant people who have lived and events that have occurred over the past few centuries it's like I'm faced with solving the riddle of the sphinx when trying to follow a normal conversation.'

Mai gave him a sympathetic smile. 'I know it can be hard. But it's good that you get to see Earth world as it is now and the modern way of life. And you can always go back to Aurum to refuel your batteries. What I mean by that is...'

Arthur held up his hand. 'Batteries. Maynard told me that electric vehicles need to charge their batteries. And Sophie told me that her mobile phone and many other devices also need their batteries charged. They are a store of energy. So, I assume you are saying that sometimes I will need to replenish my own store of energy.'

She laughed. 'Exactly!'

'Perhaps our trip to Camelot tomorrow will be the fuel boost I need!'

'Don't forget many centuries have passed since you were in Camelot, Arthur. It's much different than it was when you lived there.'

***

Mai repeated her warning to Arthur and Maynard the next morning as they prepared to leave. 'You must remember that the Camelot we are visiting today bears very little resemblance to the Camelot that you all knew.'

Arthur squeezed her hand. 'I know, my love. But we must see it for ourselves. As we have the chance to take a look around without other visitors, I'm hoping we can find a sense of the old Camelot as it was in our time.'

Before Mai could comment further, there was a knock on the door. 'Osric! Did you have a good night?' Alora asked as he came in.

Osric had a wide smile on his face. 'What a night! I have not enjoyed a full moon run so much since, oh since I was a young lad!' he enthused. 'And now we are to visit Camelot! Are we all ready to go?'

Natalie Delta and Radu were already waiting beside a tall metal gate at the entrance to the site. Natalie held out her hand. 'I'm so pleased to meet you. I was so excited when Radu told me that you three visiting historians have a special interest in King Arthur.'

She was still talking as she unlocked the gate and led them inside. Arthur's steps slowed as they entered the site and he looked around him. 'There's nothing left but a crumbling shell, is there?'

Natalie's smile froze briefly. 'Well, after so many hundreds of years, we feel we've been very lucky with our finds so far. We've been able to map out most of the main rooms of the original castle and, once you've had a look around outside, I'll take you into the museum to show you the artefacts we have discovered over the past ten years. You might be pleasantly surprised to see what we *do* have in our collection.'

Osric pointed to a broken line of cobblestones. 'Is that where the portcullis would have been?'

Natalie stepped forward. 'Yes, it is actually. Well spotted! And over here we have the remaining wall of what must have been the kitchen area.'

'Ah, yes, you can just make out the old fireplace by the blackened stones.' Osric nodded.

Natalie talked animatedly as she pointed out various features, leading them further up the hillside, with Osric stopping to ask questions along the way. Maynard dug his hands into his pockets and followed them silently.

Arthur stood still, looking around in dismay at the remnants of walls and piles of stones. 'There is nothing left. There is no Camelot anymore.'

Mai frowned and looked at Radu. 'I knew it would be hard for them to see this. I've had hundreds of years to come to terms with it. For them, it's as if they left Camelot only weeks ago. Maybe this wasn't such a good idea.'

Suddenly a mist descended around them. As it cleared, Radu saw that the scene was transformed. Arthur still stood a short distance before them, but now he was dressed in full battle dress, holding a sword in one hand and a metal helmet in the other. Behind him loomed a huge, grey stone castle. Through the open drawbridge, people could be seen scurrying around the courtyard. A man shouted as several young boys led horses into the courtyard and soldiers wearing chain mail and helmets appeared. One of the soldiers barked out orders and the others quickly mounted and moved into formation. Once the men were assembled, the commander looked towards Arthur. Arthur raised his face to the sky and silently mouthed a prayer before turning and walking towards the one riderless horse which skittered and pranced as two boys held tightly on to its reins.

Mai wiped a tear from her face as the scene faded.

Natalie's voice was heard as the present-day scene came back into view. 'Ah, there you are, Arthur. Shall we take a look inside the museum now? I bet Radu can't wait to show you the gold and ruby brooch he unearthed only a short while back. It hasn't been seen by the public yet, so you're getting a sneak preview!'

As Mai walked forward to join them, Radu caught her arm. 'What happened to Arthur just now? And his clothes? And who were all those people?'

Mai's eyes widened. 'You saw it?'

'Yes!'

'That was one of Arthur's memories of Camelot. It was the last time Arthur rode into battle. I was watching from the window of the great hall as they left that morning.' She squeezed Arthur's hand. 'You did find something of Camelot here today!'

He turned to her, his face a blank mask. 'I saw Camelot as I knew it.' He spread his hands to take in the ruins around him. 'It's gone now. There's nothing left of the kingdom I once ruled.'

Radu approached him slowly. 'Come to the museum and see how we treasure and value the legacy you left us. For us, you will *always* be King Arthur of Camelot.'

Natalie showed them into the exhibition room. 'As fellow historians, we are happy to let you handle the items, as long as you wear these special gloves.'

Osric pulled on a pair of white cotton gloves and picked up a piece of pottery. 'Fancy having to wear gloves to handle the dishes that we used every day.'

Radu stroked a long plank of wood. As he did so, he felt a tingle in his fingers. An image of a table flitted through his mind. People were seated at it; Osric among them.

'Does this bring back any memories, Osric?' he held out the plank.

A smile spread over Osric's face as he turned it over. 'This is part of the Great Hall table. Ah, we sat down to many a fine meal at this table.'

Maynard stopped in front of part of a shield which was labelled as belonging to a knight. He peered closely at it. 'That was never used by a knight,' he exclaimed.

'According to our researchers, this kind of shield was often used by a knight,' Natalie countered.

'Similar kinds were used by knights, but not this one,' Maynard continued. 'Can you see the forge mark in the corner? A blacksmith burnt that image onto it. It belonged to a soldier who could neither read nor write, hence the image. A knight would have had his initials engraved.'

'Oh,' Natalie faltered. 'We'll have to take another look at it.'

She looked nervous as she noticed the smile that played on Arthur's lips as she pointed out the prize of their collection – the ruby brooch. 'Do you think maybe we have mislabelled this article, too, Arthur?'

'No, something like this definitely belonged to someone of royal blood. It would have been a much-cherished possession.'

'I'm so glad you agree.' She lowered her voice. 'You know, we can't actually prove this, but most of our team believe it could have actually belonged to King Arthur himself.'

'Yes, I believe you could very well be right.'

Radu frowned as he picked up the ruby brooch. 'It feels flat, somehow,' he whispered to Osric as Natalie and Arthur moved away.

Osric nodded. 'Don't forget, it's a replacement.'

Not long afterwards, Natalie glanced at her watch. 'I'm afraid it's time to open the site to the public now.'

Arthur took her hand and gave a slight bow. 'Many thanks for a most enlightening tour.'

'The pleasure is all ours!' Natalie replied. 'We are always happy to meet other historians with similar interests to our own. We must keep in touch. Radu has all the details of our website. You could send us a link to your own website.'

Mai quickly intercepted as Osric was about to reply. 'We'll do that. Thank you again.'

'This has been the best day of my life,' Radu said as Alora drove them back to The Coterie.

Osric and Maynard were discussing the pieces they had seen in the exhibition and wondering what had happened to many of the valuable items that had been in the castle as they set out for their last battle.

Radu looked thoughtful. 'I wonder what happened to all those stable boys? Many of them looked younger than me. Would they have had to work for the next king?'

Osric frowned. 'How would you know that?'

'I saw Arthur's memory. He was dressed for battle and it took two stable boys to hold his horse still. I suppose you were there with the rest of the knights, waiting for Arthur. I couldn't recognise you under the helmets.'

'I thought only magically touched could see the memories of another Magical one,' Alora commented.

'That's true,' Mai agreed.

'And Radu knew about my connection with the piece of wood from the table,' Osric commented.

'So…I could be Gifted?' Radu whispered.

Mai took his two hands in hers and closed her eyes. 'There is a growing spark of magic in you. You have been mixing with the Gifted and Magical; you were able to cope with Aliki's changing in a very responsible manner. And now reading the fragment of table…you may very well turn out to be Gifted. Are there any signs of Gifts in your parents?'

Radu frowned. 'My mother doesn't seem to be. I don't know about my father. My parents split up when I was five and I haven't seen much of him since then. He last visited us three years ago.'

'It would be interesting to find out more about him,' Mai said.

'In the meantime, how about Radu joins us at the Coterie on Saturday mornings and learns more about being Gifted?' Alora suggested.

Radu let out a long breath as Mai nodded. 'But there will be strict rules and regulations; you can't let anyone else into your secrets or the secrets of any other Gifted members of our community. Not even your mother if she shows no sign of being Gifted.'

'I can do that! Oh! The best day of my life just got even better!'

As he moved next to Alora to discuss his first visit to the Coterie, Mai sat down next to Arthur who was sitting quietly at the side of the room. 'How did you find today's visit to Camelot?'

He rubbed his face. 'The memory I had when I stood outside where the gates of the castle once stood were so vivid! And the reality of how Camelot is today was like a knife through my heart.'

Mai put her arms around his shoulders. 'Maybe the visit wasn't such a good idea after all.'

He gave a wan smile and patted her hand. 'No. It was a trip we all had to make.'

'What about planning something cheerful for tomorrow?' Alora suggested.

'Actually, I am ready to go home, to the castle in Aurum,' Arthur said. 'I do not feel at home in this modern world.'

'I agree with you, Arthur,' Osric added. 'I must admit that I find the new Earth world rather overwhelming at times, and would like to return to the slower pace of Aurum.'

Maynard cleared his throat. 'Even before we came to Earth world, I felt this is where I belong. I have spoken to Bert and Venna. They have agreed to take me on as an apprentice mechanic at their garage. I can also rent the flat above their workshop which will be vacant at the end of this month; if I can stay here with you until then, Alora?'

'Certainly,' she replied. 'You're most welcome. When does your apprenticeship start?'

'Tomorrow.'

'Strike while the iron is hot!' Alora laughed.

Mai took Alora to one side as the men said their goodbyes. She told her of the young lad who had resisted the freeze charm.

Alora nodded. 'That must be Callum Hunt. The boy Sophie told you about. He's been showing a bit too much interest in the Gifted students at the school.'

'We must keep a careful eye on him.' Mai frowned. 'He could cause us trouble in the future.'

'I'll spread a warning around The Valley.'

'We will meet again, soon, Maynard, either here or in Aurum.' Arthur shook his hand as they were preparing to leave.

'Indeed, Sire. I will always be ready to stand by your side whenever you should have need of me.'

'Me, too!' Radu added.

Chapter Twenty

'Oh, it was so good to wake up in my own bed here in Aurum this morning after the excitement of the past week,' Osric commented as he poured a cup of tea and sat down with Mai the next morning. 'Is Arthur not up and about yet?'

'I think he's still asleep. The week's events have tired him out.' Mai put her cup gently on to the table and looked at Osric. 'He seemed out of sorts after the visit to Camelot.'

'Don't worry, Mai. He needs to adjust to this new life and find his own place in it. It will happen. Give him time.'

'I hope you're right. Are you going to see Peridot this morning? She'll love the book you bought her.'

Osric stood up, grinning. 'I do hope so.'

He was whistling as he arrived at the small cottage where Peridot lived. Through the French windows, he could see her standing in front of an easel. She was wearing a paint spattered shirt and cotton trousers. Her brow creased as she ran a critical eye over her work and she absently rubbed her cheek, leaving a dark blue streak. A warm smile lit up her face when she looked up and saw him.

'I hope I'm not disturbing your work?'

'Not at all. Come in, Osric! You're back from Earth world sooner than I expected. How was your trip?' She laid her brush and palette to one side and wiped the paint from her hands.

'Earth world holds many surprises! So many new things; at times it was quite overwhelming. Myself and Arthur were ready to return to the peace of Aurum after less than a week.'

'Come and sit down and tell me all about your trip.'

Her eyes widened as she listened to his stories of their trip. 'Oh, how I would love to visit Earth world and see some of those sights!'

'I found this in a book shop in The Valley and thought it might be of interest to you.' Oscar held out the brown package.

'Oh, Osric, this is beautiful! I have often wanted to know more about the artists and their stories behind the paintings Vinnie brings here. There is always a brief description, but this is so much more detailed. Look, Starry Night, by van Gough. One of my favourites. And this one...' Still holding the book, she gave him a warm hug. 'It's such a thoughtful present, Osric. You're so kind.'

'I'm glad you like it.' He cleared his throat. 'It wasn't just the peace and quiet that drew me back to Aurum, Peridot. I missed your company very much.' He took her two hands in his. 'You are on my mind all the time. I cannot see my future without you.' He took a step back as Peridot wiped a tear from her cheek. 'Oh, if my declaration is unwelcome, please tell me. I would never want to cause you any distress!'

'No! It's most welcome!' she laughed. 'I was so afraid that when you went to Earth world you'd like it so much you'd want to stay and make your home there. And I wouldn't see you again.'

Osric shook his head. 'My home is wherever you are. I knew that from the moment I set eyes on you.'

As he leaned forward his lips gently brushing against hers, there was a knock on the door and Saffron and Lupe came in. Saffron laughed as she saw the bright green flush on Peridot's face.

A smile spread across Osric's face. 'Peridot and I are...an item.'

'At last! Everyone else has seen this coming for a while now!'

'We must speak to Brunswick and Holly before we make it known to everyone else,' Peridot said.

'Yes,' Osric agreed. 'They must be the first to know the news, officially that is, anyway.'

Lupe drew in a sharp breath. 'Mmm, I don't envy you, Osric. I don't think Brunswick has a very high opinion of shifters!'

'Osric is my choice. And he'll soon win Brunswick over,' Peridot insisted.

***

'Lupe was right; Brunswick didn't seem all that keen at first and he even made a joke about wishing Peridot had chosen a goblin partner,' Sophie related the whole story to Sage as they walked to school a few days later. 'Holly was quite cross with him and said that Osric was a fine partner for Peridot.'

'How do you know all this?' Sage shook her head in amazement.

'Mary came back from Aurum last night. She's been staying with Mercy most days when she isn't working at the library lately. They heard all about it from Holly herself at Pine's Diner. Holly is arranging a celebration for the two of them on Saturday evening and everyone is invited. We'll have to go!'

'Yes, I'm so glad things have worked out for Peridot and Osric. They seem made for each other,' Sage agreed. 'I could be ready to leave about noon on Saturday. What about you and Paris?'

'I'll be ready. But Paris won't be joining us. He's going to a different party on Saturday.' Sophie paused. 'Actually, we had a bit of an argument last night. I wanted him to come to Aurum but he said it was his Non-Gifted friend, Mike's, twenty-first party on the same day and he felt he had to go to *his* party.'

'Well, a twenty-first is an important birthday.'

'So is the celebration for Peridot and Osric. Since he started at uni Paris has started to change. He seems more into NGs now. I prefer to put my Gifted and Magical friends first.' Sophie sighed. 'I feel we're drifting apart.'

'I'm sure things will be okay, Sophie.'

'I'm not so sure. Paris has applied to study for a year at a university in California in September. He's so excited about it.'

'Well, that *is* exciting news, Sophie. But that doesn't mean he's moving there for good.'

'He also said if it was half as good as it sounded, he wouldn't rule out living there in the future.'

Over the next few days, Sage noticed that her friend was quiet. One lunchtime, she was toying with her food as Sasha and Layla joined them at their table.

'You look tired today, Sophie. Too much late night revision? Or too many late night phone calls to Paris?' Layla asked her.

Sophie shrugged.

'Things are going okay for you two, aren't they? Only, I read an article in a magazine the other day that said around seventy-five percent of relationships end in the first two months when one of the pair leaves home to start college or uni, and that...'

Sage gave her a cold look. 'I don't think Sophie really cares what you read!'

As Sage and Sophie walked home that afternoon, Sophie's mobile beeped. She pulled it from her bag. 'Paris is making a quick visit home this evening. He wants to meet up later.'

'That's great news! He probably wants to make up after your argument.'

Her friend shook her head. 'I don't think so.'

Sage resisted calling her until late that night, but the call was sent straight to voice mail. 'Perhaps it isn't good news.'

The following morning, Sage noticed the slump in her friend's shoulders as she met her on the way to school.

'Not good news, then?' she ventured.

Sophie shook her head. 'Me and Paris have split up.'

'Oh, Sophie, I'm sad to hear that. Maybe it's just a temporary break.'

Sophie shook her head. 'No. He's been different since he left The Valley. When I asked him was there a crux near the Californian uni, he didn't even know. I told him I didn't think I could live away from The Valley and Aurum. And he said he was going to keep an open mind.'

'You might feel different, too when you go to uni next year.'

'That's what I was afraid of, so last night I emailed them to defer my place until next year. I don't know if I will go at all, actually.'

Sage raised her eyebrows. 'Well, maybe a gap year would be a good idea. We still have to get through our exams; let's just deal with that for the moment.'

'And trips to Aurum will keep us going.'

At lunchtime, as they joined Aliki and Radu in the canteen, Sophie groaned as Layla, Sasha and Callum headed towards them.

'I heard that you and Paris were in the café last night,' Layla began.

'Yes.' Sophie interrupted. 'And you might as well know, we've split up.'

Layla gave a sympathetic smile. 'I hate to say I told you so, but...'

'Then don't say it!' Aliki interrupted sharply.

The smile froze on Layla's face. 'Actually, I was just trying to be supportive...'

'Yeah, right...'Aliki scowled at her.

Radu cleared his throat. 'Hey, did anyone see the programme on fungi last night? It was absolutely fascinating. Did you know that they've now discovered a fungus that can break down plastic? Brilliant news for the future of the planet, isn't it?'

Callum stared at Radu. 'Isn't that just amazing? I'm so sorry I missed that programme. Have you any other fascinating facts about fungi?'

'Actually, I was really intrigued to learn that fungi are in a kingdom of their own, but are actually closer to animals than plants.'

Callum tutted. 'Intriguing!'

Aliki gave a loud laugh and hugged Radu. 'Oh, Radu, only you would try to head off an argument by making small talk about fungi! You're priceless!'

He blushed as she kissed his cheek.

Callum glared at them both. 'Are you ready to set up the field for the year sevens, Aliki?'

Still laughing, she got up and grabbed her sports bag. 'Yes, I'm ready, See you later, guys.'

'I told you, Sasha,' Layla said as she watched them walk away. 'Callum definitely has his eye on Aliki. He sees you as a serious rival, Radu.'

Radu looked puzzled. 'Aliki and I are just friends. I don't think Callum would think we're more than that.'

He shook his head as Layla began to list the occasions she had noticed Callum's growing interest in Aliki.

Chapter Twenty-One

The following Saturday, Sophie put thoughts of Paris out of her head as they stepped through the portal where Sylvan was waiting for them on Abraxus.

'Mai is with Peridot and Osric adding the finishing touches to their house extension. Arthur is at the castle with Maynard, who didn't want to miss today's celebrations,' he explained as they climbed on to the dragon. 'Flavia is cooking up a storm and said she'll be glad of your help.'

The girls could hear a buzz of voices coming from below as they stepped down from the dragon. 'I'm off to help out with transport arrangements; see you later in the square,' Sylvan called as Abraxus rose up again.

Leaving their bags in their room, Sage and Sophie hurried down to old kitchen. It was hot and steamy, with the sounds of bubbling pots, knives chopping and plates clattering in the background. Flavia gave them a brief greeting as she pulled a large tray of bread rolls from the oven. 'Just in time, can you girls put these rolls into that flat basket over there. Thank you. Lacey, you can put the next tray in the oven now. Flora, have you whisked the sweet toppings? Good. Sophie, leave Sage to do the rolls, and help Flora complete the sweets. Is that Brassion in the cart outside? Lichen, tell him to back it right up and then start loading the baskets onto it.'

After several hours, the final baskets were loaded onto to the last cart and Flavia wiped her brow.

'The food looks amazing,' Sage said. 'Well done, Flavia.'

Flavia sat up straight. 'I know Pine and Holly are putting on a fine show of goblin food for the celebration; but I want everyone to remember that Peridot is fae, too;

and there'll be enough to keep fae and everyone else, satisfied.'

Sophie cleared her throat. 'The food looks really good; Flavia and I know a lot of hard work went into it all. I just wondered why you don't use a bit of magic to make it easier?'

'Hrumph!' Flavia exclaimed. 'And have Pine telling everyone that fae can't do real cooking like goblins can? No, thank you!'

Brassion put his head around the door. 'We're ready to go now, Flavia. Flame and Flora are coming with us to set everything out.'

'We'd better get changed,' Sage said.

'I definitely need a shower and a change of clothes.' Sophie flapped her damp t-shirt. 'I don't think I'll get many dance partners like this!'

The square was bustling when they walked down with Maynard, Mai and Arthur a short while later. Mary and Mercy were already there adding the finishing touches to a multicoloured banner of flowers with the letters O and P intertwined in the air. Two fae children each holding an end to the banner, fluttered from side to side as Mercy guided them.

'A little to the right, no, not that much…that's it; perfect.' Mercy clicked her fingers and the banner was fixed in place.

At one side of the square, Flavia was standing with her hands on her hips, casting a critical eye over the tables set out with fae fare.

'It looks wonderful,' Mai assured her as Flame and Flora added the last sprinkle of brightly coloured sweets to the display. 'Now, you three need to go and get changed.'

As the three fae orbed and disappeared from sight, on the other side of the square Pine came out of the Diner, holding back the door and watching anxiously as four young goblins manoeuvred a large table outside. 'Gently now…careful…okay…leave it just there.' As the boys moved away, she pulled back a cloth and gave a tweak here and there to the display. She stood back as people standing nearby moved forward and gasped.

At first sight, the table top held a picture of a mountain pine forest, with trees in different shades of green layered against a background of mist and clouds. Closer inspection showed that this work of art was entirely edible, from the tree trunks and branches, to the blue green mountain mists and the swirling patterns of the pine cones.

'Pine! This is amazing!'

'I've never seen anything like it!'

'You've excelled yourself this time!'

She gave a modest smile. 'We goblins wanted to do our best for Peridot.'

Sage and Sophie exchanged looks and glanced back at Flavia's display.

There was a shout as a wooden cart drew up beside Pine's Diner and two shifters jumped down, unloading tables and several large cooking pots.

'Well, there's going to be plenty of food for everyone,' Sage commented.

Chrysta moved forward to help set up the rough wooden tables between Pine's Diner and Flavia's tables. She lowered her voice, glancing to her left and right. 'Fae and goblin food is lovely to look at, but shifters need something a bit more substantial. And we don't want to forget that Osric is shifter.'

By now the square was full of people. A group of fae were singing and playing soft music in the background. The hum of conversation and music stopped as Brunswick and Holly stepped out of Pine's Diner. Brunswick held up a hand.

'Thank you so much for coming here today to celebrate with Peridot and Osric. We know you all wish them the best in their future together.' He stood back as the couple appeared and a cheer went up.

Osric cleared his throat. 'Thank you for joining us today. This is the happiest day of my life, knowing that Peridot will be beside me from now on.'

'This is the second happiest day of my life,' Peridot said. 'The first was when you told me, Osric, you wanted us to spend our lives together!'

Another cheer went up as several young fae and goblins circulated with trays of Meadowsip and Greenade. When everyone had a glass in their hands, Holly raised her own glass. 'To the happy couple!'

'To Peridot and Osric!' Everyone raised their glasses.

'And now, please help yourself to the magnificent spread put on by fae, goblin and shifter,' Holly said, gesturing towards the laden tables.

Saffron came to stand next to the girls, sighing as she watched Lupe and several other shifters pile up their plates. 'I don't know where they put it all!'

'It all looks delicious,' Sophie said, taking a plate for herself. 'I've never seen half of the dishes here before. The chefs have done themselves proud today.'

'A bit of healthy rivalry?' Mai nodded towards the Diner where Pine and Flavia were standing next to the goblin table. Flavia had a tight smile on her lips.

She turned as Osric and Peridot slowly made their way through the crowd, stopping to shake hands with well-wishers every few steps.

Sophie clasped Peridot's hands. 'I'm so happy for you both!'

'Yes, you make a lovely couple.' Sage agreed.

The two girls watched as Arthur and Maynard stepped forward to give their congratulations to the couple.

By the time most people had finished eating, the goblin band had started to play more lively dance music

and Zephyr and Brassion cleared the square. A cheer went
up as Peridot led Osric to the centre and they began one of
the slower goblin dances. Soon most people had found a
partner and the tempo quickened. Sage nudged Sophie,
smiling at Mai who was demonstrating the steps to Arthur
at the side of the square.

Sylvan appeared and took Sage onto the dance floor
just as Brassion approached Sophie. 'I hope you remember
your goblin dances. Shall we?' She felt a pang as she
remembered the last time she had danced with Paris, but
she smiled and held out her hand. 'I'd love to.' She was
surprised to find herself quickly remembering the steps and
soon found herself enjoying the dance.

After several goblin dances, the musicians changed
places with a fae group. Sophie stood with Brassion and his
friends as the fae dancers drifted past.

'They're so elegant, aren't they?' she commented.
Two of the girls nodded in agreement, but Brassion
shrugged. 'I prefer something a bit more lively myself.' He
turned as someone shouted his name. 'Hey, they're
organising a game of "Hunt". You can't beat a goblin at
camouflaging! Count me in!'

Sophie watched as he joined a group of youngsters
who were organising themselves into two teams. One team
sat down while the other disappeared into the darkening
grassland bordering the square.

'Be careful, Smoke, we don't want any injuries
today,' Petra called out.

He grinned. 'It's okay, we're playing the tamer
version.'

'Let's hope they stick to the tamer version,' she
commented to Sophie.

The two of them made their way towards Flame and
Flora, who were helping Flavia to serve out food on the fae
table. Sophie picked up a cake. 'This is delicious! I've

never tried so many different kinds of fae, goblin and shifter foods before.'

Flavia nodded. 'Yes, we've all done our best.'

'It's all delicious but Pine is certainly the winner on presentation today,' Petra said.

Flavia stiffened. 'Well, yes, she may have the edge on presentation *today*.' She noisily stacked a pile of empty plates and headed for the Diner kitchen.

Flora giggled. 'I bet she won't have the edge on presentation next time.'

'Why don't you and Flame go for a dance while we take over here?' Petra suggested. 'Zephyr and his friend are over by the musicians.'

Flora was quick to take up her offer, dragging Flame behind her.

'Flame isn't usually reluctant to dance with a handsome young man, is she?' Sophie said as she helped a young goblin to a slice of cake.

Petra shrugged. 'I don't know her very well, only what I heard about her and Samar.'

'I'm glad that ended well. Maybe she has really learnt her lesson now.'

'Yes, though I did hear that she has been seen near the Dark Forest a few times lately.'

'Why would she go there?'

'I'm not really sure...' Petra looked up as Chrysta approached her holding a crying Cairn. 'Oh, someone is getting tired. It might be time to head for home.'

'You go,' Sophie said. 'Most people have finished eating; I can manage here.'

Petra jiggled the baby in her arms. 'Thank you, Sophie. I'll find Grey. Chrysta, make sure the youngsters don't let their game get out of hand, won't you?'

Flavia appeared at the table. 'I see there's hardly anything left here. I did notice there's quite a bit of goblin fare left. She looked up as Vinnie, Arthur and Maynard walked by. 'Can I tempt you with anything here, gentlemen?'

Arthur shook his head. 'I really couldn't eat another thing. You have done us proud today, Flavia. As have all the cooks.'

'Ooh, I think I might be tempted,' Maynard said, accepting a slice of cake. 'I must admit, I do miss your cooking, Flavia.'

Flavia raised her eyebrows. 'I'm surprised you have decided to settle in Earth world, Maynard. I hear it is a very busy and noisy place to live.'

'One gets used to it. There are so many wonderful things in the modern world. I took a plane ride from London to Edinburgh, Scotland the other week. It was an amazing experience.'

'I've seen pictures of planes but I've never wanted to actually ride in one! You know where you are orbing or on a dragon; but relying on a mechanical device in the air? No, thank you!'

Sophie smiled. 'Growing up in Earth world, I must admit, I take all these things for granted. However, coming to Aurum and being surrounded by magic; that's a different thing altogether!'

'Yes, you can get used to most things,' Vinnie agreed. 'Aurum is my home, but I also enjoy the modern inventions Earth world has to offer.'

'I totally agree with you, Vinnie. And may I say the words I never believed I would ever utter?' Maynard spread his hands. 'I find it just as easy to embrace and accept magic as it is to accept the wonders of modern technology. In fact, now, I feel quite honoured to be "magically touched".'

'Well, that certainly is progress!' Sophie laughed.

By this time, Mai, Osric and Peridot had joined them and a discussion developed on the pros and cons of each world. As Osric and Maynard defended the place they preferred to live, Peridot confided in Sophie. 'I was so scared when the three of them set off for Earth world. If Osric had seen things as Maynard does, I could have lost him for good!'

'You didn't need to worry. Osric loves Aurum. And he loves you. So, you're both in the right place.' Sophie sighed. *'It can't work out if you don't both agree on the right place to be, can it?'* ran through her mind.

***

Back in Earth world, the same thoughts continued to whirl around in Sophie's head. Sage tried to keep her distracted as the last few weeks of term were filled with the excitement of the coming Christmas celebrations.

Sage gave a nervous cough as she walked home with Sophie one afternoon. 'I had a text from Paris last night. He's hoping a few of us can meet up over the Christmas holidays. He's home on Friday and he suggested Saturday evening.'

'Yeah, he texted me, too. I told him I won't be able to join them. But you should go, Sage. You and Paris are good friends. You know you don't have to choose between us.' Sophie stopped and faced her. 'And you don't need to keep trying to cheer me up with your yellow auras. I'll get over this.'

'Oh, sorry. I just hate to see my best friend looking so sad.'

'I told Paris I'd already made plans to go to Aurum on Friday. Could you let Sylvan know so someone can meet me at the portal?'

'I'll send him a shimmer via Jay.'

Sophie smiled as she stepped through the portal into Aurum on Friday and found Sylvan waiting for her on Abraxus.

Sophie stroked the smooth snout of the dragon. 'It's so good to be back.'

At the castle, Mai welcomed her with a hug. Vinnie, Peridot and Osric arrived shortly afterwards as Flavia bustled around in the kitchen. Soon they were seated at the large kitchen table while Flavia put large steaming dishes in front of them.

'Come on, Arthur,' Flavia urged. 'Fill your plate up. You're hardly more than skin and bone these days.'

'I always do your dishes justice, Flavia,' he smiled. 'You remind me of Sanda, the cook back in Camelot. Do you remember her, Osric?'

'Aye, I do that. And just like you, Flavia, Sanda was always telling Arthur to put some meat on his bones.' Osric patted his stomach. 'But she never told me that!'

As Sophie listened to the chatter around the table, she noticed that Arthur seemed preoccupied.

After the table was cleared, she joined him in a window seat where he sat strumming a guitar.

'I didn't realise you played the guitar.'

'One of the goblins from the stable lent it to me. It's somewhat similar to the lute a bard taught me to play when I was a boy.'

'That's a sad tune you're playing.'

'It's the story of a young boy who leaves his village to seek adventure. But as the years go by, he realises no place feels like home and that nothing can fill the homesickness in his heart. But when he goes back to his village, everything has changed and he no longer fits in there either.' Arthur gave a sad smile. 'It reminds me of my own situation.'

'But you have a lovely home here with Mai and friends who care about you.'

'I do realise that. I would not want to be anywhere without Mai and all the company that surround me. But still; I look at Osric, he has settled in well and is devoted to Peridot. Maynard has found his niche in Earth world - Jay told me he now owns and drives his own motor vehicle.'

He spread his hands. 'As for me? Once the king of my own realm; what am I now?'

'There must be a role for you, Arthur.' Sophie stood up and walked towards the Pendragon family shield that hung above the fireplace. 'What is it that Radu said about your family name?'

The others looked up and listened as she continued. '*Pen* in Welsh means head or chief and *dragon* can mean an actual dragon, so Pendragon means Chief Dragon or Head Dragon. Some people say it is figurative and it means Chief Leader or Chief of Warriors. But I think after all that has happened to you, waking up after hundreds of years and finding yourself in a land filled with dragons, the first meaning is the most accurate. You were born to lead dragons! Your destiny is to be a fearless dragon rider!'

Arthur shook his head. 'I have only ever ridden a dragon one time and that was under duress...'

'Well, you could give it a try,' Sylvan commented. 'For our beginners, we use dragons much smaller than Abraxus and Mimosa.'

'This is definitely your role in this new life, Arthur,' Sophie continued. 'Your family shield says it all!'

'Don't you have a beginner riders lesson tomorrow, Sylvan?' Mai asked.

'Yes, we do. And we have several young dragons that need riders.'

Sophie's eyes shone. 'Could I have a go, too?'

'You're most welcome.'

Osric raised a hand. 'And I'm ready for a new challenge.'

'I'll have three dragons ready for tomorrow morning,' Sylvan continued, ignoring Arthur's protestations.

'That's a great idea,' Mai enthused.

Chapter Twenty-Two

'We're standing on the hillside which leads down to Lower Meadow,' Sylvan told the small group the next morning.

Arthur felt a breeze on his face as a dragon flew overhead and landed by a group of animals further down the slope. His eyes widened as he looked down at the spectacle below. The vast range of colours and hues made a shimmering kaleidoscope in the sunlight as young goblins and fae led different dragons to their waiting riders. There were soft growls and whinnies and occasional puffs of smoke rising up in the morning air. 'When we lived in Camelot; I was taught that dragons were ferocious creatures that only wanted to eat us. I must admit these animals are beautiful to look at but they still seem rather formidable.'

Mai smiled. 'They are indeed beautiful creatures, and look how gentle they are with the young grooms.'

'There are so many different sizes and colours,' Sophie added.

Sylvan pointed to a young woman who was riding a dragon towards them. 'Ah, here's Cora, she's taking the beginners' class today. She'll have selected the best rides for you. Mai and I will leave you to it, Cora.'

Cora beamed at them as she slid to the ground. 'I'm so glad to have you here today. Dragon riding is one of the most exciting things you can do. Let me introduce you to Nythe.' She stroked Nythe's long, golden head, noticing the look of alarm that spread over Arthur's face. 'He is a fully grown golden racer, but don't worry, the dragons you'll ride today are much younger and smaller. Before you get to meet them, I'll tell you about the set up here.' She pointed down the hillside. 'Straight ahead is Lower

Meadow where the dragons start and end up. It's where the goblins prepare them for their rides and where you rub down your mount after your ride. Over there to the right,' she indicated a square shaped enclosure, 'is Course One, the circuit for beginners. Straight ahead, next to Course One, are the changing rooms and showers. Behind them you can see two long courses; Course Two and Course Three. They are the practise lanes for riders who are planning on dragon racing later. Then over to the left is Upper Meadow. This is where you go when you have finished Course One successfully and you are preparing for Course Two. It's a more informal area where you can practise particular skills and there are always several coaches on hand to help you. Even riders who have begun Course Two go there for a bit of a breather every now and then. There's an invisible ceiling on all the training courses so the dragons cannot fly too high and each rider will wear a slow-landing charm so you won't hit the ground too hard if, or rather, *when*, you fall off. Any questions so far?' She waited for a moment before continuing. 'And now Nythe will help me demonstrate how to mount and the way you should sit.' She patted the dragon's snout and he settled on the ground. 'You swing yourself up like this.' She swung a leg over his back at the base of his neck and pulled herself on to him. Once she was seated comfortably, she made a clicking noise and the dragon stood up. 'When you're airborne, lean forward so your body is as close to your mount as possible. And when the dragon swoops, move your body in the same direction so you remain seated. You can hold on to the sash to balance yourself.' With another set of clicks, the dragon gently tilted to one side and she demonstrated the move. 'Hand movements are very important. To tell the dragon to slow down, press lightly with your fingertips on their neck. To speed up, use the heels of your hands.

'The dragons we have selected for you today are all good natured and they are familiar with course one. As you can see, each dragon has a sash. Their riders wear a tabard in the same colours. If you fall off, stay low and make your way to the start of the course. The helpers will bring your dragon back to you so you can remount and continue. When you have had enough, just make your way back to the Lower Meadow and someone will be there to help you. Now, let's go and introduce you to your dragons!'

As they made their way down the hillside, Sophie noticed that by now most of the dragons had been claimed by their riders and were being ridden to the different courses. A young goblin was standing near three dragons.

'Fern has your dragons ready for you. Thank you, Fern. Sophie, this is Shell. He's a lovely smooth ride,' Cora told her. The goblin gave Sophie a tabard as Cora got Shell to lower himself to the ground. Sophie patted the dragon's glossy blue scales and looked into his indigo eyes. 'Hello, Shell. Aren't you a beauty?' She smiled as she pulled herself on to his back.

Osric looked a little less confident as he was helped onto the second dragon. He patted her light brown neck. 'She feels much wider than a horse!'

Cora smiled. 'Don't worry; Gilla will look after you.'

Arthur cautiously stroked the long, purple snout of his dragon as Fern introduced him. 'This is Hectas; I think you'll both get on well together.'

'Just remember, I'm a raw beginner, Hectas,' Arthur mumbled as he climbed on to his back.

Cora ran through the basic moves and watched as each new rider followed her instructions.

Sophi gave a cry as her dragon began to tilt and she felt herself slipping. 'Lean in close a little sooner, Sophie. Osric, wait until you are airborne before giving Gilla the signal to go faster.'

'I didn't realise I was,' he murmured.

'Heels faster, fingers slow down,' Cora smiled. 'Don't worry, you'll soon get it. Now, I think it's time to head for the course.'

Sophie eagerly moved forward as they entered the gateway while Arthur kept his eyes firmly on his dragon's head. One by one, each dragon lifted off the ground and settled in behind the others already in flight.

Sophie gave a gasp as she heard the swish of Shell's wings and saw the ground become a blur beneath her. She leaned forward and glanced around her. Several riders were disappearing ahead of her with Arthur following them, frowning in concentration as he neared the first bend. Just behind him, Osric gave a shout as he slipped to the ground and rolled to the side of the course. Sophie clung on tightly as Shell glided around the bend and smiled in triumph as she headed for the straight once more. However, her feeling of victory was short lived as she felt herself slip from Shell's back at the second bend.

'Are you okay to remount?' a fae asked her, bringing her dragon to the start of the course.

'Oh, yes!' Sophie quickly remounted. There was a look of determination on her face as they approached the bend and Shell tilted to the right. As they headed back on to the straight, she began to enjoy the ride.

Arthur was beginning to feel more relaxed as he completed a lap and he urged Hectas to go faster along the straight run. All was going well until two dragons ahead nearly collided and to avoid them, his own mount veered suddenly to one side and Arthur found himself flung to the ground. As he stood waiting for his dragon to be brought back to him, he spotted Sophie grinning broadly as she sped past him.

'Come on, Hectas!' he urged as he remounted. 'Let's show her what we are made of!'

There was a clear path ahead as they both neared the next bend and each one steeled themselves to remain seated. Exchanging looks of triumph as they headed back onto the straight, both riders vied for the lead position. At the next bend it was Arthur who was smiling as Sophie slipped to the ground with a frustrated cry.

'Four falls is enough for me,' Osric said, brushing the dust from his jacket as he joined Mai and Sylvan in the viewing area. They watched as two more riders left the course.

'They're still going strong,' Mai said as Sophie and Arthur once again sped past them.

'I'm very impressed with their first attempts,' Sylvan commented. 'I think their dragons will tire out before they do.'

Arthur and Sophie were the last of the riders to leave the course. Their friends found them breathless and covered in dust, but beaming happily as they rubbed down their sweating animals.

'That was the best experience ever!' Sophie enthused. 'You were amazing, Shell.'

'Indeed, it was a most exhilarating experience,' Arthur agreed, smiling as Hectas clucked happily over the treat he held out for him. 'You have made me revise my opinions on dragons, Hectas.'

'Can we book another lesson for tomorrow?' Sophie turned to Sylvan 'I'm not leaving until the afternoon.'

As they waited for Sylvan to book them in for the next day, they watched the dragons amble away to join the others in the paddock.

'All set for tomorrow,' Sylvan said as he re-joined them. A frown creased his brow as there was an angry snort from the paddock. 'Magenta!' He hurried towards the top of the field where a young dragon cowered as a larger, brightly coloured youngster hissed at him.

'Magenta! Leave him! Now!' Sylvan waved a hand at her. She issued a small stream of smoke at him before she backed up and settled down on the hillside, her ears flattened against her head. The second dragon flew to join the others who had grouped together lower down in the meadow. One of the older goblins calming the herd looked up at Sylvan. 'She's getting worse. We can't do anything with her and we're afraid she might hurt one of our youngsters one of these days.'

Sylvan shook his head. 'I don't like to do it, but we might have to isolate her.'

Mai's brow creased. 'Are you sure there isn't another way? I do feel sorry for her; it wasn't her fault she lost her mother so young.'

Arthur watched as the young dragon fluttered her bright scales and shot a defiant look at Sylvan. 'She really is a beauty.'

'Yes, she is, but a menace to the others,' Sylvan continued. 'She lost her mother to guide her and now she seems beyond training. None of our dragon riders are willing to take her on.'

'Not even Rubio?' Mai suggested. 'He manages Fire Raiser, her father.'

'Fire Raiser is a full-time job for Rubio.'

'Let's go and have a word with the older riders. Perhaps we can persuade someone that she's worth the effort.'

Still talking, they made their way back down the hillside, unaware that Arthur was not following them. He watched as one by one the goblins and fae shook their heads when Mai and Sylvan spoke to them, then he turned and walked uphill. Magenta gave a warning rumble as he neared her. Pulling a handful of treats from his pocket, he held them out. She backed up, the rumblings growing louder.

'Hey, I'm not going to harm you. Look, I'll put these here on the ground so you can reach them.' He stepped back and waited as Magenta eyed him warily. After a moment, she moved forwards and scooped up the treats, casting wary glances at him as she did so.

'What makes you so angry, Magenta?' he said softly putting a second handful of treats on the ground and smiling as the rumbling faded. 'Is it because you feel like you don't fit in? I know that feeling. We could be friends, you know.' He put a third handful on the ground nearer to him and as she stepped forwards to scoop them up, held out his hand to her. Her eyes flashed and a stream of smoke poured from her mouth. With a painful cry, Arthur grabbed his arm, falling back onto the ground.

Hearing his cry, Mai and Sylvan rushed towards him followed by Osric and Sophie. Still breathing smoke, Magenta hovered above him before turning and disappearing into the sky.

'What happened?' Mai cried crouching down beside him.

Sylvan sat on the other side of Arthur and peeled a layer of burnt clothing from his arm. 'Bring me Mercy's box, quickly,' he called out to one of the fae youngsters hurrying towards them. 'This is a step too far. I'll see about getting Magenta isolated as soon as possible.'

Arthur grimaced as he tried to pull himself into a seated position. 'No, it wasn't her fault. I rushed her and frightened her. It was I who was in the wrong.'

By now the fae had returned and was opening a white box. Sylvan grabbed a ceramic bottle and poured a generous amount of liquid onto a thick bandage. 'This will sting at first, but it will soon heal your wound.' He gently wrapped the bandage around Arthur's arm.

'What were you thinking of, Arthur?' Mai asked as she watched the pain ease from his face.

'Magenta let me get quite near to her. I could see it in her eyes; she's just a headstrong youngster flexing her muscles. She's not as confident as she presents herself.'

'She's a dangerous youngster,' Sylvan insisted.

'Not if someone can get through to her. I rushed things today, but I believe I can win her trust if I take things slowly'

'I hate to say this, Arthur, but I think you might be out of your depth in this situation. You were badly hurt and it could have been worse,' Osric pointed out.

Arthur looked at Mai. 'Come on, love. You know she deserves a chance. I really do believe I can get through to her if I take things slowly.'

Sophie took a deep breath and broke the uneasy silence that followed. 'I think if Arthur Pendragon feels he can do this; then he should be given the chance.'

'As long as Magenta doesn't cause any further injury to any living creature, including you,' Sylvan added firmly.

Mai gave a nervous smile. 'Well, if you're determined, Arthur.'

'Let's hope I haven't frightened her off and she returns tomorrow.'

Later that evening, back at the castle, Vinnie and Peridot listened as Sophie and Arthur talked enthusiastically about the day's experiences.

'Dragon riding is absolutely amazing!' Sophie said. 'I can't wait to go back tomorrow!'

Osric smiled and shook his head. 'It was indeed an experience, but I think I will stick to horses in the future.'

Peridot held up the scorched remains of Arthur's jacket. 'It looks as if your experience with Magenta was not so amazing.'

'It was entirely my own fault. She is very nervous and I alarmed her by moving too quickly.' Arthur noted the look of concern on Mai's face. 'I won't make the same mistake again.'

'It's a long time since I rode a dragon. We often used to go for a ride when Aurum was first established, didn't we, Mai. How about we take out two dragons tomorrow while Arthur and Sophie continue their lessons?' Vinnie suggested.

Mai nodded. 'What about you, Peridot?'

Peridot grimaced. 'I haven't ridden a dragon since I was at school. I must admit, I agree with Osric, I am more of a horse rider!'

'As an experienced rider, can you give me some tips on taking the corners?' Arthur asked Vinnie.

Sophie nodded. 'Yes, it's easy to get into the swing of it on the straight, but it's hard to stay seated when you have to turn.'

'You need to know how far to lean to one side as you reach the bend. It's something that comes with practise,' Vinnie said. 'If you fall off, it usually means you've leant over too far.'

'So, you learn with hindsight!' Arthur joked.

'It's also important to build a bond with your dragon. As they become used to you, they will learn to adjust their moves to help you to work well together,' Sylvan added.

'Tell us about how you became so good at dragon riding,' Sophie said.

As the conversation continued, Mai looked at the rapt expression on Arthur's face. 'I think Arthur has found a new interest in life.' She smiled as Osric nodded.

When Sophie came into the kitchen the next morning, she found Arthur already pouring three mugs of coffee.

'Help yourself to some toast and eggs,' Mai told her, placing a tray on the table. 'We're all going to need a good breakfast this morning.'

Arthur helped himself to a generous portion. 'I'm going to see if I can use some of the tips Sylvan gave us last night.'

'Today, I'm going to complete at least two laps without falling off.' Sophie stated as she picked up her own plate.

'Don't ask too much of yourselves, it is only your second lesson!' Mai paused. 'And, Arthur…'

'I know. Be careful around Magenta. I promise, I'll not do anything rash, my love.'

Mai stopped herself from reminding him once more as she watched Arthur and Sophie follow Cora into the beginners' field later that morning.

Vinnie raised an eyebrow. 'Mai, don't forget that Arthur faced many dangers as king of Camelot. Come on, let's enjoy our ride this morning. Let's fly over Lilac Brae. It looks so beautiful from high up.'

'Then we could continue to the mountains,' Mai agreed. 'I haven't enjoyed that view for a long time.'

Sophie and Arthur watched them soar into the sky. 'I wish I could fly like that,' Sophie murmured.

'You will be able to if you keep practising,' Cora told her. 'Today you want to concentrate on keeping your balance at the bends. Remember, lean forward, grip tightly, using your legs and your arms…'

Sylvan was smiling broadly as Shell and Hectas landed gently in the cooling off area a few hours later.

'I did three laps without a fall!' Sophie exclaimed.

'You both show real talent.'

Arthur wiped the sweat from his brow. 'I feel as if I was really getting somewhere today. Can you sign me up for lessons for the rest of the week?'

Sophie pouted. 'If only I didn't have school tomorrow! Still; we have the Christmas break coming up and I can be here Thursday morning. Can you book me in then, Sylvan?'

They chattered about the morning's lesson as they rubbed down their dragons. Leading Hectas to the meadow, Arthur caught sight of a red flash on the hillside above him.

'She's back!' He smiled, feeling in his pockets for the dragon treats. Sylvan frowned as he watched Arthur make his way to where Magenta was settling herself down. Two other dragons moved away from her, but she seemed unaware of them as she watched Arthur approaching.

'I'm sure he'll be all right,' Sophie said, a slight tremor in her voice.

Several fae and goblins were also focused on Arthur as he neared the brightly coloured dragon.

'Lovely to see you again, Magenta,' Arthur said quietly as he crouched down on the grass, scattering a handful of treats on the ground in front of him and backing away slightly. 'No surprises today. Let us just get to know each other.'

With one eye on Arthur, the dragon leaned forward and gobbled up the treats, giving a gurgle of approval.

'I feel that we can be good friends, but we need to set some boundaries and rules.' Arthur gave her a solemn look. 'I won't get too close to you until you are ready for it; and you must treat the other dragons and their minders with respect.' He pulled out a second handful of treats. 'Agreed?' Magenta looked down the hillside and back at Arthur. He smiled and scattered the second handful of treats. 'I'm taking that as a yes.' He stood up and took a step backwards as Magenta waited to lean in and scoop them up. 'Now, don't prove me wrong and make me look foolish in front of everybody. I'll see you tomorrow.'

Walking back down the hillside, he stopped and turned as he heard a soft rumble. He watched as Magenta rose into the air, circling once before heading into the distance.

Mai and Vinnie were with the others as he reached the lower meadow. Mai hugged him.

'It's going well,' he said. 'Slowly, but well.'

Chapter Twenty-Three

'It was absolutely amazing!' Sophie told Sage on the phone that evening back in Earth world. 'Riding the smaller dragons is so different to riding on Abraxus or Mimosa. My dragon, Shell, is a real beauty.'

Sage smiled as she listened to her friend's eager description of her dragon riding experience. 'Sylvan said that you and Arthur had a real flair. Arthur's already told him he's hoping to take part in the dragon races at the next Annual Celebrations. Mai was really pleased to hear that, although she wasn't too happy with his interest in Magenta. That dragon sounds quite dangerous.'

'Yes, her father is Fire Raiser and she's definitely a chip off the old block but Arthur isn't going to give up on her. I envy him being able to go riding every day. I'm going to get in as many lessons as I can between now and the end of June. I'm heading back to Aurum on Wednesday evening, once we break up.'

'You're not going to spend all the holiday there are you, Sophie?'

'No, I'll be back here for a few days over Christmas, but I'm planning on going back to Aurum after that.' Sophie lowered her voice. 'This is just between you and me for the moment, Sage, I really think I could be a dragon rider. I'm going to practise as much as I can over the next few months and hopefully take it up full time once we finish school in June. I really need to build up my stamina and strength. I'm going to ask Aliki for her advice tomorrow.'

'Hey, slow down. You've only just tried it out. See how things go,' Sage urged her.

There was a moment's silence. 'Anyway, how did Friday evening go?'

'It was good to see Paris and his friends again. They're all enjoying life at uni. Paris wondered if you'd like to meet up, just the three of us, before he goes back to uni.'

'Not really, not just yet.'

The next morning the two girls met Radu and Aliki on the way to school. Sophie told them how she had enjoyed dragon riding and asked Aliki for advice on building up her strength and stamina.

'If you'd like to sign up for a long term plan, you could do me a favour, too,' Aliki said. 'I need a student to work with me for six months as part of my Personal Trainer course. We could work on building up individual muscle groups and also on your overall stamina.'

'That sounds exactly what I need.'

'Great. Meet me in the gym before lunch and we can work out what's best for you.'

In the canteen that lunchtime, Aliki sat down next to Callum. 'Sophie has agreed be my student for the Personal Trainer course starting in January. Have you chosen someone? You have to sign up for it before this term ends.'

'I've yet to select my victim.' He narrowed his eyes. 'What do you say, Henry? Do you want to be super fit in the New Year?'

'No thanks. I'm keeping my head down and revising for the next few months. I'll be using most of the Christmas break to revise for the physics and chemistry mocks.'

'I'm glad I've finished with physics and chemistry,' Brigitte commented. 'That Periodic table! Why is gold AU? Why not G or even Go – go for gold! Easier to remember!'

'Actually, Au is for Aurum, which is Latin for gold,' Radu told her.

Sophie raised her eyebrows. 'Hmm, Aurum means gold. I like that.'

Callum frowned at her.

'Why do people bother with Latin anymore? It's just a dead language,' Layla said.

Radu looked at her. 'Well, it's actually really useful when you're studying archaeology. Ancient Greek is another useful language.'

'Ancient Greek is for Geeks!' Callum laughed. 'And let's face it; you are a super Geek, Radu!'

'We all have to face up to what we are at some point, Callum.'

The smile froze on Callum's lips as Radu's eyes held his.

Layla sighed. 'Apart from revision plans, anyone know of any good parties over the holiday?'

'Marianne is holding her seventeenth at Zuma's. No alcohol allowed - officially anyway,' Callum said.

'I've an invitation for that; but Zuma's.' Layla grimaced. 'Do you remember Brandon's sixteenth there? What a washout!'

As they continued to discuss the best party venues, Aliki turned to Sophie. 'I heard that you and Mary are heading back to Aurum over the holiday. My parents have booked us in at the hotel for a few days after Christmas until the New Year. Mary gave us the shifter potion when we got our visas from Alora.'

'Nan, Grandad and me are planning on a trip there for New Year's Eve, too. Axel has told Grandad he'd look after Jet, Adam and Elvis,' Sage said. 'Mai said they don't really celebrate Earth world events over there, but the goblins are always up for a party.'

Radu sighed. 'I'd love to visit Aurum.'

'Why don't you?' Alora said. 'You're eligible for a visa now.'

'What would I tell my mum? I wouldn't be happy lying to her. I feel like I'm hiding enough from her as it is.'

'Hmm, you could come with us for a holiday for a few days,' Aliki suggested. 'We don't need to say where we're going exactly. I'm sure my dad could talk her round.'

'You can't deny the Gifted side of yourself, Radu, can you?' Sophie added.

His brow creased. 'That's true…maybe later on. I wouldn't like to leave Mum on her own over the Christmas holiday.'

'What are you lot planning?' Callum looked over at them.

'I bet they're planning the party to end all parties!' Layla sniggered.

'Who cares about parties when there's dragon riding?' Sophie said as they made their way to afternoon lessons. 'You've just got to try it out, Sage. Why don't you come to Aurum with me on Wednesday and join us on Thursday morning?'

'Yes, I could do that. I'll have to come back Friday; we've Dad's cousins coming to stay this weekend.'

***

'Remember to lean forward and keep your body as close to your dragon as possible especially when they swoop. Hold on to the sash to balance yourself and stop yourself from slipping off.' Cora instructed Sage and two young goblin learners later that week.

Sage drew a deep breath as she followed the other two dragons onto the course.

'Not too fast, Sleek!' she cried as they began to pick up speed. She had just begun to get used to the rhythm of Sleek's movements when they reached the first bend and she found herself tumbling to the ground.

'Thank goodness for the slow fall charm,' she muttered as she crouched down and hurried to the start of the course.

'Don't forget to tilt your body at the turnings,' said the fae as he brought Sleek back to her and helped her remount.

This time as they neared the bend, Sage leaned into the smooth, yellow neck of her dragon, clinging on tightly. 'We did it!'

Her relief was short lived as they gained speed and Sleek headed for a space between two other dragons. Once again, she clung on tightly, fixing her eyes on his neck as they sped past. At the next bend, she groaned as she slipped once more to the ground.

'Are you ready for another go?' the fae grinned as he brought Sleek to her.

'Yes, I am! I'm going to do a full lap before I give up today!'

With aching arms and legs, Sage finally turned onto the last straight and headed Sleek towards the gate. She was glad when a young goblin came to help her rub down Sleek and lead him away to the meadow.

Mai and Cora approached her.

'I thought I'd come and see how you were getting on,' Mai said. 'You did very well for your first time.'

'You certainly did,' Cora agreed. 'Arthur and Sophie won't be finished for a while. Why don't you go the viewing area and watch them? I've got to get back to the Lower Meadow for a while.'

Sage and Mai sat down to watch as Arthur weaved in and out of the other riders, hardly slowing down at each bend.

'He makes it look so easy,' Sage said.

'Yes, Sylvan says he's ready to go up to the next level already. I'm so glad that Sophie convinced him to give it a try.'

'I think it has been good for Sophie, too, to take her mind off Paris.' Sage turned to Mai. 'It looks as if the fortune cookie didn't get it right that time.'

Mai shrugged. 'Maybe it was the wrong boy next door or maybe the timing wasn't right. Paris paid us a visit two days ago. He's enjoying his university course and is very excited to have the opportunity to study in America.'

'That seems to mean more to him than his Gifted friends and his own talents.' Sage narrowed her lips.

'Don't judge him too harshly. Many of his friends and family are Non-Gifted. And he is very close to his Non-Gifted mother. Whereas, Sophie is close to her Gifted mother and is also influenced by her Aunt Mary.'

'I suppose so; it just seems that he's throwing away something so valuable. What if he loses his talents?'

'I think he needs time to sort out what he wants from life.'

'Sophie seems to know what she wants,' Sage commented as they watched Sophie fly past. They held their breath as she successfully negotiated a bend and increased her speed along the straight. She grimaced a moment later as Shell dived beneath a cluster of dragons ahead of them, sending Sophie tumbling to the ground. 'Ooh, hard luck, Sophie!'

'Sophie told Sylvan that she wants to take up dragon riding full time when she finishes school. He thinks she has the potential to make a good rider.' Mai smiled. 'It will be lovely to have you both here next year.'

'I'm really looking forward to spending more time here,' Sage agreed. 'Ah, it looks as if all the riders are finished for today.'

They walked down the hillside and found Arthur and Sophie with the other riders rubbing down their dragons.

'Isn't dragon riding just the greatest feeling, Sage?' Sophie enthused.

'I did enjoy it, but I don't know if I'll ever get to be as good as you,' Sage said.

'When we're here next year we'll both be able to get lots of extra practise in. But Arthur is definitely going to be the champion!'

'I won't stop until I am.' His smile broadened as he looked uphill to where Magenta was landing. Another dragon moved slowly away as she settled, but she did not pay any heed to him. 'Ah, good, Magenta seems calmer these days. I'll go and speak to her for a while.'

Sylvan joined them and watched as Arthur made his way uphill. 'He's not only a talented rider, but he seems to have a way with Magenta when no-one else could communicate with her.'

Mai nodded. 'She does seem to seek out his company these days and let him get quite close to her now. I just hope her new attitude lasts.'

'I think it will.' Sylvan gave a wry smile. 'But we always keep an extra supply of healing potions from Mercy on hand these days!'

Back at the castle, over lunch Sophie, Arthur and Sylvan continued to talk of various strategies to improve their riding.

Arthur looked up at Mai and gave a grin. 'Sorry, I promised we'd talk about something else for a change. What have you in mind for this afternoon?'

'I have to take some things down to the hotel, if anyone wants to join me,' Mai said. 'It's really busy at the moment now the Earth world schools have closed for the Christmas holidays.'

When they arrived later that afternoon, Saffron greeted them with Flora by her side

'Wow, it is busy today!' Sophie commented.

Saffron nodded. 'We've had to take on quite a few new workers for the next few weeks. Flora has worked here since the hotel opened and now Flame has completed her gossamer time, she has joined us too.'

'Isn't Samar working here, as well?' Sophie asked. 'Do they get on okay?'

'They don't see much of each other,' Saffron told her. 'Except when they need Samar to move heavy stuff. Most evenings, Samar joins Malbeam on the Dark Forest tours. I hear he's a very good tour guide.'

Just then, Osric drew up in a goblin carriage and a group of Earth world visitors got down. The older passengers made their way to the outdoor café while some of the younger ones joined a group of young fae and goblins playing hide and seek around the trees and bushes in the square.

One of the girls shook her head. 'How can we find you when you're so good at camouflage?'

A goblin sprang up behind her, giggling. 'You must look very carefully!'

A young fae looked up her face breaking into a smile as she saw Arthur. She flew towards them. 'Arthur! I saw you riding Hectas this morning. And you on Shell, Sophie'

'Ah, Wisp! You did indeed. And I saw how skilfully you rode Orma.'

Arthur and Sophie were quickly surrounded by youngsters. Mai watched as Arthur threw his head back and laughed as one of them said something, then tousled the youngster's hair.

'It's so good to have the old Arthur back, isn't it, Osric?'

'It certainly is, Mai. Arthur had to look harder to find his role in this new life, but now he has definitely settled down in Aurum.'

A tall, dark-skinned young man was listening to their conversation as Sophie and a goblin discussed dragon riding manoeuvres.

'You're a dragon rider?' he asked her. 'Do you live here in Aurum full time?'

'Well, I'm not exactly a full-time resident just yet.' Sophie explained how she planned on moving to Aurum once she had finished school in the summer. 'In the meantime, I'm going to spend as much time as I can here and get in as much practise as possible.'

A wistful smile played on the young man's lips. 'Aurum is such a wonderful place, isn't it? We're only here for a few days and already I feel I'd be happy to live here permanently.'

'Dareem, the goblin carriage is leaving in a few minutes. Jenna and Father are keeping our seats for us.' A young, dark-skinned woman dressed in a green silk sari was walking towards them.

'My sister, Nyla,' Dareem said.

'Hi there, Nyla. I'm Sophie. I hope you enjoy the tour.' She watched as the brother and sister made their way towards the carriage, noticing how the sun picked out green glints in their black hair and dark skin.

As the carriage moved away, Flame appeared in the doorway of the hotel.

'Ah, there you are, Flame.' Flora waved to her. 'I wondered where you'd got to.'

'Just tidying up a few things,' Flame replied, seeming flustered as she spotted Mai.

Sophie caught sight of a figure behind her who disappeared back into the hallway out of sight. She noted the frown that flickered across Mai's face.

Chapter Twenty-Four

Sophie slowly pushed her clothes into her bag a few days later.

'I wish I could just stay here until the end of the holiday.' She remembered how excited she had always felt about previous Christmases. This year, putting up decorations and Christmas shopping hadn't been so much fun. The present she had ordered online for Paris over a month ago now lay pushed to the back of her wardrobe.

Mai appeared in the doorway, watching as surreptitiously Sophie wiped a tear from her cheek.

'I'm not trusting any more fortune cookies!' She gave a weak smile.

Mai gave her a hug. 'As I said to Sage, maybe Paris was the wrong boy next door, or maybe the timing was wrong; but things will work out for you in the end; I know they will. Look at me. I had to wait a long time to find my perfect partner!'

'Yes, but I'm mortal; I don't have several hundred years to find someone!' Sophie replied as they made their way to the kitchen.

Arthur put a mug of tea in front of each of them. 'I'll miss you on the morning rides, Sophie. It will be good for both of us when you're here full time.'

'What do your parents think of you plans?' Mai asked.

'Hmm, actually, they know I'm not going to uni next year, but I haven't told them my latest plans about training to be a dragon rider yet. Mum really enjoyed her trip here last month. I hope she'll understand why I want to live here and how important dragon riding is to me.'

'Don't forget to think about how your father and brother will feel, too. They're Non-Gifted but they're still a very important part of your family, Sophie.'

'You're right, Mai. Since I got my Gift, I get so excited about magical stuff that I do forget that it must be hard for Dad and Gary living with Gifted ones in the family. I need to make more of an effort.'

These thoughts were running through her head as she pushed open the back door to her family home later that day. There was the smell of spices in the air and Christmas carols were playing in the background. Her father looked up and smiled at her.

'Ah, you're back, Sophie.' He put the finishing touches to a tray of mince pies and slid them into the oven. As he leaned down to set the timer, Sophie noticed the deepening frown lines on his face and the streaks of grey in his black hair. She gave him a hug.

'Hi, Dad. It's getting very Christmassy around here!'

There was the sound of heavy footsteps on the stairs and her brother came into the kitchen pulling on his jacket. 'Hi, Sophie. I'm off to get my last Christmas present. Something for Aunt Mary. Have either of you any ideas?'

'I need to get something to go with Sage's present,' Sophie said. 'I'll come with you. We can look around together.'

'Can you pick up a box of Christmas crackers while you're there?' their father asked. 'I forgot to put them on the list your mum took with her this morning.'

Sophie enjoyed looking around the shops with her brother and was pleased when he confided in her about a girl he liked that would be at a party at a friend's house the following day.

'How do I know if she's interested in me?'

'Well, see if you like the same kind of things. Find out what kind of films she likes, or what kind of music. Mind you, I might not be the best romantic advisor.'

'I'm sorry about you and Paris. He's the loser.'

Sophie nudged his arm. 'Thanks, Gary. I'm lucky to have a brother like you.'

'Even though I can't jump around the place or ride dragons?'

'Because you put up with family members who *can* jump around the place and ride dragons!' She laughed and then turned a serious face to him. 'Do you get tired of being surrounded by Gifted people? And hiding all this stuff from Non-Gifted friends?'

Gary frowned. 'I never really think about it. It's always been like this. I'm not the only NG in a Gifted family in The Valley, so I do have friends who understand that I need to let off steam when it gets a bit too much.'

'Do you ever wish you were Gifted, too?'

'Not really. Well - okay - yes. When I listen to you talking about Aurum and dragon riding, I do. And I think it's unfair that the NG members of a family are kept out of an amazing place that is such a big part of life for the Gifted family members.'

'Yes, that does seem unfair.'

'Why do they have those rules? We're hardly a threat to the Gifted and Magical, are we?'

Sophie shrugged. 'It goes back to when Magical folk and creatures suffered terribly at the hands of ordinary people. Aurum was created as a place where ordinary people can't go, so they feel safe there.' She paused. 'But things have changed a lot lately. Maybe there will be a time when our families can visit.'

Over the next few days Sophie made a big effort to pay more attention to her Non-Gifted family and friends and to appreciate their company and her time in Earth world. She even made a conscious effort not to use her Gift or to talk about dragon riding though she was pleased when Sage suggested they spend an afternoon at Alora's and she could chat with her Gifted friends about the other side of her life.

Sophie was humming to herself as she packed her bag for Aurum a few days later. After kissing her mother goodbye and hugging Gary, she climbed into the car next to her father. Mary was waiting outside her house with a large suitcase and a basket when her father drew up. As usual, she chattered nonstop on the drive to the outskirts of town.

'I've a selection of herbs that I'm sure will interest Mercy; some I dried over the last two months. And I put in two of the older potion books from the Alternative Archives at the library. It's a pity that Denise isn't coming with us today.'

'Denise and I are going to a New Year Eve party by ourselves for the first time in ten years! Gary is staying at his friend's house and Sophie is busy. We won't even have to worry about you popping by with the latest gossip, Mary.' Sophie grinned as her father winked at her.

Mai was waiting for them when they crossed into Aurum. Mary made her way to Mercy's cottage while the others went to the hotel where Aliki and her parents were waiting in the foyer, chatting to Sage and her grandparents.

'We've put you all on the first floor in adjoining rooms,' Lupe told them as he led them to the lift.

'How about you unpack your bags and meet down in the lounge for tea and cakes in half an hour?' Saffron suggested.

'We'll head over to the castle now,' Sage said. 'We can all meet up at Pine's later this evening.'

Sophie sighed as she put her bag down on the bed and looked around the room that felt as familiar as her own bedroom in Earth world. 'Oh, it's so good to be back. But I did enjoy Christmas with the family and seeing all our relatives. Mai made me think about things.' She told her friend about Mai's gentle reminder to consider the Non-Gifted among her family and friends. 'You know, this is the first time I've ever asked Gary how he felt about our family dynamics. I was so caught up in developing my Gift I forgot about how Dad and Gary must feel. I'm going to make a big effort to be more understanding of the NG side of my family from now on.'

'Does that mean you're reconsidering going to uni?'

'No way! I'm still planning on living here and training to be a dragon rider. But I'll definitely make sure I make time to see my family and friends in Earth world. And be more patient with them.'

Mary waved them over as Sage, Sophie, Arthur and Mai entered Pine's Diner that evening. 'You must try one of Pine's latest pastries. They're absolutely delicious.'

'And the green tea is very refreshing,' Ellen added.

'I'll go and take a look and get a selection of cakes and tea for us,' Sophie said.

She was holding a tray of tea, pastries and cakes when she heard a familiar voice behind her. 'Oh, Dareem, you're still here.'

'My sisters and father returned to India as planned but I managed to persuade my father to let me extend my holiday until New Year's Day, Earth world time. I've been helping Osric in the goblin stables and I'm really enjoying myself. I've joined him taking groups out riding in the afternoons. You'll be dragon riding most days, won't you?'

A smile spread over her face as she nodded. 'Well, I'd better take these back to our table. I'll see you later.'

Sylvan and Zephyr had joined the others and were discussing the following day's plans.

'So, is it just Aliki and Sage down for grass surfing tomorrow morning?' Zephyr asked.

'We knew you'd be dragon riding, Sophie,' Sage told her. 'Nan and Grandad are going to the Art Museum.'

'And there's horse riding in the afternoon, led by Osric and Dareem,' Aliki said, looking at the pamphlet.

Aliki's mother looked at her husband. 'I'd like to go on that, what about you?'

For the next few minutes, as pastries and teas were enjoyed, the following day's activities were decided on.

***

Sophie felt the usual tingle of excitement as she reached the meadow the next morning and Shell raised his head, giving a gentle snicker as he spotted her. Fern smiled. 'He's pleased to see you, Sophie.'

Sylvan turned to Arthur who was mounting Hectas. 'You're moving on to course two preparation today, Aren't you?'

'I certainly am.'

Sophie settled herself on Shell's back and patted his neck. 'Come on, boy. Let's see if we can catch up with Arthur.'

An hour later, Sophie frowned as she watched a fae bring Shell back to her after a third fall. '*This* time I *will* make the five laps!'

She urged Shell forwards and braced herself as they approached the first bend, taking a deep breath as they started onto the second straight. Two riders ahead of them moved to one side as Shell overtook them. At the second bend Sophie flattened herself against the dragon's neck, clinging tightly as he leaned to one side. Her heart was beating fast as they cleared the fourth bend, feeling her grip loosen as they headed along the final straight. 'I must hold on!' she whispered, but despite all her efforts, she slipped to the ground. Jumping up, she clenched her fists and fixed her eyes on Shell. Seconds later, she landed with a bump on his back and clinging to the sash, sped past the assessor to the finishing line.

200

'Five laps all within the time!' the goblin timekeeper shouted. 'Well done; you're ready for course two.'

Sylvan rode over as Sophie dismounted. 'Well done! I knew you could do it.'

She shook her head. 'I didn't. I fell off just back there.' She noticed the puzzled look on his face. 'I Transposed.'

The goblin gave a low whistle. 'That's pretty impressive.'

'But it doesn't get me onto the second course.'

'You'll get there, Sophie, but maybe not today. Why don't you have a rest now and try again tomorrow?' Sylvan patted her shoulder. 'Give Shell a rub down then take the goblin carriage back to the castle.'

Sophie bit her lip. 'I'll do that. I think we've both had enough for today, haven't we, Shell?'

Seated in the carriage, surrounded by chattering young goblins, Sophie felt her mood lighten.

'You're from Earth world, aren't you?' a girl asked her.

'Yes, but I'm planning on moving here once I've finished school in the summer.'

A boy turned to her. 'What's Earth world like? I'd love to go there.'

Sophie described her small town with its old-fashioned, stone cottages and the surrounding green countryside and sea views. 'The Valley is actually very pretty but some of the bigger towns and cities are not so nice, certainly not as beautiful as Aurum.'

The boy nodded. 'Maybe, but I'd like to be able to go there and see for myself.'

The girl raised her eyebrows. 'I wouldn't! My grandmother used to tell us about the dreadful treatment goblins and Magical people had to put up with on Earth world before Mai Lin created Aurum.'

The boy looked down at his hands. 'If our green skin didn't make us stand out; we would be free to travel to Earth world just like the fae and other Magicals can now. It doesn't seem fair.'

'That's true.' His friend nodded. 'Even here in Aurum, we don't have any special talents like most of the others. We're like the Non-Gifted of Aurum.'

Sophie shook her head. 'That's not true at all! All the people in this carriage are training to ride dragons; not all the people of Aurum can do that. And I'm sure there's a goblin talent...'

'Which is?' the girl waited.

Sophie bit her lip for a moment, then exclaimed. 'You can camouflage! No-one can ever spot you when you camouflage because you're so good at it!'

'Hmm, that's true. It's great for playing games as kids, but is it a useful skill in everyday life? Orbing certainly is.'

Sophie's brow creased. 'Well, I'm sure there are plenty of ways you could use camouflaging.'

'Yes, maybe you're right there,' the girl looked thoughtful.

The boy pursed his lips. 'Oh, come on, Posy.'

Shortly afterwards, they arrived at the goblin stables. After a chat with Dareem, Sophie set off for the castle. As she walked, she went over the last conversation she had had with Paris. She had complained that he didn't seem to value his Gifted side and Gifted friends so much since he had started university. His reply was that he was planning a future living and working in Earth world and his priorities had changed. 'I love Aurum and our friends there, but to me it seems more a place for a holiday, a break from my real life.'

'To me, it is a huge part of my life,' Sophie had countered.

Paris shook his head. 'You've hardly seen anything of *this* world. Don't you want to see a bit more? I can't wait to go to America next year. It's the opportunity of a lifetime.'

'You might even decide to settle down there.'

'Who knows?' He shrugged. 'Maybe you'll decide to settle in Aurum.'

Sophie remembers how her stomach fell and there was a lump in her throat. She swallowed. 'It looks as if we're heading in different directions.'

Paris looked up at the sky blinking rapidly. 'Maybe we need a break.' His voice sounded gruff and not much louder than her mumbled agreement.

She brushed a tear from her cheek as she looked up and saw Sage waving from the kitchen doorway. The next minute, she was hurrying down the path towards her.

'Oh, we are *so* glad to see you,' she cried. 'You always come up with the best ideas! And we definitely need inspiration today!' She pulled her bemused friend into the kitchen where Mai and Flavia were seated at the large table.

Mai looked up, a smile spreading across her face. 'Ah, Sophie will have a winning idea. If anyone can come up with something, Sophie can!'

'Now, it's got to be impressive and really unusual – something that Pine would never even think of,' Flavia announced.

'She's talking about the fae food for the New Year Eve party,' Sage explained.

Sophie let out a long breath as three pairs of eyes fixed themselves on her expectantly. 'Oh, I don't really know much about food...'

'Oh, come on now, you have the best ideas about everything.' Flavia's smile was strained. 'We can't let Pine win again! I've heard she's got something even bigger planned for this party.'

'Those little pastry parcels you make are really delicious...' Sophie ventured. Flavia shook her head. 'Or that amazing pasta dish...'

'Too much like shifter fare. We need something to really stand out.'

Sage passed her a long, handwritten list. 'These are the ideas we already thought about, but Flavia wasn't really taken with any of them.'

Sophie's eyebrows rose as she scanned the long list. 'Looks like you've covered everything here. I don't know if I can think of anything else. All I seem to think about these days is dragon riding, I'm afraid. Not much use, really.'

There was silence as Flavia's face froze.

'I'm sorry I couldn't help.'

Suddenly Flavia stood up, leaned over the table, grabbed Sophie's shoulders and gave her a firm kiss on her forehead. 'Perfect! I knew we could count on you! A dragon theme!' She grabbed a pencil and a clean sheet of paper, muttering to herself. 'And I'll need extra helpers...'

'Anything we can do?' Sage offered.

'No, not you girls. I mean proper fae cooks. I'll go to Faeville straight away.' She stood up, orbed and sped out of the window.

Mai let out a long breath. 'Thank goodness you came to the rescue, Sophie.'

'I don't know how I did.' She spread her hands.

'Let's just be thankful that you did!'

The next few days quickly passed by. Flavia spent most of her time in the old kitchen, not letting anyone else enter, except for her specially selected team of fae helpers; all of whom had been sworn to secrecy over the planned fae table. Several times a day, carts would draw up outside the kitchen and youngsters would hurry inside carrying covered baskets. One of the boys was limping as he entered the kitchen. 'I nearly lost my footing on the mountain top picking these!'

Flavia spun around and held her finger to her lips. 'Never you mind; it'll all be worth it.'

On Monday evening, New Year's Eve in Earth world, there was a feeling of excitement in the air as people made their way to the square in Goblin Glen. The place was filled with the sound of laughter and music as Sage and Sophie made their way down to meet Jim, Ellen and Aliki and her family.

The door to Pine's Diner was closed, but through the windows Sophie could make out Pine and several goblins moving around a large table.

'I wonder what Pine has planned for this evening?'

'And what Flavia has in store, too.' Sage gestured towards a large tent on the opposite side of the square with the entrance laced shut.

Petra and some of the shifters were setting out huge iron pots on their own table.

'Aren't you involved in the food contest?' Mai asked her.

Petra shook her head, laughing. 'Presentation isn't high on the shifters list when it comes to food. As long as it tastes good and there's plenty of it, we don't get any complaints!'

The square grew quiet as the doors to Pine's Diner opened and a large table was carefully wheeled out. Pine made a few last minute tweaks, then stood back as people moved forward to see her latest display.

Once again, Pine had chosen a verdant scene, but this time, it was a three-D display. In the back ground were mountains, decorated with tiny green iced biscuits to represent trees. A river of Greenade snaked through a valley of lime coloured cheese into a lake. Different shades of green vegetables decorated each side of the river and a carpet of light green cakes appeared to be the grass in the valley. Dark green shades of scones and bread rolls made up a pathway on one side.

'What a spread! Well done, Pine,' a woman commented.

She beamed. 'Goblin chefs can be very creative.'

Flavia appeared. 'That really does look impressive, Pine. My compliments!'

'I can't wait to see what the fae table holds,' she replied.

Flavia nodded to one of her helpers who was waiting in the tent doorway. 'Come and take a look. It's a bow to all our dragons, and of course to our own Arthur Pendragon.'

There were several gasps as the tent sides were pulled back to reveal the fae table. The centrepiece was a selection of small savoury pastries interspersed with carved radishes and spring onions set out in the shape of a dragon. Below his feet, shredded lettuce and other green leaves represented grass. From his mouth streamed coils of delicate noodles while above his head, brightly coloured fruits and vegetables were arranged to make a rainbow. Layers of blue fruits and cakes made up the sky, with tiny puff pastries grouped together as clouds. A large pizza sun gleamed in different shades of yellow in the sky. Two lines of delicate sweet cakes sparkling like jewels framed the masterpiece.

'It's a work of art!' Sophie exclaimed.

Flavia beamed with pride. 'Fae chefs can be creative, too!'

'It looks almost too good to eat!' Aliki commented.

Flavia frowned. 'Oh, no! It's all there to be eaten! The biggest compliment will be for you to enjoy the food.'

'I recognise the blueberries, but what are these indigo fruits, Flavia?' Ellen asked her. 'And the bright yellow ones? I've never seen these before.'

'The indigo fruits are from the Mountain Royal trees, and the yellow ones are from the Sol Gorse that only grow in the south of Aurum,' she told her.

This time it was Pine who wore a tight smile as she nodded. 'Well done, Flavia.'

No-one seemed willing to take the first plateful of food from either Flavia's or Pine's display, until Petra gave one of the shifter children the go ahead.

'I thought Meadowsip was the best taste ever, now I'm not so sure,' Sage commented, biting into a small pale, flaky pastry. 'This is so delicious!'

'A special fae recipe. Even the best goblin chefs can't imitate it!' Flavia said, giving Pine a quick glance.

In the next hour, there were murmurs of praise as food from all tables quickly disappeared.

'Time for the dancing to start,' Sage nodded as the goblin musicians set up their instruments.

'Look, there's Brassion and Lychen and their neighbours,' said Sophie, making her way towards a group of goblin youngsters.

'We're probably the best dancers around here these days,' Brassion was saying.

'I see you're still as modest as ever, Brassion,' Sage laughed.

One of the girls nodded. ''He's been here a few months and already he knows everything!'

'I'm a quick learner!' Brassion winked at her. He turned as Dareem joined them. 'How about you? What are your dancing skills like?'

Dareem shrugged. 'I know a bit of goblin; a bit of fae.'

'Well, they're clearing the square now, so everyone find a partner!' Reed said.

Sylvan appeared and took Sage's hand. A goblin girl grabbed Brassion's hand. 'You'd better be as good a dancer as you say you are!' As the others partnered up, Dareem turned to Sophie. 'May I have this dance?'

Flame danced by with Kyte and Brunswick and Holly skilfully wove their way around the floor. Peridot and Osric were at the edge of the crowd slowly demonstrating the steps to Ellen and Jim who watched closely. Mercy led Mary through the basic steps, then they both joined the other dancers. Sophie exchanged a smile with Sage as Ellen led a reluctant Jim on to the dance floor.

Dareem turned out to be a good dancer and light on his feet. He persuaded her to try out one of the more difficult goblin dances, both laughing as she struggled to master the quicker steps.

'Dragon riding is easy compared to this!' Sophie gasped as the music ended.

The goblin musicians had put down their instruments to a loud round of applause. They were replaced by a two fae players as the floor cleared and fae couples stepped forward.

'You must find a partner,' Sophie said as she saw Dareem sway to the music. 'I know exactly who that could be!' She grabbed his hand and pulled him towards Peridot and Osric. 'Peridot, how about you dance with Dareem? You both have fae blood.'

'Go on,' Osric urged her. 'I think you deserve a partner who knows what he's doing.'

They stood and watched as the dancers glided effortlessly around the floor.

The was a round of applause when the fae dances came to an end. Arthur nodded at Osric and they made their way to the musicians' seats. Osric sat down and picked up a guitar propped up nearby. Arthur held up his hands. 'Well done to our musicians and to our goblin and fae dancers. This next dance is for everyone; it's one that was very popular in Camelot in our previous life. We'll give you a brief demonstration.' Osric began to play a soft melody as

Arthur walked towards Mai and held out his hand, giving a slight bow. She smiled and bobbed a curtsey. Holding hands and standing a distance from each other, they walked several steps forwards before taking steps apart and back together again. They repeated this several times, then turned away from each other and linked hands as they turned in the opposite direction, pausing for a moment before Arthur put his hands on Mai's waist and with her lightly holding his shoulders, they whirled around back to their starting point.

'Come on, now!' Arthur said. 'See how easy it is?'

Quickly goblin, fae and Gifted partners lined up behind them and the dancing began again. After a while, one of the goblin musicians took over the guitar playing from Osric so that he, too could enjoy a dance with Peridot.

Sophie felt quite breathless when the music finally stopped. With two cold drinks in his hands, Dareem led her to a bench at the edge of the square. Taking a grateful sip, Sophie turned to him. 'After all the dancing, this is just what I need!' She sighed. 'I can't believe it's nearly time to go back to Earth world. This next two terms will be busy, revising for the exams.'

Dareem nodded. 'I'm going to be busy at university; I've got behind with my assignments over the holiday.'

'What are you studying?'

'Accountancy. Our family has a large jewellery business in the capital. My parents want me to work with Nyla in the accounts department of the family company. Jenna works on the design side.'

'That sounds interesting.'

Dareem shook his head. 'I will really miss this place; I'd much rather be working here in the goblin stable than in the family business, if I'm honest. How do your parents feel about you becoming a dragon rider?'

Sophie's brow creased. 'I've not exactly told them yet. They know I really enjoy dragon riding, but not that I intend to take it up as a career. I'll have my work cut out to persuade them.'

They were just getting ready to re-join the others in the square when they heard a woman's voice nearby. Sophie looked around but a large bush hid whoever it was from view.

'You danced with her twice!'

'She's just a friend. You know I would much prefer to dance with you, but…'

The woman sighed. 'I know.'

'I'd much rather make things public; you know that.'

'I would too, but what if they disapprove? Where would we go?'

'We'll be fine. Things will work out.'

There was a rustle as the pair moved closer together. 'We're going to have to say something soon. It's sheer luck that we haven't been spotted up to now.'

The woman gave a long breath. 'Yes, we'll have to.'

'Go back to the others now. I'll see you later.'

There was a flash of a red dress and red hair as the woman hurried back and was lost among the crowd.

Sophie stood up and looked to see who her partner had been, but there was no-one there. 'That was definitely Flame, but I don't know who she was with. Whoever he is, he's a very fast mover. Let's go back to the square. It must be nearly midnight.'

They made their way through the crowds where they could see Sage and her grandparents standing chatting with some other visitors from Earth world. Suddenly, someone in the crowd shouted and pointed up into the dark sky. Four brightly coloured fae were flying up above them, staying close together. They stopped and then slowly moved apart, each holding the corner of a giant, white net. For a few moments they hovered in the air, then all at once they flicked the corners of the net and a cloud of flower petals cascaded down onto the crowd below like a gentle, sweet-smelling snowstorm. Delighted gasps and cries went up. Some turned their faces upwards to be caressed by the gentle storm while several of the youngsters ran and jumped, shouting and laughing as they snatched the petals from the air.

'What a beautiful ending to the holiday,' Ellen smiled and squeezed Jim's hand.

Sophie and Sage exchanged smiles as they nodded in agreement.

Chapter Twenty-Five

Back in Earth world, Sophie groaned as she turned off the alarm clock several days later. The first day back at school in January was always hard and the next few months were going to be particularly challenging. She had already pencilled in her next trip to Aurum in her diary, but she knew she wouldn't be able to spend as much time there as she would like .

As she and Sage joined Aliki and Radu by the lockers that morning, other students were hurrying inside out of the cold weather.

'I hate January!' Layla complained. 'They should ban this month. It's bitterly cold and full of mock exams! Ugh!'

'It's not so bad,' Sasha countered. 'I'll be glad to get the mocks over and done with. The sooner we start; the sooner we finish.' Her phone pinged and a smile lit up her face as she looked at the screen.

'You've got your love to keep you warm,' Layla joked as Sasha moved away, texting as she went. 'She's met a boy who works in the new discount shoe shop in town. Hopefully, it won't last too long.'

'Why not?' Aliki asked.

'Who wants to plan a future with a shop assistant?'

'Well, if we didn't have shop assistants we wouldn't have shops, would we?' Radu pointed out. 'I think everyone has to find the job that suits them, whatever it is.'

'I agree with that,' Sophie nodded solemnly.

Layla pouted. 'Well, I picture myself in a well-paid job in ten years' time. Maybe I'm just more ambitious than you lot are.'

'I don't think I'm going to become rich through archaeology.' Radu laughed. 'But that's what I want to do.'

'It's your Camelot exhibition on Saturday, isn't it, Radu?' Sage said brightly.

'It's not exactly *my* exhibition.' Radu smiled. 'But I am really looking forward to it. A bit nervous though; I hope we get a good turn out. My mother is working on Saturday but she has promised that she'll pop in at some point.'

'Are you going to Radu's museum exhibition on Saturday?' Aliki asked Layla who shook her head. 'Not really my thing, I'm afraid.'

'What about you, Callum?' she asked him as he came in through the door

'A bit too geeky for my taste.'

'Well, I'll definitely be there with you and I'm going to make sure that everyone knows that you unearthed the ruby brooch.' Aliki pulled a brochure from her bag. 'It's a pity they didn't include a photo of you.'

There was an air of excitement in the school as rumours that Arthur himself wanted to visit the museum exhibition quickly spread amongst the Gifted students. Callum's ears pricked up as he overheard the name Arthur mentioned by Aliki and Radu as they got ready for the Sports for All session that week.

'You know, I might just take a look at this exhibition, Radu,' Callum said. 'It could be interesting to see what kind of things you lot get up to.'

Radu looked pleased. 'There are details by each exhibit explaining where we found the items and the research we carry out to ensure the authenticity of each find.'

Layla yawned noisily as she pulled on her trainers. 'I think a bit of retail therapy will be my Saturday outing. Much more fun, don't you think, Sasha?'

'Actually, David was really impressed to hear how Radu is involved with the Archaeological Society. We're going to go to the exhibition during his lunchbreak on Saturday.'

'David almost walks on water these days - in his discount shoes!' Layla sniped as she jogged down to the race circuit.

'Lots of people have shown an interest in this exhibition,' Sophie commented. 'And not just G...'

'Not just what?' Callum raised an eyebrow.

'Not just geeks! Hey, I bet I can do a faster lap than you today. My PT has been working wonders on my fitness levels!'

Callum followed her to the track, a smug smile on his face. Fifteen minutes later, he was pushing himself to stay ahead of her, his lungs ready to burst. Somehow, he managed to get over the finish line seconds before her. Breathing heavily, they both collapsed to the ground.

'Hey, you gave me a run for my money there!' he gasped. 'How did you improve so quickly?'

Sophie pushed her damp hair from her forehead. 'With Aliki's help, and I get in as much practise as I can at the weekends.'

Callum sat up. 'Where do you actually go at the weekend?'

'Usually to see friends.'

'But where do these friends live? I never see you around town.'

Sophie smiled and stood up. 'You will this Saturday; I'll be at the museum. See you there.'

On Saturday morning, Radu walked around the exhibition hall again, looking at the different items displayed. On one side were different kinds of armour and weaponry. Down the centre were three long glass cases. The first one held a selection of kitchen utensils, cooking pots, ceramic bowls and knives. Most were incomplete fragments, but alongside the case were sketches and text to explain what they would have looked like and how they would have been used in earlier times. The second one was filled with farming equipment of the time, ploughs, scythes and the remains of a wooden cart wheel. Again, sketches and text brought the articles to life. Radu paused at the third one where items of personal jewellery were displayed with a description of each piece and its possible owner. He smiled as he read: *'Gold brooch with design in rubies used to fasten a cloak. This was most likely to be owned by a noble person, or even royalty.'*

He looked up as Aliki walked towards him. 'Do you think we'll get many visitors? And what will they make of it all? I know that these fragments of centuries old articles are really exciting for me and the others in the Archaeological Society; but will they impress anyone else?'

'They will if you tell them a bit about the background and how you discovered them,' Aliki assured him. 'I wasn't too interested in all this stuff until your enthusiasm made me see them in a new light.'

She smiled as she led her parents into the crowded hall an hour later. Radu was deep in conversation with an elderly couple who were asking him several questions about the articles in one of the glass cases.

Sophie and Sage arrived and made their way from one display to another. Sophie pointed to metal fragments beside an artist's impression of a whole shield. 'That shield looks very much like the one in the Great Hall, doesn't it?'

'And where would that be?' A voice made them look up. Callum stood behind them.

'Don't creep up on us like that!' Sophie laughed.

'So where have you seen the other shield?' he repeated.

'We heard about someone who's really into this period of history. They made a scaled version of a castle of this time,' Sage answered. 'They wanted everything to be as close a match as possible.'

'Oh, look, your grandparents are here with Mary.' Sophie grabbed her friend's arm and pulled her towards them.

Callum watched them greet the older couple. He turned and made his way towards Radu who was surrounded by a group of students from their school. As they moved away, he stepped forward.

'Hi, Callum.' Radu smiled. 'I wasn't sure if you'd actually come today.'

'I wanted to see this precious discovery of yours.'

Radu's smile widened. 'It's just over here. It's a brooch believed to be used to fasten the cloak of a nobleman as it is made from gold and encrusted with rubies.'

'And you just dug it up in the soil?'

'Well, we had mapped out an area in the grounds of the castle and we each had a plot to concentrate on, and after six weeks, I came across the brooch. It was very exciting!'

Callum peered at the brooch. 'Six weeks? A lot of work for one brooch. And you don't even get any money for it.'

'Money's not everything, Callum.'

At that moment, Aliki led Jim and Ellen over to them.

'Is this the brooch, Radu?' Ellen asked. 'Oh, my word! What a find! You must be so proud of yourself.'

Callum moved back as they peered into the glass case, asking questions about other items also displayed. He looked around the packed hall and noticed a door marked

"Staff Only" nearby. Making sure no-one was watching him, he went over and tried the handle. The door clicked open and he slipped inside, closing it behind him. Around him were several long wooden tables. One had containers of broken pottery, with different coloured pieces separated; another had an assortment of metal fragments and a third scraps of faded materials. With his hands in his pockets, he walked around, pulling a face as there were no items that looked even vaguely valuable. As he passed the table with broken pottery, he heard a strange sound, as if someone was sweeping up broken glass. His eyes widened as he turned round. Different shards were moving together, building an image in the centre of the table. Slowly a woman's face appeared. Her long, black hair was tied up in an elaborate old-fashioned style, with tendrils framing a white, oval face. Blue eyes were accentuated by fine, arched eyebrows; her nose was straight and regal. Finally, full, red lips appeared, and as Callum stood frozen, unable to tear his gaze from the image, they tilted into a cruel smile. With a cry, Callum stepped back, tripping over a pile of wooden crates and falling to the floor. The next moment, the door was flung open and a man appeared as he scrambled to his feet.

'What are you doing in here?'

'I …I…' Callum pointed at the pottery image and frowned. The image had disappeared with the fragments divided into different coloured piles once more. 'I … felt dizzy, it was so hot in the hall. I wanted to go outside but I took the wrong door.' He rubbed absently at his wrist.

The man's brow creased and he pulled a chair forward. 'You are looking rather pale. Here sit down for a minute and I'll get you a drink of water.' As the man filled a glass, Radu appeared in the doorway.

'Callum? What are you doing here?'

'Is he a friend of yours? He found the hall a bit stuffy and he mistakenly thought that this was the way out,' the man explained, handing the water to Callum. 'Perhaps you could show him the actual exit when he's got his breath back.'

Radu noticed how Callum's eyes kept darting towards the pottery shards as he sipped the water.

'I'm so sorry. The heat got to me. It's pretty crowded out there,' Callum said. 'So, this is where you do all the real work?'

The man looked around and nodded. 'Yes, this is where we bring our discovered treasures and piece them together. It takes a good long while, but the feeling you get when you can reconstruct the original item is so rewarding.'

'It must be hard to know how to put everything together. I thought some of those bits of pottery look like a woman's face.'

'No, those are part of a floral border. You can see a section of it completed in the exhibition.' He pointed to one of the larger pieces. 'I can see why you might think that, though. This leaf shape could almost be someone's lips, smiling.'

Callum shuddered and stood up. 'I'd better get going. Sorry again.'

'Yes, and I think I'd better lock this door in case anyone else mistakes it for the exit.'

Before he followed them out, Radu's gaze swept around the room. Nothing seemed out of place, but what had upset Callum?

A woman dressed in fitted black trousers and a black, leather jacket watched as the two boys walked towards the exit. Despite the overcast sky; she wore dark sunglasses. Smoothing her long, black hair from her pale face, she studied the brochure in her hand. A smile tilted her red lips as she located the case containing the ruby brooch and she strode forwards. A frown creased her brow as she looked at it. She pushed her sunglasses up into her hair and fixed her vivid blue eyes on Radu who had returned to his display.

'That isn't the original article, is it?'

'Of course,' he answered, a slight blush tinging his cheeks. He was relieved to see Aliki arrive with Sasha and David at that moment.

'Of course, it is!' Aliki repeated his words firmly. 'Everything here is carefully authenticated by experts.'

The woman gave the group of young people a cold smile and carried on to the next display case. At that moment, a commotion at the entrance door made her draw a sharp breath. Arthur and Mai Lin had entered accompanied by Maynard. A woman wearing a lanyard had walked forward and greeted them warmly. 'Arthur, Maynard and Mai,' she shook their hands. 'I'm so glad you could make it to the exhibition.'

Pulling down her sunglasses once more, and using the crowd to shield her from their view, the woman made her way to the exit. A scowl curled her lips as she gave them a final glance before hurrying from the building.

Standing outside the main door, Callum pulled up his jacket collar and took a deep breath. 'Maybe it was just my imagination. I'm getting a bit carried away with all this magic stuff,' he muttered to himself. 'That old guy and Radu didn't see anything weird.' He took a deep breath. 'I need to get back to some normal people.' He pulled his mobile from his pocket. 'Hey, Roy? Where are you? The café? Okay, I'm on my way there now.' He stumbled as a tall, slim woman dressed in black pushed past him. 'Hey, watch where you're going!'

She swung around, catching her falling sunglasses, a furious expression on her face. 'Just get out of my way!'

Callum flinched under her icy, blue glare as she swept past him and hurried on.

'The exhibition went really well, Radu,' Aliki said giving Radu a hug as the last of the visitors left the museum. 'Callum had a bit of a cheek going into the staff area, didn't he? I bet he was hoping to find something worth a bit of money!'

Radu pursed his lips. 'Maybe that's what he intended, but something really shook him up.'

'Nearly getting caught?'

'No, there was more to it than that. I couldn't see what had set him on edge, but something definitely had.'

***

At school on Monday, Radu was glowing with the praise he was given by both staff and pupils for the success of the exhibition. At lunchtime, Sage patted his shoulder as she joined the others at the canteen table. 'Everyone was very impressed. Well done, Radu.'

'Everyone except for one woman. She actually asked Radu if his ruby brooch was genuine, can you believe that!' Sasha said.

Sage frowned. 'I didn't see her.'

'She looked like a model; tall and slim with long, black hair and striking blue eyes. She was dressed in black. Very beautiful, but very stuck up!'

'Oy, Callum, you nearly spilt your coffee on me!' Layla complained catching his cup as it tilted dangerously.

Callum didn't seem to hear her. 'What woman?'

'Just one of the visitors, I suppose,' Sasha continued. 'She couldn't have been anyone important; not like that man, Arthur. The museum staff made a big deal out of him and his friends being there.'

'Arthur?' Callum looked at her. 'When did he arrive?'

'Just after you left. You didn't stay that long, did you?'

'Well, Callum wasn't going to waste all his time in the museum, was he? He joined us at the café. We had a real good laugh, didn't we, Callum?' Layla said. Her expression soured as he once again seemed oblivious to her.

'You could have introduced me to your friend Arthur, Radu.'

'I couldn't. You'd already left.'

'Next time, then. I'd definitely like to meet him.'

Radu shrugged.

Chapter Twenty-Six

The next week went by quietly as Sage, Sophie and their friends had most of their time taken up with schoolwork and exam preparation. By the weekend, the two girls were glad to escape to Aurum.

When Sylvan took them to the castle that morning, Peridot was sitting with Mai, Saffron and Lupe in the kitchen. There were photos spread out on the table.

'Maynard sent some pictures of his new car,' Lupe explained.

Sage let out a low whistle as she looked at the sleek sports car. 'Wow, that's quite a car!' She picked up one of the photos, on the back Maynard had scribbled a message. *"Anyone want to join me for a spin in this beauty?"*

'Are you interested, Lupe?' Saffron asked.

'Not really. I had enough of fancy cars with Nefarus.' He stood up. 'We'll have to get back to the hotel now; we've a group of Gifted from France arriving this morning.'

Sophie went to change into her riding outfit and left with Sylvan shortly afterwards. Peridot looked at the photos with a wistful look on her face. 'I must show Osric these photos. He might want to take up Maynard's offer. I don't want him to feel trapped in Aurum just because I can't go to Earth world.'

Sage turned to Mai. 'Is there a spell so goblins could visit Earth world safely? Give them some kind of camouflage?'

She frowned. 'Not one that I know of; but there could very well be something in one of the spell books. There are too many books to look through, but I'll speak to Mercy. She's very good at sorting spells. If we could categorise them, we might find one that we could tweak.'

Peridot's face lit up. 'Oh, that would be wonderful! I could go to Earth world with Osric!'

'There are a lot of spell books to look through, Peridot. It will take a long time, even with the sorting spells.'

'Could I help?' Sage asked. 'I'd love to look through your spell books, Mai.'

'I'd definitely be glad of your help.' Mai smiled. 'We could ask Mercy to teach you some of the sorting spells to begin with. Let's go and see her now. She'll be glad to hear that I've finally decided to tidy up the spell room!'

As they were setting out for Mercy's house, Sophie was brushing the dust off her jacket as she picked herself off the ground yet again. She sighed as Shell flew back to her. 'Arthur is already on course two and I'm stuck here on course one.'

'Well, he does ride every day. Are you ready for another go?' Cora watched as Sophie climbed back onto Shell. 'I know you can do it, Sophie. You're a future dragon rider, remember?'

She smiled as she saw the look of determination on her face.

'Yes, I am. I can do this!'

Both Cora and Sophie were on tenterhooks as Shell cleared the final corner and headed for the last straight. Even the goblin assessor was holding his breath as they neared the finishing line.

'Yes!' he cried. 'Five faultless laps within the time! Sophie and Shell have completed course one!'

Several of the younger riders gathered around her as Shell landed in the Lower Meadow.

'You did it, Sophie!' a goblin girl said.

A boy beamed at her. 'You were brilliant!'

'I hope I can be as good as you one day!' another girl commented.

'Congratulations, Sophie. That was very impressive.'

Sophie spun around to see Dareem standing smiling at her.

'Hey, what are you doing here? Are you having another break from uni?'

He raised his eyebrows. 'I'm having more than a break. I finally admitted what I've known for a long time now; studying accountancy and working in my father's jewellery business is just not for me. This is where I really want to be so I've moved here permanently. I'm working with Osric at the goblin stables, and I've just signed up for dragon riding lessons, too.'

'Wow! So, your parents were okay with that?'

'My mother was totally against it. My father wasn't too happy, but he could understand how I felt.'

'Maybe your mother will come round to it over time; when she realises how serious you are about it. Anyway, it's your life at the end of the day.' She let out a long breath. 'My parents think I'm only taking a gap year from Earth world. That gives me a year to persuade them that I really want to be a dragon rider.'

Dareem grinned. 'Perhaps between us we can work out a way to keep our parents happy.'

'That would be great!'

They looked up as Arthur led Hectas into the grooming area.

'I hear congratulations are in order,' he patted Sophie's shoulder. 'I knew it wouldn't be too long before you completed course one.'

'Like you, Sophie is a natural dragon rider.' Cora beamed as she joined them.

They looked up as there was a soft whinny. Magenta had landed on the hillside nearby. Arthur nodded at her. 'I'll be with you soon, Magenta, once I've rubbed down Hectas.'

'She's so much calmer these days. You've worked wonders with her, Arthur,' Sophie commented, watching Magenta settle down patiently.

'Yes, she is, but she still won't let me ride her. That's what I hope will happen soon.' He laughed as Hectas pushed his snout into his hand. 'Don't worry, Hectas, I'm still planning on riding you in the dragon races later this year. Are you hoping to train as a rider, too, Dareem?'

'I don't know about that; but I do want to know how to ride a dragon. Most of the little kids here learn to ride at school. It seems to be a bit like learning to drive in Earth world.'

Arthur shuddered. 'I don't think I would ever like to drive one of those motorised machines. Have you seen the speed that Maynard's new car can travel? It's unnatural!'

Dareem laughed. 'I'm sure there was a time when you would have said the same about dragon riding! Motor vehicles aren't so bad when you get used to them.'

'I would put my trust in an animal, be it horse or dragon, before any machine,' He added as he watched Hectas take to the sky.

As the two men continued their banter about the merits and setbacks of motor cars and dragons, Sophie looked down the hillside. There were only a few dragons remaining on the lower slopes now. Three young dragons play fought together. Two young goblins were rubbing down Abraxus, as he basked in the sunshine. Olid, Zephyr's dragon stood under the shade of a tree while Zephyr groomed him. He picked up a bucket and took it to a nearby tap, stopping to chat with another fae rider. Sophie watched the two young goblins leave Abraxus and run to Olid. Her brow creased as one of them clambered onto the dragon's back. Both youngsters were laughing until suddenly Olid rose up and began to beat his wings. The would-be rider screamed in alarm which made Olid become even more agitated. His companion gave a cry for help as the dragon rose from the ground.

'Look!' Sophie grabbed Arthur's arm. They watched in dismay as Olid circled several times then headed upwards, picking up speed as he went. Zephyr, Cora and several of the other coaches spoke quickly together, looking around to see which animals they could use to pursue Olid and his young rider.

'They're leaving the training area!' Sophie gasped. 'They're already outside the height limit! We have to do something quickly.'

Arthur ran towards Magenta. 'I really need your help, Magenta. We must go after the youngster.'

Her eyes flashed nervously for a second before she lowered herself to the ground and let him climb on to her back.

Sophie clenched her fists. 'I can do this.' She squinted at the diminishing figure of Olid and took a deep breath. A moment later, she crashed onto the dragon's back, grabbing hold of the sobbing goblin boy to steady them both. With her sudden landing and the boy's shrieks of fear, Olid let out a snort and flew faster still.

She patted the youngster's back. 'You must calm down. You're frightening Olid. Take a deep breath.' The shuddering sobs gradually died down to soft moans, but the boy's grip on her sleeves remained tight. 'That's better. Now we just need to get Olid to take us back to the training grounds. You're Jaden, aren't you; Smaragda's brother?'

He nodded. 'Are you going to make Olid turn around now?'

Sophie gave him a tight smile. Despite using all the signals she had learnt on Shell, Olid continued to speed ahead. 'Don't worry, we'll soon be heading back.'

A line of trees appeared ahead and Olid flew past them until they were flying over a dusty stretch of land with a few bedraggled clumps of grass scattered here and there. Sophie felt her throat go dry as she realised where they were. The barren strip of land just before the White Mists. Leaning forward, she pressed her fingers into the dragon's neck once again and whispered. 'Slow down, Olid. Please slow down.' For a moment, it seemed as if Olid was finally responding to her command and she held her breath as his speed began to lessen. Her hopes were quickly dashed as Jaden jerked upright and pointed to the swirling mass ahead. 'The White Mists! We are going to go to After world! Help us! Somebody help us!'

At his sudden movements and shrill cries, Olid pulled his head up in alarm and increasing his speed once more, flew straight into the thick cloud.

Following behind them on Magenta, Arthur could just make out the shape of Olid as he disappeared between the trees. A sudden shout made him look around. Sylvan was standing on the ground, waving his arms wildly. Arthur guided Magenta to the ground. 'What is it? I don't want to lose sight of them.'

Sylvan was tying the end of a rope to a branch of the tree. 'They've entered the White Mists. Are you going to follow them? You may not survive.'

Arthur narrowed his lips and nodded.

'You'll need this if you're going in there.' Sylvan held out a wooden spool wound with the rest of the rope. 'Fasten this to your belt.'

He saw Arthur's puzzled expression. 'It's Ariadne's silk thread. It will help you to find your way back out of the White Mists.'

As Arthur secured it to his belt and remounted Magenta, Sylvan looked at him. 'And remember...'

'Don't sleep. I know.' He clicked his tongue and Magenta rose into the air.

Sophie felt an icy chill hit her as they entered the White Mists. She wiped away the droplets that clung to her face and hair and peered around her. Everything was hidden in the thick clouds. She could hardly make out the shape of Jaden who had wrapped his arms around her and was sobbing softly.

'It's okay, we'll just get Olid to turn around and we can make our way back out of here.'

There were occasional grunts from Olid as he swooped first one way and then another; seeming as confused as they were about which direction to take.

Sophie was alarmed when Jaden's grip grew slack. She leaned down and realised his breath was slowing down. At the same time, she felt an overwhelming urge to close her own eyes and relax. With an enormous effort she shook her head and grabbed the boy's shoulders. 'No, Jaden! You mustn't sleep!' Tears sprang to her eyes as he murmured and nestled closer to her. 'Hey, what's that? I saw something. We have to shout, Jaden. Help! Help! We're over here!'

Jaden pulled his head up slowly. 'I can't see anything.'

'Over there! Shout, wave your arms!'

For the next few moments, they both shouted, Jaden weakly waving an arm. Sophie fought back the urge to weep and give in to the waves of tiredness that engulfed her. Just as she felt she couldn't keep up the pretence any longer, Jaden stiffened. 'Listen!' A faint cry sounded in the mist and Olid gave a low growl.

'We're over here!' Sophie called; her voice muffled in the mists. She gave a cry of relief as she heard a man's voice and the throaty grumble of a dragon.

'It's Arthur. I can't see you. Magenta will lead you and Olid to safety. Keep talking so we know you're behind us.'

Olid turned towards the sound of Magenta's growls and clucks, making his own guttural utterances in response.

'I've never been so glad to hear a dragon's growl before!' Sophie gasped. 'Stay awake, Jaden! We'll be out of this soon.'

'Your sister is waiting for you, Jaden,' Arthur called out, his own voice sounding slurred. 'Don't go to sleep, don't let her down.'

Jaden rubbed his eyes. 'No, I won't.'

Sophie willed the dragon to keep moving forward as she heard his laboured breath and his struggle to beat his wings. 'Olid needs some encouragement, Jaden. We must keep him going.'

'Come on, boy.' Jaden's voice was hardly more than a whisper. Sophie gently shook his shoulders. 'That's it. Come on, boy. Come on, Olid. You can do it.'

'You can do it,' Jaden mumbled.

After what seemed like hours, Arthur gave an excited cry. 'We're nearly out of the mists!'

The next few moments went by in a blur for Sophie as they moved into the barren ground that bordered the White Mists. She was vaguely aware of voices and felt someone take Jaden from her stiff arms. Another person caught her as she began to slip from the back of the dragon. She heard a woman say her name and a cup of pungent liquid was brought to her lips. 'You have to drink this, Sophie. It will clear the mists from your body.' The liquid stung her throat and she retched, white bubbles of mist pouring from her mouth. Again, the cup was placed at her lips and once again she expelled a cloud of misty bubbles. She coughed, feeling the tightness in her chest begin to loosen. Slowly, she was able to focus on the faces around her. Dareem stood close by as Mercy peered into her eyes. Behind her Arthur grimaced as he drained a similar cup and coughed up plumes of mist. He patted his chest and turned to her. 'How are you feeling, Sophie?'

'I'm okay.' Sophie pulled herself to a seated position. 'Where's Jaden?'

Arthur pointed to a green carriage where Sage was settling Jaden onto his mother's lap; his father and sister seated close by. Sophie watched as she surreptitiously flicked her hands above their heads. There must be plenty of emotions to capture there. 'He's fine. Mercy's remedy has cleared all the mist from his body and Sage has worked wonders at calming the whole family down. I think Jaden is ready for a good night's sleep now.' He looked back at Sophie as she gave another cough. 'Are you sure you're all right?'

Sophie took a deep breath and nodded. 'I'm fine.'

He patted her shoulder. 'I'll help Zephyr see to the dragons.'

She looked up to see Sage hurrying towards her. 'Are you okay? We were so worried about you!'

She nodded, pulling herself up onto shaking legs and was grateful that Sage was there to support her. Mai joined them as Arthur neared Magenta who was pacing in a small circle, fluttering her wings. Zephyr was crouching down next to Olid, who lay listlessly on the ground.

'I do hope the dragons are going to be okay.' Mai frowned. They watched silently as Arthur cupped Magenta's mouth and poured in several drops of liquid. The dragon threw back her head and let out a stream of fire, smoke and mist. She shook her head, resisting as Arthur tried to repeat the action. 'Come on, girl, this will help you!' He managed to make her swallow another mouthful before she stepped back and once again expelled a long flame interspersed with large, white bubbles of mist high into the air.

Dareem smiled. 'I think Magenta is recovering.'

They looked around as Zephyr came running up. 'Olid won't take the liquid. He's fading fast.' He grabbed a new bottle from Mercy and raced towards his dragon, who was breathing raggedly. Zephyr gave a strangled cry as he held the bottle to Olid's mouth and watched the liquid dribble to the ground. 'We need help; we must hold Olid's head back to make him swallow this.' He hurried towards a group of young men standing by the goblin cart.

Arthur knelt down and stroked Olid's neck. 'Come on, Olid. Don't give up now.' He looked up as Magenta nudged him away and pushed her snout against Olid's body, making a guttural sound. Olid gave a slight shiver, but remained on the ground. Magenta repeated the guttural sound, then threw her head back and sent a plume of fire into the sky. Everyone waited, but Olid lay still, hardly breathing.

Magenta circled the other dragon, then hit his side with a plume of fire. Olid gave a whimper, briefly lifting his head from the ground. At that moment, Zephyr returned with three young men.

'Hey, are you going to watch as Magenta sets about Olid while he is in such a weak state? She could kill him!'

As he stepped forward, Arthur grabbed his arm. 'No, she is trying to help him. Look.'

Her guttural murmurings were getting louder as Magenta circled Olid, ending up in front of him. This time, she sent a flame straight into his face. He roared in pain and pulled himself to his feet. Magenta threw back her head and sent another flame skywards. Olid lowered his head, his sides trembling. Slowly, he looked up and opened his mouth. A long stream of smoke and sparks mixed with bubbles of mist trickled out. With another growl of encouragement from Magenta, Olid steeled himself and sent a stronger flame mixed with mist into the sky.

'That's it, Olid!' Zephyr cried as his dragon gave a roar and expelled a final strong flame interspersed with bubbles of mist. He looked at Magenta. 'You were right, Arthur. Magenta saved his life.'

Arthur patted Magenta's neck. 'She's been a true hero today.'

Dareem gave a sigh of relief. 'I have to drive the goblin carriage back to the Glen. Jaden and his family must be ready to go home now.'

Mai turned to Sophie and Sage. 'I think it's time we headed back home, too. Take my hands.'

Flavia was waiting for them in the castle kitchen. She pulled Sophie into warm hug. 'I'm so glad to see you. When we heard you'd gone into the White Mists...' She broke off and bit back a sob.

'Yes, it gave us quite a scare.' Mai nodded. 'Anyway, Sophie, have a shower and get changed.'

'Call me if you need any help,' Sage added.

Flavia dabbed her eyes with her apron. 'I've got some hot soup ready. You must be hungry.'

When Sophie returned to the kitchen a short while later, Saffron and Peridot were there.

'We were so worried about you!' Saffron pulled her close.

'Everyone in Aurum was so worried – the White Mists!' Peridot shuddered.

'Still, you're here now. And everyone is safe.' Saffron pushed back her chair. 'I promised I'd go back and let everyone know how you are, Sophie.'

Mai also stood up. 'I'm going to go and see how Arthur and Zephyr are. I know they're reluctant to leave until they're sure Magenta and Olid have fully recovered.'

Sophie tried to hide a huge yawn behind her hand.

'And you're ready for bed. I'll stay here until you get back, Mai,' Flavia announced, sitting down at the table with a cup of tea beside her.

'I must admit, I do feel tired.'

As soon as Sophie's head hit the pillow, she fell into a deep sleep. The rays of the sun slanting across her bed the next morning told her that she had slept in later than she had intended. Dressing quickly, she made her way to the kitchen to find Mai, Sage and Peridot there.

After greeting them, she turned to Mai. 'Has Arthur already left for dragon riding?'

She nodded. 'We decided to let you have a lie in after the excitement of yesterday.'

'How brave you were!' Peridot placed a cup of tea in front of her. 'You're the talk of Aurum today.'

'Arthur is the one who did all the rescuing,' Sophie countered. 'I've a lesson booked on Shell this morning. I should be there now.'

'Don't worry,' Mai told her. 'Sylvan said he would get one of the young goblins to exercise him today.'

Just then, there was the clatter of horse's hooves in the yard and a knock on the door.

Saffron opened it to find Jaden, Smaragda and their parents standing there.

'We've come to say thank you to Sophie and Arthur for saving Jaden,' the mother said. She stepped forward and grabbed Sophie's hands.

'I'm so glad I was able to help. And both of us are grateful to Arthur and Magenta, aren't we Jaden?'

His father put his hands on his son's shoulders. Sophie saw the muscles in his jaw tighten. He cleared his throat. 'We can't thank you enough. Or apologise enough. I took the two youngsters up to see the dragons. I let them out of my sight for a moment, and...well, you know the rest of the story.'

His wife continued. 'Both Jaden and Smaragda want to apologise and have promised they're not going to climb on another dragon unless it is during proper, supervised lessons.'

Jaden blushed and nodded furiously. 'I'm so sorry, Sophie. Mum and dad told me that you put your life in danger for me. I'll never do that again, ever!'

'Well, all's well that ends well,' Mai said. 'There's hot tea in the pot and I'm sure we still have some of Flavia's biscuits left.'

As they sat down at the table, there was another light tap on the doorway and Dareem appeared. 'I'd just tethered the horse when I heard the mention of tea and biscuits.'

Mai smiled and handed him a cup of tea. As he sat down, he turned to Sophie. 'I'm glad to see you've recovered from your ordeal. That Transposing you did, it was amazing!'

She sighed. 'I keep thinking, what if I'd missed Olid's back, or even worse, knocked Jaden off!'

Dareem squeezed her hand. 'But you didn't.'

'I don't think I'd be much use riding today, but I would like to see Shell before I leave for Earth world.'

'Once I've taken Jaden and the family back to Goblin Glen, I planned to ride up to the training grounds to book my lessons for the week. You and Sage could both come with me, if you like.'

Mai looked over at them. 'That's a great idea, girls. And you could remind Arthur that we're meeting Osric and Peridot at Pine's Diner this lunchtime.'

Once the goblin family were dropped off home, Dareem turned the cart around and they headed uphill to the training grounds.

Sophie smiled as she saw Shell enjoying a rub down from Reed, one of the young goblins that she knew was especially fond of him. Shell looked up and snickered when he saw her. Further up the hillside, Arthur was talking to Zephyr as he rubbed down Hectas.

'You look as if you've had a good ride, Reed. I'm afraid I slept in today,' Sophie said as she patted Shell's neck.

'I'm not surprised; no-one is. We're all so impressed with your bravery yesterday.'

'Arthur had to come to our rescue. And look at him now, it looks as if it's all in a day's work for him!'

Reed nodded slowly. 'King Arthur. Once a king, always a king.'

Arthur looked up and smiled as Dareem and the two girls made their way towards them. 'I don't know where you get your energy from,' Sophie commented. 'Mai said you got back late last night and you were up early again this morning.'

'We wanted to check on Magenta and Olid. They seemed all right when they flew off last night, but I'll be happy when I see how they are today.'

At that moment, the beat of leathery wings made them all look up. The two dragons were circling overhead and landed gently on the hillside. Zephyr grinned at Arthur and both men hurried towards them.

They watched as the two dragons stood closely together as they approached. Magenta's ears flattened as Zephyr came near but she remained still as Olid gave her a gentle nudge.

Zephyr grinned as Olid nuzzled his pocket, looking for a treat. 'You seem to have recovered from your ordeal. Okay, you've earned these.' He pulled out a handful of treats, which quickly vanished.

Magenta froze when Zephyr turned to her, her red scales quivering. Olid gave a low purr as Zephyr gingerly held out another handful of treats. 'And you've earned a treat, too, Magenta.'

'It's okay, he won't harm you,' Arthur reassured her. Magenta paused then snatched up the treats, taking a step backwards.

'Wow, that's progress!' Sophie whispered. 'Magenta is finally ready to make friends!'

Chapter Twenty-Seven

Back in Earth world that evening, Sophie slowed down as they neared her house. 'I don't know if I'll mention this weekend's events to Mum and Dad. It might put them off my planned gap year.'

'They're bound to hear about it from someone sooner or later, and probably an exaggerated version,' Sage pointed out. 'I think you'd be better off telling them yourself first.'

'Will you come in with me and stick up for me?'

Both girls took a deep breath as Sophie's mother opened the door. 'Hi there, I thought I heard voices. How was the weekend?'

'Well, we had a bit of an adventure, actually...' Sophie began. 'I could really do with a cup of tea.'

Ten minutes later, her father sat wide eyed as she finished her story. 'I was never in any real danger, though. Arthur was right behind me, wasn't he, Sage?'

Sage nodded rapidly. 'Yes, right behind you.'

Her mother drew a deep breath. 'Let me get this straight; you actually Transposed onto a dragon while it was flying? And then you went into the White Mists – which is the last step before After world?'

'After world?' her father repeated. 'You mean...death?' He clutched his wife's shaking hands. 'Well, that's it. No more Aurum for you. It's far too dangerous.'

'But, Dad...'

He shook his head. 'I know you need to practise your Gift, but you can do that at Alora's from now on.'

Sophie stood up. 'Aurum isn't any more dangerous than Earth world...'

Gary appeared in the doorway. 'What happened?'

'Your sister has been risking her life this weekend; that's what's happened,' his father said.

'Sophie took some risks to rescue a small boy, actually,' Sage clarified. She gave a brief summary of the events.

Gary frowned. 'Surely, you're proud of her, Dad? I bet you would be if she did the same thing here in the normal world.'

'Exactly. You wouldn't be proud of me if I just stood by and let an innocent child perish, would you?' Sophie pulled a mournful face.

There was a tap at the door and Mary came in. 'I've just heard about your rescue mission from Jay at Alora's! Sophie, what a hero you are. Oh, you must be so proud of your little girl!' She hugged her tightly. 'You have such a great future ahead of you, young lady. Not many Gifted can actually Transpose onto a moving target, let alone a dragon.'

'Yeah, go Sophie!' Gary punched her shoulder lightly. 'We're all proud of her, Aunt Mary.'

Sage smiled at her friend as she left later that evening. 'I think Mary and Gary are winning your parents over, Sophie.'

Over the next few days, Sophie was astonished to hear the exaggerated versions of her weekend escapades repeated to her by Gifted students at school.

'You were so brave!' a girl whispered to her as she put her books in her locker. She saw Callum walking towards her as the girl left. He fell into step with her as she headed for her next lesson. 'You seem to have quite a few admirers this week, Sophie. What have you been up to?'

'Nothing much.'

He bit his lip. 'It's not something you've done at school, so I'm assuming something happened at the weekend. Where *do* you spend your weekends?'

She shrugged. 'With friends.'

'Yes, but who are they and where are they? Why are you so secretive? What have you got to hide?'

'I've got physics now. See you, Callum,' she said, pushing open a classroom door.

He clenched his fists as the door closed behind her. He was determined to find out more about Sophie's secret life.

The following Saturday, he was standing near Sophie's house while it was still quite dark. He stepped back into a nearby driveway as he saw her leave the house. She looked back at someone and shook her head. 'I promise you, there'll be no adventures this weekend!'

Making sure there was a good distance between them, he followed her. As expected, she made her way to Sage's house and the two girls headed out of town. When they were close to the portal, Sage put a hand on Sophie's arm. 'Just walk past. We're being followed by Callum.'

Sage smiled as two tourist coaches appeared on the hill. 'Just in time. Quick cross over.' Once the coaches had hidden them from Callum's view, she nodded. 'Get ready to Transpose. I'll see you at the portal.'

She grinned as they both reappeared at the portal at the same time. Holding hands, the two girls hurried through.

Sylvan was waiting as the two girls stumbled into Aurum.

'It looks as if someone is after you.'

Sage rolled her eyes. 'Callum was following us. We managed to shake him off but I don't think he'll give up easily. If he follows a less experienced Gifted to the portal, he could cause problems.'

'We'd better let Mai know about this.'

Mai listened as Sage aired her fears about Callum. 'I'll speak to Alora and we'll make sure we keep a careful eye on Callum. We'll increase the security on the portal to keep out unwanted visitors.' She noticed the look of alarm in Sophie's eyes. 'Keep us informed on anything else you notice about him or anybody else, but don't worry too much. Now, enjoy your weekend in Aurum.'

'I'm going to. I promised my parents that this weekend was going to be a quiet one and I'm just going to concentrate on my riding! Are you going up there now, Sylvan?'

He nodded. 'Yes, I'm taking a new beginners' class today while Cora puts you through your paces on the Upper Meadow, ready for course two.'

'I'm going to spend the morning with Mercy, going through your spell books, Mai,' Sage said. 'She's going to teach me some of the basic sorting spells.'

Seeing Shell waiting for her in the training grounds, Sophie soon forgot about Callum. She was excited about moving on to the next level.

Several riders were taking a leisurely ride around the perimeter of the Upper Meadow. Spaced out around the centre of the field were three posts. A rider had positioned herself at a distance from one of the posts, then flew towards it, slowing down before looping around and heading back to the starting point.

Cora nodded. 'Well done, Zelen. Try again, this time building up your speed.'

Zelen nodded and repeated the manoeuvre, sliding to the ground as she went around the post. She stood up and shook her head.

'Remember your posture,' Cora called out. 'Try again.' She then turned to Sophie. 'Your turn now. That's your post, over there. Take it slowly at first.'

Sophie faced the post and urged Shell forwards. As they neared the post and Shell turned back, she felt herself slipping to the ground.

Cora gave her an encouraging smile. 'Try taking the loop at a wider angle to start with. That's it, nearly there...ooh.' She watched as she picked herself up and remounted Shell.

'I just can't get the hang of looping back! It's so much more difficult than the corners on course one.'

'And they seemed impossible to you at first, but you got there in the end.'

After several more unsuccessful attempts, Sophie gave a cry of frustration.

'Forget about the posts for today and join the others on the perimeter, just as a reminder that dragon riding is fun!' Cora suggested.

Sophie gave a wry smile and patted Shell's snout. 'You're right, Cora.' She soon felt her mood lift as they flew at a leisurely pace around the perimeter, chatting to a young fae who had also recently moved up a level.

'Hey, Sophie; had enough of falling off for one day?' Sylvan flew up beside her.

The fae's mouth opened. 'You're Sophie? The one who rode into the White Mists to rescue a young goblin?'

'Well, it wasn't *quite* like that...' she began.

Sylvan held up a hand. 'Don't be so modest, Sophie! You're our hero!'

The fae waved to another girl behind them. 'Pink, come and meet Sophie, the one who rescued Jaden from the White Mists!'

By the time she was ready to go to the Lower Meadow to rub Shell down, Pink and her friend had brought several others over to meet her. Her attempts to give a realistic account of her part in the rescue was dismissed. She was relieved to see Sylvan making his way to the front of the group.

'Here, I'll finish up with Shell. Dareem is leaving for Goblin Glen in a few moments, if you want a lift back.' He gestured towards Dareem who was standing next to a green carriage. Sophie nodded eagerly, bidding goodbye to her new admirers and made her way towards it.

'You're the latest hero!' Dareem said as he helped her onto the seat beside him.

Sophie groaned. 'I've been trying to play it down. Mum and Aunt Mary are coming here later in the week. I don't want this to make Mum think that a gap year in Aurum is dangerous.'

Dareem shrugged. 'Perhaps there'll be a new story by then.'

When they reached Goblin Glen, she slid down and watched Dareem lead the horse to the paddock. The sound of familiar voices made her look up. Casper and Rhandra were dismounting from a pair of goblin ponies. 'Hey, Sophie, we've been hearing all about you rescuing Jaden. And the White Mists!'

Sophie shrugged. 'Believe me, most versions are greatly exaggerated.'

'We're heading to the hotel for lunch. Why don't you join us and fill us in on all the details?'

'I'd love to. I'm meeting Sage there.'

They fell into step together; Casper told Sophie about their activities. 'Last night we went to see the latest show at the Fae theatre. First thing this morning we visited the Goblin Museum of Art.'

'I decided we'd done enough arty things, so I put us down for the pony trek,' Rhandra added. 'And after lunch today, we're going to the new pool that Mai created behind the hotel. You should join us.'

Sage was already sitting at an outside table and waved them over as they neared the hotel.

'I'm so hungry,' Sophie said as she sat down. She gave a quiet groan as two goblins stopped by their table.

'You're the Transposer who rescued the young goblin, aren't you?'

'Well, not exactly single-handedly.'

'I said it was her, Mum,' a fae was pulling her mother towards them.

'You're really brave,' the mother smiled. 'You even faced the White Mists!'

Casper shivered dramatically. 'Oh, my life! The White Mists!'

'Actually, Arthur saved us from the White Mists,' Sophie protested. Her face fell as two more people headed towards them and she gave a sigh of relief as Flame strode up to their table.

'Okay. Even Superheroes have to eat! Give her a bit of space!' She put a basket of crusty bread on the table and glared until Sophie's admirers went back to their table. 'I hope you're hungry because Flavia has excelled herself today. She's gone for an Italian flavour. I heard her tell someone that her pasta is a secret recipe from a fae that lived in Rome for over a hundred years. Shall I bring a selection of dishes?' She reached out to put a jug of cold water in the centre of the table.

'That's a pretty wristband, Flame,' Rhandra commented, touching the broad woven band she wore. 'Very unusual rusty colouring. And what's the inscription?'

Flame pulled her hand away and shrugged. 'Oh, it's just a pattern. I'll get your dishes now.'

Sophie whispered to Sage as Flame headed for the kitchen. 'I bet it's a love token from her latest admirer!'

'I wouldn't be surprised,' Sage laughed.

The conversation died down as they all tucked into a selection of pasta, pizza, salads and dips.

Casper soaked up the last of the pasta sauce from his plate with a piece of bread. 'That was absolutely delicious. The best so far.'

'You said that last night's meal was the best so far.' Rhandra giggled.

'And it was. The food here just gets better and better!'

'Can I get you anything else?' Flame said.

'If I eat another mouthful, I will sink straight to the bottom of the pool this afternoon,' Casper groaned.

'Oh, the new pool! It was a great idea of Saffron's. It's very popular with the visitors and residents. I'm going there with Flora and some of the other hotel workers when we finish the lunches today. Some of the guests have said it's as good as any of the Caribbean beaches in Earth world,' Flame commented. 'See you there later.'

'Are you coming for a swim, too?' Casper asked Sophie and Sage as he stood up.

'Yes, we'll meet you down there,' Sage replied.

After collecting their swimsuits and towels; the two girls made their way to the pool.

'Flame was right, this is a beautiful place. It's like being on a beach,' Sage remarked as the two girls put their bags down beside Casper and Rhandra who had spread a rug out under one of the palm trees that offered shade from the sun. The pool was a large, oval shape framed by a wide, sandy boundary. At one side, several youngsters were happily building sandcastles or paddling at the water's edge. Gentle waves sparkling in the sunlight lapped the shore. Further out in the deeper waters, several wooden platforms had been anchored. Some of the swimmers had pulled themselves on to them and sat with their feet dangling in the warm water, while others dived and swam nearby.

The sound of laughter made them all look up. A group of young people had arrived and were setting up a game of volley ball nearby. Sage spotted Flora and Flame, Samar and three young goblins from the hotel. Rhandra stood up. 'Shall we join them?'

Soon they were organised into two teams with a mixture of fae, goblins, shifters and Gifted in both teams, each using their particular skills to gain points. As a fae dropped the ball down between the teams, Sage flew upwards to hit it. Before she could do so, Rhandra appeared in front of her, laughing as she carried it down to the ground. Camouflaged in a leafy shrub beside the makeshift court, a goblin suddenly sprang forward, taking Rhandra by surprise and making her drop the ball. With a shout of glee, the youngster shot the ball over the net.

After a while, hot and out of breath, they stopped for a rest. Mai and Arthur arrived as they took a break for a cold drink and were quickly persuaded to join the game for the second half.

'This is so unfair,' Arthur said as Mai grabbed the ball from him and soared upwards. 'I'm no challenge to your magical wiles. I'm a mere immortal!'

'Let me give you a hand,' a shifter shouted, hoisting him up to return the ball across the net.

'Ha, the benefits of teamwork!' Arthur laughed as Mai gave a playful pout.

He was still smiling as his team were the final winners.

'Flame is certainly attached to her wristband, she's not even taking it off to go in the water,' Sage commented as she watched several of the players heading for a cool dip before they headed back home.

'And it looks like she's started a fashion trend,' Sophie added. 'Samar is sporting one, too.'

Mai looked up with a frown. 'They are both wearing wristbands? Oh, dear; I had no idea it would get this far so quickly. I'll have a word with them. And I'd better speak to Delbert before he hears it from someone else.'

'Do you think they have exchanged love tokens?' Sophie asked.

'If only it was just an exchange of love tokens!' Mai said as she made her way towards Flame. From the fae's expression, she was not happy with the conversation but she gave a quick nod as Mai beckoned Samar to her.

When Sage and Sophie arrived back at the castle later that afternoon, they were surprised to find Samar and Flame in the kitchen. Flame's face was pale and her eyes were red-rimmed. Samar strode backwards and forwards across the kitchen floor.

'Are you okay?' Sage asked softly.

Flame bit her lip, her face creasing as she shook her head.

Samar stopped and faced the two girls. 'It was bound to come out sooner or later.'

'So, you're a couple?' Sophie said.

'Yes, though whether we can stay here in Aurum now is the big question.' He grasped Flame's hand. 'Whatever happens, we'll be together.'

They all looked around as the sound of loud voices was heard.

'You suspected something and yet you did nothing about it?' A man's voice said angrily.

'Banning youngsters from doing something is likely to have the opposite effect,' Mai retorted.

'We'd better leave you to talk,' Sage said, heading for the door.

Flame held out her hand. 'Please stay and stick up for us. We've done nothing wrong; all we did was fall in love.'

A moment later, the door was flung open and Delbert strode in his eyes narrowing as he looked at Samar. 'What did you think you were doing?'

'Calm down, Delbert,' Mai said, putting a hand on his shoulder.

'Calm down? How far have things gone?'

'They've clearly exchanged blood,' Mai looked at the wristbands they both wore.

'And...' Flame put a hand over her stomach.

Delbert slumped into a chair with a loud groan. 'No, no!'

'We're going to stay together, here in Aurum, or take our chances in Earth world if we have to,' Flame said, her voice wavering.

Samar put his arm around her shoulder and nodded.

'Is there any reason why they can't stay in Aurum?' Sophie asked. 'Is it a crime if they've fallen in love?'

'Haven't you ever been in love, Delbert?' Flame raised her chin and held his gaze.

Delbert pinched the bridge of his nose. 'Oh, yes, I have loved.' His voice faltered and he walked towards the window. They waited silently as he gazed out at the gentle rolling hillside in the distance. Finally, he sighed. 'Yes, I have loved. She was everything to me. And my love destroyed her and all that mattered to me. Even after all this time, it's difficult to talk about it.'

Mai gestured towards the blank wall. 'Would it be easier to show us your memories?'

He closed his eyes for a moment, then spread his hands and an image appeared on the wall.

Two figures were sitting on a grassy bank beside a river. The man was clearly Delbert, but a much less serious version of the man they knew in Aurum. His partner, a young woman giggled as she plucked the petals off a daisy. 'He loves me, he loves me not, he...' Delbert pulled it from her fingers and continued. 'He loves her; he loves her even more; he loves her to the ends of the earth; he loves her for all eternity!' She leaned forward and kissed his lips gently. 'For all eternity!'

The scene faded and was replaced by another image of Delbert seated behind a desk in a wood-panelled room. The sound of his quill scratched across the paper as he wrote on a sheet of thick parchment. His brow furrowed as he paused to read over the words he had written, before he dipped his quill into the inkwell and continued writing.

There was a rustling sound and he looked up, his expression softening as the young woman wearing a long, full skirted dress approached him and put her arms around his shoulders, resting her chin on his head.

'Are you still writing? Can't you take a break for a while?'

'Just give me a few minutes to finish this chapter, Solia. It's important that I get all the facts recorded while they are still fresh in my mind. I need to make sure the truth is preserved for future generations. Vampires and shifters are often seen in a bad light, when not all of us are as we have been painted.'

'Who will read all these books you write?'

Delbert finished a sentence and put down his quill. 'At the moment, very few other-worldly people have had access to them. But I'm hoping to house them in a library available to all of our kind in future years.'

Solia leaned down and kissed his cheek. 'How did I ever get to win the heart of someone as clever as you, Delbert. I hope our child will inherit their father's brains.'

'And their mother's beauty and kindness,' Delbert added. He swung her on to his lap. 'And are you taking it easy as Aubria advised?'

'Yes, I am.' She sighed. 'My sister never had to rest up for half the day when she was expecting a baby.'

'Your sister had a fae baby. You know it's different for you, expecting a vampire/fae child. Aubria says it is very unusual, and you must take special care. She is an experienced midwife and we must take heed of her advice.'

'I know, but don't forget, Aubria also said I need to get outside in the fresh air.' She walked towards the large window and looked out at the distant mountain tops silhouetted against the blue sky. 'The day is too beautiful to stay indoors.'

'It looks a wonderful place to live,' Sophie commented.

Delbert gave a short laugh. 'Yes, in the milder months it was beautiful indeed; but in the winter it became treacherous.'

The image changed again, and now the view from the window was very different. A thick blanket of snow covered the ground and bowed down the branches of the trees. Overhead, the sky was a threatening, gunmetal grey.

'The stormy weather hit us so suddenly that year. I wasn't ready for it, though I should have been.' His lips narrowed. 'The baby decided to come early. Aubria, the midwife, was in the village nearby, but the road was cut off by snow and no-one could get through. I could see that Solia was in distress, so I decided the only thing to do was to go and fetch Aubria myself. I would carry her up to the castle. I left our young maid with Solia, hoping that she could hold on until we returned.' His voice cracked. 'We came back as quickly as we could but it was a difficult birth. Aubria did everything she could but I lost Solia and my child that night.'

There was silence for a while. Mai went to stand beside Delbert and rub his shoulder. Samar pulled Flame closer to him.

Delbert cleared his throat. 'I was overcome with grief and hid myself away for many years. If it hadn't been for Vinaconsuella coming into my life; I would not be here today. She gave me a new reason to carry on. I hadn't been able to save my own child, but I could do everything in my power to help her.

'I vowed that no-one would ever have to endure such pain again. Over the years, I wrote a new book for my future library. It was a warning to all non-humans on how they should interact. I emphasised the dangers of vampires and fae becoming close.'

'You kept this from us all, Delbert,' Mai said. 'I've always trusted your judgement over the centuries. Are you telling me now that these ideas that you presented as facts were based solely on your personal experience?'

He shook his head. 'As I said before, there were few children born to vampire and fae parents. I found evidence of five others. And three of those ended sadly.'

'What about shifter and fae? You were against that, too, weren't you?' Sage asked.

'Shifters and vampires often live alongside each other. I was afraid if a shifter brought a fae with them to live near vampires, it could also lead to disaster. It seemed sensible to keep them apart, also.'

A heavy silence descended on the room once more. Sophie noticed Sage slip something from her pocket and flick the air just before Flame stood up and put her hands protectively over her slightly rounded stomach. 'Well, we're going to prove you wrong! That was a long time ago. Things have changed. We're going to have a perfectly healthy baby, aren't we Samar?'

He gave a nervous smile as he stood beside her. 'If anyone can do it, you can, Flame. But we need to have a midwife who is experienced in vampire/fae births to look after you.' He turned to Delbert. 'You said you found out about two such children who survived. We need to find one of their midwives to look after Flame and our baby.'

'It was a very long time ago, Samar, hundreds of years. I don't know where they are now.'

'We know someone who *is* good at researching the past...' Mai began. She looked up as there was a gentle tap on the door and Vinnie and Peridot entered. 'And here she is.'

'What's happening here?' Vinnie said, looking at their faces.

'We need some hot tea,' Sophie said, standing up. 'And biscuits.'

When she returned to the table with a tray, Vinnie was talking to Delbert.

'Delbert, you must give me all the information you have about the midwives you spoke to.'

'I can't remember their names off hand, but I have details of them in my study at home. They were both living in Romania at the time.'

'I have several contacts in Romania who might be able to help me.' Vinnie turned to Flame and Samar. 'I'll leave here tomorrow morning. We'll find you a midwife as soon as possible.'

Peridot stood up and hugged Flame. 'We're all here to look after you and your baby.'

'Yes, we'll all be here to help you.' Mai nodded.

Chapter Twenty-Eight

It was dark when Vinnie stepped out of the taxi in front of the Royal Hotel in Brasov, Romania, the following day. The doorman greeted her and picked up her suitcase, leading her inside. The woman behind the reception desk looked up and smiled.

'Vinnie, welcome. It's been too long since your last visit. I've put you in your usual suite.'

'Thank you, Sorinah. It's lovely to be back.'

In her room, she kicked off her shoes and let her feet sink into the deep pile carpet. The large four-poster bed and the old-fashioned oak furniture seemed so familiar. When Delbert had travelled, he had always insisted on first class accommodation and now she continued to enjoy it. Pushing open the shutters, she looked out at the starry night sky. All was still except for the lights of the occasional car making its way slowly along the steep road that cut through the forested hillside flanking the town. Vinnie leaned forward and listened to the sounds of the night creatures as the rest of the hotel guests slept. A scuffling in the trees at the foot of the hillside made her run her tongue over her lips. With a smile, she sprang up onto the balcony wall and leapt onto a branch of a nearby tree. Pausing to ensure that no-one was watching, she swiftly made her way towards the forest.

The first light of dawn was just becoming visible as she showered and dressed the next morning. She sat down at the desk, pulled out her notebook and looked at the names she had written down. The details she had were from several hundred years ago and anything could have happened to these women in all that time. She hoped she would be able to locate at least one of them if not both. Picking up her bag, she pushed the notebook inside. The market place would be waking up by now and she hoped she could find someone who might be able to supply information on these special midwives.

'Early potatoes, spring cabbage, freshly picked this morning!' a stall holder shouted out as Vinnie made her way through the stalls.

Stopping for a moment, she admired a selection of colourful flowers.

'They remind us that spring is here,' the stallholder said. He held out a single daffodil. 'For a pretty lady on a sunny day!'

'Thank you.' She smiled, feeling a pang as she recalled how Timur would present her with a single flower or a small bouquet so many years ago.

'Vinnie!' A voice brought her back to the present. She looked around to see a stooped old woman, dressed in a faded cotton dress with a ragged apron tied around her waist. She found herself embraced in a warm hug.

'Tassa! You're back in Brasov again. Last I heard, you were in Albania.'

Tassa scowled. 'Yes, the curse of being immortal, you have to keep on the move.' She tidied up the bundles of herbs on a small table beside her. 'What brings you here today? Are you on an art quest? Or maybe looking for a potion?'

Vinnie shook her head. 'I'm looking for these two midwives.' She opened her notebook and read out the names. 'Izabela Aurel and Yetta Ion.'

'I don't recognise the names, but you could speak to Lina. She lived here at least a hundred years before me.' She pointed a gnarled finger up the cobbled street towards a tall, dark, stone building. 'Three years ago, she returned and opened a health food store just past the Town Hall.'

Vinnie thanked her and left as a middle-aged woman came to the stall, picking up different bunches of herbs and haggling over the price with Tassa.

It was easy to locate Lina's shop from the wooden sign with her name carved on it hanging above a wide glass doorway. Inside there were aisles of modern-day health foods – tins, dried packets and fresh produce as well as some older remedies that Vinnie recognised from centuries ago. She made her way to the cash desk where the young girl pushed a mobile phone into her pocket and gave her a bright smile.

'Is Lina here today?' Vinnie asked her.

'Yes, do you have an appointment?' the girl frowned. 'Lina doesn't see reps by the way.'

'I'm not a rep. Could you tell her that I'm a friend of Tassa's?'

The girl went through a doorway and reappeared with a young woman dressed in neatly pressed, navy trousers and a light blue shirt. 'You're a friend of Tassa's?'

'Yes. She thought you might be able to help me locate one of these women.' Vinnie held out the page.

Lina's eyebrows raised. 'Come into the office.' Sitting down behind a desk, she gestured to the chair opposite. 'You're a vampire, aren't you? Have you need of a midwife?'

Vinnie shook her head and explained about Flame and Samar and Delbert's fears for them. 'He found out that these two women specialised in such offspring, but tragically too late to save his own partner and child, many years ago.'

Lina tapped the desk. 'The last I heard of Izabela; she was living in a remote village in Spain. But that was over three hundred years ago. Yetta Ion also left Romania long ago, but she does visit occasionally. The last time was about ten years ago and she stayed at La Paloma Hotel in Bucharest. Aleko Parsel, the owner, retired just over seven years ago, but he still lives in the hotel's penthouse suite. He might be able to give you some information on her.'

Vinnie thanked her and left. As she made her way back to her hotel, she dialled La Paloma Hotel on her mobile phone. She told the receptionist that she was trying to trace a family friend and she hoped that Mr Parsel would be able to help her, asking if she could call and see him. When she mentioned Yetta Ion's name, Aleko quickly came to the phone himself. They arranged an appointment for the next day.

Vinnie was impressed when she entered the hotel lobby the following afternoon and looked around her. A huge chandelier was suspended from the high ceiling, the glass teardrops glittering in the light. A man dressed in an evening suit, sat at a grand piano in the vast foyer, playing soft background music as she walked across the polished marble floor.

A young woman in a smart tailored suit stepped forward to greet her. 'Vinaconsuella? Mr Parsel is expecting you.' She led her to a lift that took them to the top floor of the building and along a plush carpeted corridor to large double doors. A uniformed man opened them and stood aside as they entered. The woman gestured towards a sofa by a huge window that looked out over the grounds and the town below. A moment later, a tall, silver-haired man came through a doorway opposite. He moved slowly, leaning on a silver-headed cane. Vinnie judged him to be in his eighties. He held out a hand. 'Aleko Parsel, so pleased to meet you, Vinaconsuella. I have heard of you from several of my friends who collect rare antique artifacts. I dabble a little myself.'

They chatted about antiques and the different and unusual ones they had come across over the years. Finally, Aleko sat back.

'It's very interesting discussing antiques, but I think the main reason for your visit is to trace an old family friend?'

Vinnie explained how Lina had thought he might have some information about Yetta Ion.

He clapped his hands together and laughed. 'Yetta! What a woman! She brought this hotel to life when she stayed here. The last time must be nearly ten years ago.'

'I heard she was a nurse.'

'Yes, I think she had some kind of medical background. I still hear news of her now and then.'

'Do you know where she is now?'

'She lived in Rome until five years ago. I bumped into her at the opera house. She is a great lover of the arts and theatre. Last year, I heard she'd moved to Paris but I don't know exactly whereabouts.'

Soon after that Vinnie rose to leave. 'When you find Yetta, send her my fond regards. Tell her she must come and stay at La Paloma again soon.'

'I will,' she promised.

That night, back in her own hotel room as the rest of the hotel guests slept, Vinnie researched Paris; making note of the latest theatre productions and art events. Finally, she booked a flight to Paris for the next day.

Chapter Twenty-Nine

A week later in Aurum, Saffron knocked and pushed open the door of Flame and Samar's house.

In the lounge, Peridot was placing a cup of tea and a plate of biscuits in front of Flame.

'Good news,' Saffron said brightly. 'Vinnie located one of the midwives and they've just arrived at the castle. They'll be on their way to see you this afternoon.'

Flame scowled as she picked up a biscuit. 'It's not fair! Just because I'm pregnant, they're shipping in some old crone to hover over me, probably feeding me vile, so-called healthy foods and not allowing me to move!'

'Oh, I'm sure it won't be that bad, love.' Samar patted her shoulder.

'It's all right for you to say that! You won't have to put up with it!'

'Everyone just wants to make sure that you and your baby are well taken care of,' Saffron pointed out.

Samar nodded. 'She's right, love. Anyway, let's just see what the midwife is like before we jump to conclusions.'

'I've designed another dress for you,' Peridot said, pulling out her notebook. 'What do you think of this, maybe in burgundy?'

'Oh, it is rather pretty, Peridot,' Flame's eyes lit up. 'Better make it with plenty of room; I'm growing by the minute.'

The two women were engrossed in a discussion on fabric and colours, when there was a knock on the door. Mai came in, followed by Vinnie and a tall, black woman. She wore a white dress cinched in at the waist with a shiny, red belt that accentuated her curvy figure. Red, high heeled shoes completed her outfit. Loose curls framed a friendly face. Beaming at Flame, she grabbed her hand. 'Hi, there. You must be Flame. I'm Yetta.'

'Hi...Yetta,' Flame stuttered. 'You're the midwife?'

Yetta threw back her head and laughed. 'You were expecting an old crone, weren't you? No, don't deny it.' She gestured outside the window. 'Don't worry; I had my misgivings, too. Coming to some old worldly fantasy land with no internet and no technology! At least I can get to London easily from here.'

'Aren't you going to be staying here looking after Flame?' Samar looked anxious.

Yetta turned to Samar. 'Oh, you must be Samar, the father to be.' She shook his hand. 'Of course, I'll be looking after Flame, but I won't need to watch her every minute of every day. That would send us both crazy! Anyway, there's a fashion show in London in a fortnight's time. A friend of mine got me some tickets and I really don't want to miss it. Talking about fashion, that's a beautiful dress you're wearing, Flame. It really sets off your red hair.'

Flame smiled. 'Peridot designed and made it for me. It is lovely, isn't it?'

'Peridot, what a pretty name.' Yetta turned to her. 'You're obviously talented. Maybe you could come with me to the fashion show? My friend would love to meet you, he's always on the look-out for new ideas.'

Peridot spread her hands. 'I think I might have trouble blending in Earth world.'

'Oh, you mean being green? What about that old genie spell?' Yetta frowned. 'Does anybody still use that? I would imagine it could be adapted for goblin purposes. It can hide blue skin, I'm sure it could do the same for green skin, too; temporarily anyway.'

'You mean there really *is* a spell? A spell that would let goblins visit Earth world!' Peridot's eyes shone.

'Yes, it's a really old one; dates back to the "Freedom from the Lamps" ruling. Mai Lin will know about that.' She turned back to Flame. 'Now, I must say, you're looking really well. How about we have a private girly chat about your baby? Then afterwards you can show me the high life of Aurum. I've heard that Pine's Diner is the place for first class tea, coffee, cakes - and gossip!'

As the two of them went into the bedroom, Saffron smiled at Samar. 'She's quite a character, isn't she?'

***

Meanwhile, Sophie and Dareem had just finished their riding sessions and were rubbing down their dragons. Sophie hugged Shell's neck. 'This is the last time I'm going to see you for a while. I'm going to miss you so much!'

'It is only for a few weeks, Sophie,' Dareem pointed out.

'It's going to feel like forever. What if Shell forgets me?'

Arthur joined them at that moment. He patted Shell's long snout. 'He won't. I'll keep reminding him that you'll only be gone for a short time while you finish your school studies in Earth world and that you'll be back here as soon as you can.'

The dragon gave a gentle snort and nuzzled Sophie's shoulder. 'I think you understand, Shell.' She bit back a tear as she watched him glide down the meadow to join several other dragons who were ready to return to their own homes.

A glowing orb made them all look around and Sylvan materialised nearby. 'Ah, I'm glad to find you all together. The new midwife, Yetta Ion, has arrived and Vinnie and Mai took her to meet Flame and Samar this afternoon. Now they're all on their way to Pine's Diner and Mai suggested we all meet up there.'

'What is the midwife like?' Arthur asked.

Sylvan grinned. 'Come and see for yourself!'

When they reached the square a short while later, Yetta was already there with Flame and Samar, talking animatedly to a group of fae and goblins. She looked up as Mai said something to her and stood up.

'You must be Arthur, King of Camelot!' she grabbed his hands. 'I heard the rumours, but I never thought I'd actually get to meet you!' She turned to Sophie and Dareem. 'And these must be your dragon flying friends!'

She looked over their shoulders with a wide smile as Vinnie appeared with Delbert. Giving a slight bow he took her hand and kissed it. 'Yetta. It's been so long since we met. You're still as...striking ...as ever.'

'It's been too long, Delbert! And look at you, still as dapper as ever! We have so much catching up to do.' Her mouth fell open as she heard someone call out her name. 'No. It isn't. It couldn't be! Benigno! You haven't changed a bit! And here's me thinking Aurum would be a dull place!'

Several young waiters pushed some tables together and brought out chairs as they sat down, chatting and laughing.

'Well, Yetta certainly isn't an old crone, is she?' Sophie said as she sat down at a side table with Dareem.

He smiled and shook his head. 'I think she'll liven the place up a bit.'

'I'm going to miss all this for the next few weeks until our exams are over.'

Dareem nudged her arm as he saw her desolate expression. 'Hey, how about I visit you now and again over the next few weeks just to keep you updated on Shell and all the Aurum news?'

Sophie's face lit up. 'Oh, would you, Dareem? It'll make my enforced exile so much more bearable!' She sighed. 'You're right, it is just a few weeks. Then I can *really* start living the life I want to.'

'I know exactly how you feel, Sophie.' He picked up his glass. 'Here's to the next stage of your life!'

Sophie tapped it with her own glass. 'To Aurum and the future!'

About Trish Moran

Trish Moran was born in Dublin, Ireland and moved to the Midlands, UK at a young age. Her first teaching job took her to London and she later taught in Greece. After several years, she travelled to Australia and worked in Melbourne.

After over a decade outside the UK, she moved back to the small Midlands town where she grew up.

Trish has always been an avid reader; one of her friends describes her as a readaholic, nervously lining up her next book as she comes to the end of the present one. She enjoys reading a wide variety of books which includes YA – especially fantasy and stories of more down to earth dysfunctional families; adult thrillers with complicated plots; and stories with quirky characters. She loves to discover a book with a new slant and think, 'Gosh, what a great idea! I wish I'd thought of that!'

In her thirties, Trish decided she would like to try writing, and completed several (unpublished) short stories and novellas before embarking on the Clone Trilogy - YA Sci Fi; Mirror Image, Altered Image and Perfect Image, published with Accent Press.

Shrinking Violet, published with Solstice Publishing was her first venture into YA Paranormal.

The idea for the Enchanted Series came after a trip to a medieval castle and overhearing a young child saying, 'Where do the dragons and wizards live now, mummy?' And it expanded from there, with Sage Book One and Sophie Book Two.

As well as reading and writing; Trish enjoys going to the gym, walking and nature photography.

Social Media

Blog: www.trishmoranblog.com

Facebook - https://www.facebook.com/trishmoranauthor
Twitter - https://twitter.com/trishmoran99
@trishmoranauthor

Instagram – https://www.instagram.com/pfmoran99/?hl=en
pfmoran99

Amazon author page link - https://www.amazon.com/-/e/B0933BDG6F

Printed in Great Britain
by Amazon

10336522R00149